The Peter Bay

DOGWOOD PRESS

Also by Randy Pierce

Magnolia Mud
Pain Unforgiven

Kathy,
Thanks for supporting my writing! I hope you enjoy the book.

The Peter Bay

A NOVEL

signed 6/29/17

RANDY PIERCE

DOGWOOD PRESS

Copyright © 2016 by Dogwood Press
ISBN 978-0-9835386-8-4

This book is a work of fiction. Names, characters and events are a product of the author's imagination. Any resemblance to actual persons, living or dead, or events is purely coincidental. No part of this book may be used or reproduced in any manner whatsoever without written permission, except in the case of brief quotations embodied in critical articles and reviews.

ALL RIGHTS RESERVED

Library of Congress Control Number
2015960052

Printed in the United States of America

Cover design by Cyndi Clark
Swamp photo on front cover ©istockphoto.com/pateilers
Cloud photo on flap and pages ©istockphoto.com/VvoeVale
Author photo by Cheryl Pierce

First Dogwood Press edition: March 2016

DOGWOOD PRESS
P.O. Box 5958 • Brandon, MS 39047
www.dogwoodpress.com

To my siblings: Cheryl, Shonna, and Terry

In Memory of Tracy McIlwain

Acknowledgments

A BOOK IS NOT published without a lot of help. I would like to thank my wife, Cheryl, for her patience and support. Everything I do is in the hope that my children will understand the importance of hard work and perseverance. I want to thank Tiffany, Brantley, Anna, and Josh for the motivation to keep on keeping on. And to my extended family, your encouragement keeps me writing. To my beta readers, Alice Goff, Sandy Chesnut, Joey Griffin, Dustin Thomas, and Jeff Rimes, the book is much better because of you. And last, but certainly not least, I offer my sincere appreciation to my publisher and editor, Joe Lee. He deserves to have a *New York Times* best seller. The literary world is much richer because of him.

PROLOGUE

December 13, 2010

HE DROVE PAST the driveway and noticed the white Nissan sitting where it was supposed to be. As expected, the pickup was gone. He glanced in the rearview mirror. No traffic. He knew there would be none—he was in the middle of nowhere. He drove another mile, turned around, and crept toward the dim, woodsy road which was waiting. The vehicle snapped small branches as he backed it out of view from the county road. He put it in park and waited.

He looked at his watch. 6:45 a.m. The bus would be here soon. He pulled the picture from his shirt pocket and held it close to his face. That smile! And her body. Barely five feet tall, maybe a hundred pounds. She was perfect. He had coveted her for years.

He turned the key and the engine stopped. He could hear the motor popping as it began to cool. He lowered the window and listened, flinching as leaves rustled in the distance. He held his breath and squinted in the direction of the sound as he opened the door and stepped onto the pinestraw-covered road. He eased the door shut and bent low to determine the source of the sound.

A twig snapped. The sound grew closer. He exhaled as an armadillo eased into a small clearing.

The twelve-ton yellow heap pounded the dirt road as it approached its appointed stop. He heard the brakes whistle and squeak as the bus came to a halt. He eased to the edge of the road and watched the two girls walk up the steps and onto the bus. It was time. He backtracked to the car and put his gloves in his pocket, and then the handcuffs and masking tape. He didn't need a blindfold—he wanted her to know who he was. Adrenaline pumped through his arms and legs and crashed into his spine. He'd been looking forward to this day since he first saw her six years ago.

To avoid footprints he walked in the grass on the side of the road just above the ditch. The tips of his shoes were wet from the heavy coat of dew which had blanketed the southern soil. The roof of the house came into view, so he ducked into the woods and squatted to get a better look. The place was quiet. He stood and walked through a growth of small pines until he could get a more suitable angle of the house. He located what he thought to be the kitchen window, hoping to see her there. He then noticed a small dog lying on the porch. He reached to feel the bulge in his sock which would be used to distract the animal. He'd thought of everything.

After a moment, he stepped out of the trees and walked to the backyard. The windows were covered by blinds so he hurried to the west side of the house. He could hear water rushing through a pipe to the septic tank below his feet. She must be in the bathroom, he thought. He approached the backdoor and twisted the knob. Locked. He thought about the dog and knew the mutt couldn't be avoided, so he pulled a dog bone from his sock. The canine was no match for the enticement.

With the dog occupied, he gained confidence and walked up the steps, approached the door, and turned the knob. He smiled when it opened. He loved rural living—country folks were so trusting. He noticed a Christmas tree in the corner of the room when he entered the house. There were empty boxes on the floor and couch. It appeared that the family had been decorating the tree the day before.

He heard a noise and froze as a door opened and another one shut. He took two steps and peeked down the hallway. He then crept toward the back of the house and looked into the bathroom. He saw a bra hanging on a towel holder. He opened the door across from the bathroom, but closed it when he discovered it was the children's room. He eased to the next door and listened. Nothing.

His heart was pounding against the wall of his chest as he looked back down the hallway. The dog was scratching at the front door with a quiet whine. Before the whimper turned into a bark, he twisted the knob and eased the door open. She was lying in the bed on her stomach with her face pointing in the opposite direction. Her eyes were closed but she couldn't be asleep, he thought. He knelt and waited a couple of minutes, hoping he could see her body. He could detect slight movement in the covers as she breathed. Soon she would breathe no more, he thought. But first, he had things to do to her. Things he'd fantasized about for years.

He stood up and stepped to the bed, then waited to see if she would open her eyes. The curves of her cheeks matched the curves of her body. He gently pulled the tape from his pocket and set it on the nightstand. He stared at her, drinking in her beauty. She adjusted her pillow and he watched as she opened her eyes. With the quickness of a deer, he taped her mouth shut and zip-tied her arms behind her back. She squirmed as he flipped her over and bound her feet.

He ripped the nightgown from her body. Her eyes were wide as she jerked her head from side to side. He wanted to make love to her then, but it would not be safe. He reached down to kiss her and was surprised at her strength as she struggled to break free. She managed to kick him in the stomach with her knees. He then pressed her neck into the mattress and squeezed the air passage closed. He released his grip and she tried to cough, but the tape seemed to be causing her pain. He wanted her alive until he was finished with her so he removed the tape. As he bent to kiss her, she spat in his face. His jaws tightened as raw anger surged through him. The blood vessels swelled in his neck. With one punch, she was unconscious.

He covered her with a sheet, threw her over his left shoulder, and walked down the hall. As he did, he noticed that the children's bedroom door wasn't shut. How did it open? Did it open on its own? Had he closed it? Was someone there? He began to perspire. The dog was now barking and scratching at the door. He ran out of the house with her body bouncing over his shoulder like a long, thin piece of wood. When he arrived at his car, he popped the trunk, placed her inside, and drove away.

He thought to check the police scanner app he'd downloaded onto his phone. He listened to the chatter and realized that there *was* someone else in the house—someone had called 911! He pounded the steering wheel with his clenched fist and screamed. His plans had changed, and now there was only one place to go.

He drove toward the Peter Bay.

CHAPTER 1

Saturday, March 1, 2014

MEMORIES OFTEN FADED and hid in places too remote to discover without proper motivation. Sometimes a song would transport a person to a place, or to a time long gone. Or an old friend would dislodge forgotten thoughts. For Grant Hicks, walking on the same soil he walked as a child provided fertile ground for visiting his past. After all, memories were never really forgotten. They just needed a little help from time to time.

Thin cirrostratus clouds covered the sky and seemed innocuous, but Grant knew they were a precursor to the storm that would follow that night or early the next day. He'd been studying clouds lately. Not because he was interested or cared a whole lot. His motivation began with the curiosity of a child—his child. The father and son walked to the field and Grant picked the spot that had once been familiar. They lay down and looked skyward.

During the initial silence, Grant sought a parallel from the tiny droplets in the sky and humans. The cirrus clouds he'd noticed yesterday on the drive to Mississippi from Atlanta were harmless. They danced and invited earth's inhabitants to come out and play. But today's clouds had a warning in them, a cautionary prediction. Tomorrow would not be like today. Grant figured people were a lot like clouds. Some brought happiness, others carried caution, while still others came with darkness and fear. He was jarred back to reality by his son.

"Daddy, what's the sky look like to you?" Ladd asked.

Grant concentrated a moment and turned to him. "It looks like pizza dough spread too thin on a pan ... a blue pan ... and you can see the metal seeping through."

Shortly after their marriage, Grant and Jade had adopted Ladetrus. The child's mother (Jade's sister) and father were imprisoned over three years ago, but they'd abandoned Ladd long before that. Grant and Jade had enrolled him in an aggressive private preschool to help make up for lost time. He was now in first grade and ahead of most of his classmates.

Like many young people from small towns, Grant left after high school and vowed never to return. He'd succeeded in staying away for almost twenty years until the sickness and untimely death of an old friend brought him back to the place where he grew up. He was glad he returned because he met and fell in love with Jade Lott. He thought (and still did) that she was the kindest and most beautiful person he'd ever met.

"What if it was night, Daddy? What would the clouds look like then?"

"Hmm. I believe they'd look like white smoke from a far-off fire." Grant looked at his son. "The fire would be at the same place the treasure is. You know, at the end of the rainbow."

Ladd smiled. "I like coming here. You and your daddy used to come here and look at the sky when you were little?"

"We did indeed. He and I would lie on our backs on this very spot and look for clouds shaped like objects or animals."

Grant sat up with his hands extended behind him. Out of the corner of his eye he noticed that Ladd did likewise. For the next several minutes Grant shared memories of his childhood, with Ladd absorbing each detail. They became quiet when they heard a familiar voice calling from the top of the hill.

"Let's go, Ladd," Grant said. "Your mama's calling."

Grant walked toward the house and saw Jade standing in the backyard holding Ella Reese, their two-year-old daughter. Ladd ran ahead and picked wildflowers that had recently come to life and gave them to his mother. Grant looked to his right at the larger pasture that once held black Angus cattle, but now was spotted with wild shortleaf pines and dead sagebrush. He thought to himself that one day he'd clear the old field and replace the rusty fence. Fix it up like it used to be.

Ella Reese reached for her father when he approached.

"Hey, baby. Come to Daddy."

"Judge Eaton just called," Jade said. "He's on his way here."

"Really? I haven't seen him in a while."

"How long has he been a judge?"

"As long as I can remember. He say what he wanted?"

"No. Just said he wanted to drive over."

Growing up, Grant had always cherished the privacy of living at the end of this dirt road—now called Hicks Road. In 2010 he'd bought the place from Lewis and Ethel Seals, who'd purchased it from Grant's mom after Grant's dad died. The Seals, then in their late eighties, were allowed to remain on the property until they passed away. Following their deaths, Grant and Jade found every opportunity to visit and begin the home's restoration. They'd owned it outright for six months, but much work needed to be done.

Grant heard a truck door shut. He looked out the front window and saw that Judge Walter Eaton was still driving the same old pickup he'd had four years ago when they'd met for the first time (Grant had known *of* Eaton ever since he could remember, but had never met the man). He now watched Eaton stretch his back as the old man looked over the place. Grant opened the door and walked outside.

"Come in, Judge," Grant said with a wide grin. "Good to see you."

Eaton spit a chaw of tobacco into his left hand and tossed it underhand at least twenty feet toward the woods. Grant watched the wad of tobacco unravel as it neared the edge of the yard.

"Hello, Counselor."

They shook hands and walked to the porch. Eaton sat on an old rocking chair as Grant sat on the porch swing. The front door opened and Ladd ran to Grant for him to open a bottle of juice. After Grant handed the drink back to his son, Ladd walked back inside as if the old judge was invisible.

"He's growing, Counselor," Eaton said.

"Like a weed."

"How's he doing up north?"

Grant hid a chuckle because the judge referred to Atlanta as being up north. Eaton, like many southerners, had moved the Mason-Dixon line farther south as the years passed.

"He's doing great. In fact, he's way ahead of most of the kids in his class."

"What about the racial thing? That presenting any difficulties?"

A mixed-race child, Ladd looked more black than white. His natural father was African American. He and Jade's sister had lived together for years (in between prison terms). Jade hadn't heard from her sister in over three years, although Jade's mother used to call occasionally. When she found out that Jade and Grant had married and that he was an attorney, the request for loans had started. Grant agreed to the first five, but when he finally put his foot down, Jade's mother disowned her. She told Jade she'd gotten *above her raising*.

"None at all," Grant said. "We still get an occasional stare, but that's about it." He noticed that Eaton seemed to be in deep thought. "How have you been, Judge?"

"Other than being old as dirt, I'm getting along fairly well." Eaton pulled some tobacco out of his back pocket and reloaded. "Counselor, I need a favor."

Grant didn't respond immediately, recalling the last time the judge needed a favor. Grant had made the mistake of feeling sorry for a local man and agreed to represent him in Eaton's court (even though Grant practiced law in Georgia, he was also licensed in Mississippi). He thought that would be his only appearance in Greene County Justice Court, but he thought wrong. A few days later, Eaton sent the sheriff to instruct Grant to appear before him; the old judge had appointed him to represent Roscoe Gipson, who'd been arrested for bootlegging moonshine.

"What can I do for you, sir?"

"I guess you know about the murder of Lacy Hanna?"

"I recall from the paper that she went missing," Grant said. "In 2010?"

"December of that year. Not long after you and Jade got married, if I remember it right."

"Yep, we got married in October that year. But I haven't read anything about the Hanna case lately. Anything changed?"

"You haven't read the *Herald* this week?"

"Not yet," Grant said warily. "We don't get our paper until Saturday and we drove down here right after Ladd got out of school yesterday."

"Her body was found Tuesday," Eaton said. "At least her bones were."

"Really? Where?"

"Not far from the Chickasawhay River. About five miles south of Leakesville."

Grant watched the judge squint and spit a string of tobacco juice into the yard. He used his left hand to wipe the dribble from his chin. Grant didn't know Lacy Hanna, but he'd read about her disappearance in the *Greene County Herald,* the local weekly paper. Grant felt his stomach tighten as he wondered why Eaton was here. The judge finally turned back to Grant.

"Counselor, are you up for a case?"

Grant laughed. "A murder case? You know I'm not a criminal defense lawyer."

Eaton stood and spit again. "Son, this case—or this defendant, rather—is different." The judge paused. "Do you want to know who the defendant is?"

Grant was afraid to ask. He'd find out soon enough, he thought. But who the defendant was wouldn't matter anyway. He was *not* getting involved in a murder case.

"Sir, I'm the managing partner at my firm now. And we don't practice criminal law. I've had two criminal cases in my life and both were in your court. No offense, Judge, but a murder case is in circuit court with a real judge." In Mississippi, justice court judges weren't required to be lawyers. Even though the position was part-time, Grant had never thought to ask Eaton what else he'd done to earn a living. "Not to mention," Grant continued, "I'd be up against the State of Mississippi. I'd be way out of my league. There's no way I can help. I'm sorry."

With that, Grant walked down the steps and into the yard. The judge waited until Grant stood still before he spoke again.

"They arrested Ben Petty yesterday for the murder of Lacy Hanna."

Grant felt his knees weaken. Eaton, moving now, walked past Grant and patted him on the shoulder.

"Sleep on it, Counselor," he said matter-of-factly. "You can call me in the morning. We'll get together then and talk."

Grant watched the pickup ease up the dirt road and disappear over the hill. He then looked at the house, which he wasn't ready to enter. He turned and walked past the barn to the old pond that held many of his memories. He sat on the ground and leaned against the same old pine he'd leaned against as a child. He watched a rabbit disappear into the briars that covered the dam. Grant looked to his right and gazed at the stand of pine trees that were mere saplings the first time he saw Ben Petty.

He looked back to the pond and remembered Petty floating on a homemade raft which was built using two fifty-five gallon barrels tied together with wire. He smiled as he recalled the drums flipping Petty into the snake-infested pond. Then he was brought to the present when he heard Jade calling his name. He stood, brushed off his pants, and gazed at the house on top of the hill. Hearing his name echo off the trees reminded Grant of his mama calling him to supper and watching Petty escape undetected into the woods.

At first, Grant had felt sorry for Petty. Later, he wanted to hang out with him for the most compelling reason ever: he was told not to. Over time they'd become friends who needed each other. Of course, that friendship slowly became a memory after Petty moved away. Grant hadn't spoken to or seen him since he was a kid. He frowned as he realized he hadn't thought of Ben Petty in decades. Memories were that way sometimes, he surmised.

Jade looked at Grant when he walked into the house. "There you are," she said. "What did Judge Eaton want?"

Grant picked up Ella Reese and kissed her before turning to his wife. "An old friend needs my help."

CHAPTER 2

Sunday, March 2, 2014

GRANT AND JADE had stayed up late last night. Jade suspected something was up when she caught him on his laptop researching the Mississippi Criminal Code after the kids were put to bed. He finally told her the purpose of Judge Eaton's visit. He thought Jade would be excited about the possibility of spending more time in Greene County, but she seemed reserved. Grant had become a bit defensive as she questioned his ability to represent Ben Petty. At one o'clock in the morning she kissed him and went to bed.

The smell of coffee woke him. He'd fallen asleep on the couch and sat up to focus on the wall clock above the television. He'd managed a few hours of sleep, and he found Jade in the kitchen sitting at the table drinking a cup of brew.

"Morning, sweetie," he said as he kissed her on the cheek.

"Get any rest?" she asked.

"A little," he said. He poured his coffee and joined her at the table. "I haven't thought about Ben in years." Jade sipped from her cup and listened. "He and I spent a lot of time together. We fished in every pond and creek within miles of this place. It's amazing how someone that you spent so much time with as a child can leave your mind. Almost like they never existed."

"What are you going to do?" she asked.

"I'm not sure," he said. "What would you do?"

"I don't know. Doesn't it scare you to represent someone charged with murder?"

"Scared? No. Nervous? Yes." He sipped the coffee and winced as the java burned his tongue. "Anyway, I haven't agreed to do it yet."

Jade stood and placed a pan of cinnamon rolls in the oven. She set the timer and sat back down. "Do you think we'll ever move back here, Grant?"

He didn't answer immediately. He walked to the kitchen window and looked outside. He stared at the grass and remembered standing in the yard as a child and signaling to his sister Lauren when to stop turning the television antenna on the backside of the house. They only had three channels and when someone wanted to change stations, a team effort was required; Grant was the signal person, Lauren turned the antenna, and their dad told Grant when the picture was clear. If the weather was bad, they were forced to watch whatever channel was on at the time.

He finally turned back to Jade. "Move back here? Now *that* scares me."

• • •

Grant called Judge Eaton the next morning and was told to meet him at Ward's as soon as he could get there, after which Eaton immediately disconnected. That made Grant want to know how Eaton had gotten his phone number in the first place, since he had a private listing. But Eaton knew everyone around here and could probably find out pretty much anything he needed to know.

Grant had bought an old Jeep from a gentleman in McLain. He loved the vibration he felt when he held the ball on top of the stick shift and raised or lowered the gears in the machine. Jade didn't allow the kids to ride in the vehicle since the door windows were out and the front window had a spider web of glass (spawned by a bullet of some sort). Grant knew he should have had it fixed by now, but he kind of enjoyed having the Jeep to himself.

He pulled into the parking lot of Ward's and saw Judge Eaton standing outside. Ward's was the local morning hangout for old men who met daily to solve the world's problems, have breakfast, and drink coffee. Grant had grown to like the place too. He especially enjoyed the homemade root beer that had made the place famous. Eaton got into the Jeep and handed Grant a cup of coffee.

"Here you go, Counselor."

"Thanks, Judge. Where to?"

"Ever heard of the Peter Bay?"

"Nope. Where is it?"

"I'll show you," Eaton said, pointing toward Main Street. "Your daddy never told you about the Peter Bay?"

Grant said no and listened as Judge Eaton described the place, which was part of the Chickasawhay River swamp. As the story went, a local man hid out in the Peter Bay to avoid fighting in the Civil War and was never seen again. Legend had it that he was attacked and killed by an animal ... and the place was haunted. Stories were told of hunters seeing the ghost of the man, and hunting dogs would disappear when they ventured close.

Eaton directed Grant through town and onto Jernigan Road. Grant knew this road well because it led to the Hicks Cemetery, where Grant's dad was buried. A few miles later, the judge told him to turn onto a pipeline right-of-way which was head-high with weeds and underbrush. A distinct path had been beaten down by recent traffic.

"Lacy Hanna's remains were found here Tuesday," the judge said.

Grant glanced at Eaton. He was looking straight ahead. They could hear the tall grass rubbing underneath the Jeep as they crept to the end of the right-of-way. Grant drove the vehicle as far as he could and parked. The men stepped out of the Jeep into an area that had turned into dirt and mud due to the recent activity at the location. The judge walked in front. A limb whipped Grant across the brow, and he realized he was walking too close to the old man.

"Who found her, Judge?"

"A local fellow named Taylor Lee. He'd been trapping when he decided to walk into the hollow of a cypress tree to take a crap."

"I bet that scared the shit out of him," Grant said, smiling.

The judge didn't respond. They walked a hundred yards or so before Grant saw the yellow crime scene tape. He gazed at the scenery and was amazed at the grove of cypress, which had to be hundreds of years old. When they arrived at the tape, the judge stopped.

"That's where she was," the judge said, pointing. "Inside that cypress. The tree's been hollowed out for years. Ten men can walk into the base of it."

Grant focused on the tree. The opening at the bottom was indeed wide enough for a person to walk inside without bending. He looked up at the limbs that reached to the sky. He turned to Eaton. "What's the story on Lacy Hanna?"

"She was a good girl. Her husband, Ronnie, bought the Floyd farm in Neely. They moved here from Pascagoula. They wanted a quiet life in the country."

"After Hurricane Katrina?"

"No. They moved here in 2004. Ronnie bought two hundred acres of paper company land. He works at the shipyard and commutes to work. Lacy stayed at home and took care of their girls. They have two daughters."

Grant walked along the barrier of the tape. The judge stayed behind and waited for him as he explored the scene, which was nothing but rotting leaves and cypress knees. He walked deeper into the forest, almost out of sight of the judge, before returning.

"So how did they tie Ben Petty to the crime?" Grant asked.

"You'll need to talk to Sheriff McInnis," Eaton said. "There are no eyewitnesses as far as I know. Claim they have enough evidence to convict."

Sheriff Paul McInnis, elected in 2011, was the son of former sheriff Lauvon McInnis, a man Grant and Jade were still close to. Lauvon McInnis had been a resident of Greene Rural Nursing Center when Jade worked there as a nurse. After his son was elected sheriff, Lauvon moved in with him. His health had improved enough to no longer require constant care. And Paul's wife, also a nurse, took great care of her father-in-law.

The judge started back toward the Jeep and Grant followed. Before getting in, Eaton filled his jaw with Red Man tobacco. Grant slowly backtracked through the woods toward town. When they arrived at Ward's, Eaton looked at Grant.

"Will you take Petty's case?"

Grant sighed. "Judge, I can't. I'm not ready for a murder trial. And this one is capital murder. Ben could get the death penalty. He needs an experienced criminal attorney. I did some research last night and under Mississippi law, I'd need co-counsel who's actually defended a capital murder trial before." Grant looked toward the restaurant. Sensing Eaton wasn't going to respond, he turned back to him. "Understand?"

Eaton glanced at a man and woman who were walking toward the eatery. Then he looked at Grant. "They found a scrapbook in Ben's trailer."

"And?" Grant asked. "What does that have to do with me

taking his case?"

"The scrapbook wasn't about Ben," the judge answered.

"Well. Who was it about?"

"You."

"Me?" Grant asked. "Why would he do that?"

Eaton stepped onto the pavement and shut the Jeep's door. He then leaned into the vehicle. "Well, Counselor, you'll have to ask Petty that question."

Grant eased out of the parking lot and back onto Main Street. His gut was twisting along with the drive shaft of the old vehicle. He hated moral crossroads. He thought about his life and realized that he rarely had to make tough decisions. Oh, it was a difficult task managing a law firm with 150 lawyers and an additional 200 employees. But this was different. A life was at stake, and another life had already been extinguished. Grant looked at himself in the rearview mirror. He didn't know if the man looking back was a man of courage or a man of convenience, a man of principle or of shifting sand. Was he a rock or did he move with the wind?

He drove toward the farm knowing that he'd soon find out.

CHAPTER 3

Monday, March 3, 2014

GRANT HAD BEEN up this morning since four. What had been planned as a peaceful getaway at the farm (Grant and Jade had named their Mississippi home *the farm,* though neither had ever actually farmed), had turned into a stress-filled weekend. The couple had stayed up late again and discussed the pros and cons of Grant representing Ben Petty. Jade left it up to him in the end.

Grant put his cell phone in his pocket and stepped outside. The night sky was giving way to light as he walked toward the old barn. Thunderstorms had rolled through hours earlier and the ground was still soggy. The air was damp and cool so Grant zipped up his windbreaker. The barn, a converted chicken house, was long and thin. It was filled with rusty chicken feeders, rotted hay bales, and old lumber. Grant kept his Jeep in the building and climbed in. He didn't plan on driving anywhere, but he enjoyed sitting in the old machine.

When they were children, his sister didn't like to play outside and the boy nearest Grant's age lived too far away to visit alone.

The Peter Bay

By necessity, he had created imaginary games. They all centered around a ball of some sort. Grant's interest, like that of most boys, changed with the seasons.

He went back in time. He was playing for the New York Yankees in the World Series, which was tied three games apiece. The hated Dodgers had a three-run lead with two outs in the bottom of the ninth. Grant had morphed into Bucky Dent (he played shortstop too). He looked at the coach for the sign. Grant nodded his head and, before he stepped into the batter's box, he glanced at Randolph on third, Nettles on second, and Jackson on first. Reggie gave him a thumbs-up and a wink. Grant stepped into the box and tapped the plate with his bat and stared at Sutton on the mound.

Here it came—the bat connected with the ball on the sweet spot. The ball soared into the sky and, as Grant rounded first base, he watched it bounce into the woods. The crowd was on its feet as Randolph crossed home plate, then Nettles. Grant was running so fast that he almost caught Reggie Jackson as he rounded third. He glanced over his shoulder and stopped in his tracks: the baseball was flying back toward him! A voice from the woods screamed, "Run! Run!" Grant regained his composure and sprinted toward home plate, sliding in safely. The Yankees win! The Yankees win!

Still reminiscing, Grant watched the skinny frame walking toward him, the youngster hunched over like he was carrying a five-gallon bucket filled with water. His left arm appeared longer than his right. As he came into focus, Grant noticed his right arm was stuck in an awkward, bent position. The boy stopped near second base on the pretend field. Grant walked over to him.

"What's your name?"

"Ben Petty. Yours?"

"Grant Hicks." He looked at his new acquaintance. "How old are you?"

"They say I'm nine," Petty answered. "But I don't rightly know."

Grant frowned. "Why don't you know?"

"I just don't," he said. "How old are you?"

"I'm eight, going on nine."

"How do you know you're eight going on nine?" Petty asked.

Grant shrugged his shoulders. "I don't know. Mama and Daddy told me, I guess."

"Well I ain't got no mama and daddy to tell me, so I don't rightly know." Petty looked toward the house. "You live here?"

"Yeah," Grant said as he looked toward the house, then back toward the woods. "Where'd you come from?"

"I was exploring and saw you playing."

"Do you want to play ball?" Grant asked.

Petty looked at his right arm. "Can't. Arm's kinda messed up." He looked back at Grant. "Want to go exploring?"

"I can't. Mama won't let me." He pointed at Petty's arm. "Why's your arm that-a-way?"

Petty held up his right limb. Grant grimaced as he took a good look—the arm was bent at the elbow, and he couldn't fold it. Petty dropped his arm to his side and looked at Grant. "They say my daddy did this when he killed my mama."

• • •

Grant walked into the house holding his shoes. Jade and the kids were still asleep and he didn't want to wake them. He sat on the couch and looked around the living room. The knotty-pine paneled walls were dark and made the room feel small. He looked at the television in the corner and thought about turning it on. He pondered how quiet the place was. He couldn't even hear the second hand of a clock or the chirping of a bird from the branches of the large red oaks in the yard.

Grant smiled as he remembered the quietest place he'd ever

been. It was at Big Creek Baptist Church when he was a kid. At the end of his sermon, the preacher called on Dewey Coleman to pray. Coleman was at least eighty and sound asleep. Grant's family was sitting behind the Colemans and the preacher didn't know the old man was snoozing. Grant had noticed that nobody else knew Coleman was asleep either; every head was bowed and every eye was closed. He tried tapping Coleman but that didn't work, so he nudged Mrs. Coleman. She looked at her husband and then launched into the first prayer a woman had ever prayed at Big Creek Baptist Church. Today, women prayed there all the time. Mrs. Coleman was a pioneer, Grant knew, and her legend began all because the preacher had bored her husband to sleep.

Grant snapped out of the daydream when Jade walked in and joined him on the couch. She leaned her head on his shoulder. He stroked her hair and gently kissed her head. She sat up straight and looked into his eyes.

"I'm going to take the case," he said.

She leaned her head back on his shoulder. "I know."

• • •

Grant walked into the sheriff's office at 8:00 a.m. He found a group of police officers surrounding an attractive female dispatcher. He stood at the window waiting for someone to notice him. No one did, so he leaned over and spoke into the small opening at the bottom of the plexiglass.

"Is Sheriff McInnis in?" he asked.

The dispatcher told the deputies to scram and turned to Grant. "Who wants to know?"

"Grant Hicks."

"Oh," she said. "I've heard of you. My daddy went to school with you." Grant didn't respond, suddenly busy subtracting her estimated age from his. "Daddy's name is Stewart Sisco."

"Yeah. I remember him. Couple grades ahead of me." Grant smiled, relieved that perhaps he wasn't quite old enough to have a daughter her age. "He must have been a young father."

"Sixteen when he got Momma pregnant. I'm twenty-seven, in case you're wondering." She winked. "Name's Heather Sisco."

"Nice to meet you. Is the sheriff in?"

"He's in his office." She pressed a button beneath the counter, and the door buzzed and unlocked at the same time.

Grant followed the dispatcher down the hallway, trying not to watch her from behind. She wore heels with form-fitting, designer jeans. The shirt was tight and emphasized the appropriate places of her figure. Before he could look up, she'd turned to him and smiled. His face glowed red—they both knew she'd caught him.

Sisco opened the door. "Sheriff, you have company."

She stepped aside and Grant walked into the office. He'd met Paul McInnis four years ago during a visit to the nursing home to see Lauvon. Grant recalled how excited the former sheriff was when he revealed that his son would be a candidate for the office. The father and son struck Grant as very close.

"Hey, man," the younger McInnis said. "Come on in."

"Hey, Sheriff." They shook hands. "How are you? And how's your dad?"

"I'm good, and he's well." McInnis smiled. "He has a scanner at home so he can make sure I'm doing things right around here."

"How do you like being the high sheriff?"

"It has its ups and downs, but most days I love it. Have a seat."

Grant sat down and looked around the office. McInnis's digs were plain: no pictures, and several empty frames leaned against the wall waiting for photographs. McInnis was in his late thirties and even though he wasn't in the military, he wore his hair like a drill sergeant.

"Sheriff, how's Ben Petty?"

"Hasn't said a word. Just sits there."

"Has he had his initial appearance?"

"Yep. Friday. He appeared before Justice Court Judge Darryl Puckett. No bond since it's capital."

"Can I see him?"

McInnis raised an eyebrow. "You representing him?"

"Maybe. I need to talk to him first."

The sheriff stood. "Let me see if he wants to talk to you. I'll be right back." Two minutes later Sheriff McInnis stuck his head inside the door. "Follow me." Grant walked behind the sheriff and into a room with a steel door. "Y'all have five minutes."

The furniture was metal and anchored to the walls and floor. Petty was skin and bones and dressed in an orange jumpsuit at least three sizes too big. When the sheriff slammed the door, Grant jumped slightly. He took the measure of Petty, who was staring back. He'd lost most of his hair and his face was pocked like it had been beaten with a meat tenderizer. His ankles were cuffed and locked to the table legs, his left arm cuffed to his chair. His right arm hung and was as bent as Grant remembered.

"Hey, Ben." Grant waited for a response but none came. "We don't have long, so I'll get to the point. Do you want me to represent you?"

Petty didn't respond verbally but nodded his head yes.

"Okay. I'll make an entry of appearance when I leave here. Do you want to talk more now or later?"

Petty stared. Grant knew the five minutes was bleeding fast. He looked at his wrist but no watch was there (he never wore a watch, and he often wondered why he looked at his wrist as if he did). He felt his pocket for his cell phone, but he'd left it with the dispatcher. Grant stared back at Petty. Still nothing.

"Look, Ben, you're going to have to talk to me. Okay?"

A knock sounded at the door. The muffled voice of the sheriff said, "Two minutes."

Grant wondered what to ask next. He'd never done this before. "Ben, where were you when Lacy Hanna disappeared on December 13, 2010?"

Petty was staring at the table now. Still silent.

"Ben, do you realize that they're going to ask for the death penalty? Do you?"

Petty looked at Grant briefly, then turned away.

Grant stood. "I'll be back in a few days. And if you don't talk to me then, I'll have to withdraw as your attorney. Understand?"

Grant watched the crooked Adam's apple move up and down Petty's skinny neck as if he was swallowing something too large for his throat. Petty made eye contact and whispered, "I didn't kill Mrs. Hanna."

Grant stepped close and placed his hand on Petty's right shoulder. "I believe you." He tapped on the door to let the sheriff know that he was finished. He turned to Petty before he left. "I'll see you in a few days."

・・・

On the ride back to Atlanta, Grant and Jade discussed the logistics required for Grant to represent his new client. He'd meet with the firm's partners tomorrow and work out the details, which included temporarily stepping aside as managing partner of Rimes & Yancey. He figured the trial would be late summer or early fall. Mississippi's elections were next year and both the district attorney and sheriff would want a quick conviction.

Grant saw that Jade finally seemed excited that she'd get to spend more time in Greene County. Her grandmother, Lillie Lott, was a resident at the nursing home where Jade worked when she lived in Leakesville. And Jade's best friend, Edwina McSwain, still worked there. For his part, Grant was happy that he'd get to spend more time at the farm. He looked forward to fishing with Ladd at the old pond and taking Ella Reese to Big Creek to play in the shallow stream.

Grant worried, though, when he thought of Petty. He wondered if he was prepared for a murder trial—a capital murder trial. He looked out the window and frowned. He knew damn well he wasn't.

CHAPTER 4

Monday, March 10, 2014

GRANT AND JADE had no choice but to cancel their spring break reservations for Destin, Florida, as Grant's new client required his presence in Greene County. He'd spent last week researching Mississippi law and its requirements to qualify as capital defense counsel; other than being licensed in Mississippi, he met none of them. He'd filed an entry of appearance as Ben Petty's attorney over a week ago, and the preliminary hearing was scheduled for this morning. The circuit clerk had called Grant and informed him that the judge wanted to meet with him and the district attorney prior to the hearing.

Grant parked in front of the courthouse and paused before he opened the door to his Range Rover. He'd bought the vehicle for Jade for Christmas, but she didn't like driving it (especially since Grant had previously bought one for his long-time ex-girlfriend). He exhaled, opened the door, and stepped onto the pavement. He walked toward the front steps and looked up at the clock on top of the courthouse, which still wasn't working. Grant recalled that it had been nine o'clock since he was a kid.

He opened the door to the circuit clerk's office and walked in to find a woman who looked about forty. She glanced at her watch and smiled. "You're early, Mr. Hicks."

Grant offered his hand. "You obviously know who I am. And you are?"

She shook his hand. "Pertina Burnett, the circuit clerk. I was at a conference when you came in and filed your entry of appearance the other day. Judge Riley will be here in a minute. Want some coffee?"

"Yes. Thank you."

Burnett poured Grant a cup and directed him to her personal office, which was in the rear, while she attended to a young attorney who'd come in to file a lawsuit. Grant noticed that in contrast to Sheriff McInnis, Burnett had pictures on every wall and shelf. He began to look at each picture, but didn't get to gaze long.

"What in the hell are you doing with my cup?" a female voice demanded.

Grant turned to find an older woman standing in the doorway. She wasn't smiling, and her eyes were deep blue and staring hard at Grant. She had gray, shoulder-length hair.

"Excuse me?" Grant glanced at the robe hanging over her left arm. "Judge Riley?"

The judge looked athletic and Grant hoped she was a runner. He liked to run, and maybe a bond could be forged. She didn't answer his question, though, and barked in the direction of the clerk.

"Pertina, why does he have my Dale Earnhardt cup?" Burnett walked in with another cup of coffee and extended it to the judge. Riley took it and looked at Grant. "Don't use my cup again, Mr. Hicks."

Caught off guard, Grant started to explain that he didn't choose the cup, but decided to let it go. He remembered that his stepdad recently retired from Hendrick Motorsports—he and Grant's mom lived in Charlotte, North Carolina. Now wasn't the time to say so, however. He might mention it later to curry a small measure of favor, if that was possible, but his first impression was that it would do no good. Riley appeared to be tough and to the point.

"I won't, Your Honor."

She sat behind Burnett's desk. "Sit down."

"Thank you, Judge."

Riley was wearing khaki pants, flats, and a white, buttoned shirt. Grant noticed a wedding ring but no other jewelry. She leaned back in Burnett's chair and propped her feet on the desk, but before she and Grant could establish a conversation a young man with dark brown hair entered the room. He was dressed in a tailored, gray suit with a green tie. Grant noticed the cufflinks and matching pocket square.

"Morning, Judge, I brought some doughnuts. Want one?"

"You know I don't eat that crap," she said. "Meet Grant Hicks. The newest member of the Greene County bar."

He smiled at Grant. "Troy Lee," he said while shaking Grant's hand. "I'm the district attorney. Good to meet you."

"Nice to meet you, too."

Grant had to admit that Troy Lee was impressive and was surprised at how young he looked. He had green eyes and just a trace of gray in his hair.

"The purpose of this meeting is to discuss the obvious," Riley said. She stared at Grant. "Mr. Hicks, I'm sure you're a hell of a lawyer. But my law clerk tells me you have zero experience in a criminal courtroom in Mississippi. Is that true?"

"Yes, ma'am."

"Ma'am is not required unless we're in the courtroom," she said. "Mr. Hicks, Mississippi requires at least two attorneys to defend a capital murder charge and at least one has to have some capital murder experience. So who'll help you?"

Grant had no clue. He looked at Lee for help. The young district attorney seemed to read his mind. "Judge, George Brewer meets the qualifications."

"Are you kidding me, Troy?" she asked. "No-show George? Is he on or off the wagon now?"

"Judge, I think he got saved again and stopped drinking."

"When was the last time he tried a capital case?" Riley asked.

"I'm not sure," Lee said. "Been a while."

Riley turned back to Grant. "Do you know George?"

Grant *had* met George Brewer. He was giving Edwina McSwain, a volunteer firefighter, a ride to a fire back in 2010 because she didn't have a car—she had jumped in Grant's vehicle and directed him to the fire station. The fire truck was pulling out as they arrived, so they followed behind. As the truck slowed at a four-way stop, Brewer had jumped on. The truck bounced across the Chickasawhay River bridge and Grant was worried that Brewer would fall; a mile later the truck made a sharp left turn and Grant's concern became a reality. He and Edwina watched Brewer roll down a hill and into a ditch. They were the only folks who stopped to help the poor man, and Grant still remembered the sweaty alcohol smell on Brewer when they helped him off the ground.

"I've met him once," Grant said, making sure to go to his poker face.

Judge Riley looked at Lee. "Troy, I'm delaying the preliminary hearing till Friday at one-thirty." She turned to Grant. "Go find George, Mr. Hicks. You have until Friday to associate co-counsel. If you show up alone, I'm removing you as attorney and appointing the Office of Capital Defense in Jackson. Got it?"

"Yes, ma'am."

"I told you to not say ma'am unless we're in the courtroom."

Riley stood, but she continued to stare at Grant and pointed at the door. "Now go wash my cup."

• • •

Grant left the clerk's office relieved that the preliminary hearing was delayed until Friday. He walked through the bank's parking lot to George Brewer's law office. The brick building looked as if it had been built in the late 1960s or early 70s. The office shared parking space with the local bank, so Grant had no idea if one of the vehicles belonged to Brewer. He opened the front door and walked down a narrow hall. A small, engraved sign by the door at the end of the hall read: *Attorney at Law*.

Grant passed a wall-mounted water fountain with dust on the surface that had turned into dull, gray rolls of dirt. The interior walls were made of concrete blocks and were painted a pale green. Grant figured the color was the same in an insane asylum. When he arrived at the door he looked at the golden knob (which appeared new). The door, though, was old, cheap, and hollow, and a hole the size of the tip of a shoe was near the bottom.

He opened the door and walked into the waiting area. There was no computer on the desk, but an old electric typewriter was buried by stacks of deeds and other legal documents. Grant attempted to ring a bell that sat on the desk, but his first effort produced no sound. He kept working the bell until a ding drifted through the office. Nobody came.

Grant looked to his right and noticed a small library. He walked into the room and found the smell of old books pleasant. He picked up a small picture from one of the shelves. A younger, thinner version of Brewer was standing in line with a group of local officials, each wearing a hard hat and holding a shovel as they broke ground for what was to become the county health department. He heard the front door open, so he stepped back into the waiting area and sat down.

Loud lopsided steps clicked toward the door. Brewer stepped in holding a device which was shaped like a bazooka and made from plastic pipe. He was dressed in camouflage and appeared to have shaved but had missed several spots on his neck.

Grant extended his hand. "Mr. Brewer, I don't know if you remember me, but I'm Grant Hicks."

Brewer tossed some mail on the desk and shook Grant's hand. "I remember you. Thanks for taking me to get patched up when I fell off the fire truck a few years ago."

Grant relaxed. "Oh, you're welcome."

"Come on back," Brewer said.

Grant followed him down a narrow hall which opened into a larger office. The floor was covered with matted-down shag carpet. The desk was large and Grant wondered how it had fit through the door and hallway. Brewer sat in an old wooden chair which squeaked as his weight settled. On the wall behind the desk were framed pictures of him presenting checks to clients. Brewer noticed Grant looking and turned to the wall.

"Made a hell of a lot of money in this office," he said.

"I see that. Impressive."

Brewer looked back at Grant. "I know you're not here to visit, Mr. Hicks, so what's on your mind?"

"I don't know if you know, but I'm representing Ben Petty."

"This is Leakesville," he said. "Everybody knows."

Grant slid up to the corner of his chair. "I need co-counsel."

"And?"

"Your name was suggested to me."

"By who?"

"The district attorney," Grant said. "And Judge Riley encouraged me to ask you."

The bell rang at the front desk but Brewer ignored it. "What do you know about defending a capital murder charge, Mr. Hicks?"

"Please call me Grant." The bell rang again. Grant pointed

toward the door. "Do you need to see who that is?"

"No. If it's important they'll walk on back," Brewer said. He leaned up in his chair and placed his folded hands in front of him on his desk. "I haven't tried a capital murder case in fifteen years. I don't believe I can help you."

Grant looked again at the smiling clients in the pictures along the walls. "Apparently, you're a hell of a lawyer."

"Was, Grant. I *was* a hell of a lawyer. Not anymore." He stood. "Can't help you. Sorry."

Grant stood. "Well, thanks for talking to me." He looked at the plastic bazooka-looking device leaning against the wall. "By the way, what is that thing?"

Brewer finally smiled. "Technically, it's a potato shooter. But for me, it's also payment for legal services rendered." He reached to shake Grant's hand. "I know you didn't come here for advice, but I'm going to give you some anyway. Withdraw from Petty's case and take that pretty wife of yours back to Atlanta. Don't get sucked back into this place. I believe if your daddy were here, he'd tell you the same thing."

Grant walked backed to his vehicle ignoring folks who waved or said hello. He hadn't thought of what his dad would have told him or what advice he would have offered if he were alive. Grant still carried the guilt borne of youthful pride and arrogance. His dad, Michael Hicks, had refused to represent Grant's high school friend, Brandon Smallwood, who'd also been charged with capital murder. Smallwood was ultimately convicted and spent most of his short life in prison for a crime he didn't commit. Grant's father committed suicide a few years after the conviction, and Grant was so angry that he didn't even return home for the funeral. Ironically, it was Brandon Smallwood who helped Grant let go of the past. Grant wished many times that he could have forgiven his dad before his childhood hero ended his life.

The ride back to the farm was a blur. Grant's mind often

wandered as he drove; he'd sometimes drive for miles and not remember where'd he'd been. He slowed as he approached the house. He had three days to associate co-counsel. If he didn't succeed, at least he could say that he tried. Perhaps, he thought, as he looked at himself in the rearview mirror, Ben Petty would be better off if he failed.

CHAPTER 5

Thursday, March 13, 2014

FOUR YEARS AGO, on the first night after Grant finally returned to Greene County after being away since high school, an old preacher named Reverend Lollis Clark took him to supper at Rocky Creek Catfish Cottage. The restaurant was located between Leakesville and Lucedale and attracted folks from miles around. Tonight, Jade and her friend Edwina had planned a night of food and fellowship, Mississippi style. Edwina's aunt had agreed to watch Ladd and Ella Reese for the evening, and Grant admitted to himself that he was looking forward to visiting the place that had become a weekly ritual for many.

On the twenty-minute ride to Rocky Creek, Grant listened as Edwina caught Jade up on the nursing home gossip. Grant wondered to himself, once again, how Jade and Edwina had become so close. They appeared to be opposites. Jade was white, small, quiet, and found the best in the worst of folks. Edwina was black, on the large side, loud, and found the worst in the best of everyone. But the two friends were drawn to one another, and their mutual love was not in question.

Grant noticed the parking lot was full and that cars were spilling out into the highway. Edwina leaned between the seats. "These fools still ain't figured out the new parking lot."

"New parking lot?" Grant asked, pulling into the church lot across the road to allow the cars to settle in and to avoid getting rear-ended.

"Yeah, they painted the lines different and it's caused holy hell." She pointed across the highway as two cars entered the wrong way. "Oh shit!"

Edwina flung open the door and darted across the road. Grant and Jade laughed as she opened the driver's side door of an old Ford and an elderly gentleman stepped out after a brief burst of conversation. Edwina got in and drove the car to an empty spot. She then motioned for Grant to drive over.

"Classic Edwina," Jade said with a big grin. "Taking control."

"She's gonna get jumped on one of these days," Grant said. "I'd hate to see her turned loose in Atlanta."

Jade put her hand on Grant's. "I don't believe Atlanta could handle Edwina."

A young hostess led them to their table, which was in the back of the restaurant. Grant noticed several familiar faces and nodded at a man he remembered meeting at the barber shop on his last visit to Greene County. They sat down and a waitress took their drink orders.

"Grant, I hear you're representing Ben Petty," Edwina said.

"It's true. At least for the moment I am. Judge Riley may remove me tomorrow."

"Why would the judge remove you?" Jade asked.

"In Mississippi, two attorneys are required when the death penalty is on the table. And one has to have tried a capital case before. Right now, it's just me, and I haven't."

The waitress brought their drinks and took their orders. Jade looked at Edwina. "Do you know Ben Petty?"

"No," she said. "But I don't have to know him. He's guilty as hell."

"Why do you say that?" Grant asked. "Innocent until proven guilty, you know."

Edwina smirked. "He's guilty alright. Word on the street is he's some kinda pervert."

"Where'd you hear that?"

"Everybody says that," Edwina said, "and everybody at the fire department believes he did it, too."

The waitress brought hush puppies and coleslaw. Edwina dove in first. Grant remembered the first time he'd met Edwina. She'd invited herself to sit in his Porsche. When the fire alarm sounded in town, the next thing he knew he was driving her to the fire station. Grant wondered how the department let her volunteer when she had no car and didn't have a driver's license, but both of those problems had been corrected. She was now the proud owner of a maroon 1988 Oldsmobile Cutlass Supreme with mag wheels.

"Since you have your license now, do they let you drive the fire truck?" Jade asked.

Edwina swallowed and frowned. "Not yet. That damn fire chief always beats me to the truck. One of these days I'm gonna get there first. And when I do, Edwina will show those men how to get to a fire."

"By the way, Edwina," Grant said, wishing to change the subject, "how's Pete Ball?"

Grant had known of the locally famous Pete Ball most of his life. Pete, who managed to appear when you least expected him, was rail thin, at least sixty, and cross-eyed. Most people thought Pete a bit slow, but Grant knew him to have the mind of an elephant. He didn't forget a name or a conversation.

Edwina grinned, showing her two new, golden front teeth. "That fool still crazy," she said. "Last year they locked him up for trespassing or some country shit."

"Pete seems so innocent," Jade said. Grant looked at Jade and saw the worry on her face. "What happened to him?"

"They let his skinny ass out and dismissed the charges," Edwina said. "He was in there snitching on the real criminals so much the crooks threatened to kill him. The po-po were tired of refereeing. So they let him go. But that crazy fool wouldn't leave till he ate supper that night. Claimed it was his constitutional right." The catfish had arrived, and Edwina stuck a whole fillet in her mouth and looked at Grant. "Only constitutional right that white man has is to be crazy."

Grant's phone vibrated in his pocket. He pulled it out and answered the call.

"Counselor, Walter Eaton here. Can you run over to the house?"

"Sure, Judge. But we're eating right now." Grant glanced at his watchless arm. "An hour?"

The judge gave him directions and hung up the phone. After supper, Grant dropped the ladies at Edwina's house and drove the eight miles toward Sand Hill to Eaton's house. Grant thought about the earlier conversation with Edwina regarding Petty. Why would she say he was a pervert? And why did everyone think the man was guilty? Grant had practiced law for sixteen years, and he was a successful civil litigator. But this was his first venture into the criminal world. Did people really believe *innocent until proven guilty?* Or had that become a fiction—had the statement turned into a unicorn? He turned on his blinker, still not sure what he'd gotten himself into. Perhaps, he thought, he'd find out soon.

• • •

Judge Eaton's directions were easy to follow: Seven and a half miles from the Piggly Wiggly to Crooked Creek Road, turn right. Drive half a mile until the road dead-ends. Grant dimmed his lights when he saw two men sitting in lawn chairs shielding their eyes with their arms. He turned the engine off and walked toward them. The SUV's lights went out as Grant approached. He slowed his pace. Thick darkness enclosed him.

"Have a seat, Counselor," Eaton said.

Grant could see the ember of a cigarette burning as it arced toward the mouth of the unidentified man. The tip turned bright red as the fellow sucked the nicotine through the filter. The man's face glowed and Grant noticed he was wearing a cowboy hat. Grant turned toward Eaton but could barely make out his silhouette.

"Hey, Judge," Grant said, after taking a folding chair. "What's up?"

"Counselor, I want you to meet somebody," Eaton said. "He's going to help you on Ben's case."

Grant turned toward the cigarette. "And you are?"

"Mortimer Evans is the name," a man said in a gravelly voice. "But folks call me Mordiky."

"Nice to meet you." Grant looked back at Eaton. "Judge, how do you suppose Mordiky can help?"

"Tell him, Mordiky."

Mordiky thumped the still-burning cigarette into the yard. "I'm an investigator. Well, a retired investigator, rather. Walter called me and asked me to offer my assistance. So here I am."

Grant leaned back in his chair. He was finally able to relax now that the man's identity was revealed. "What type of investigator are you?"

"Spent thirty years working for the district attorney's office in Hattiesburg," he said. "Took retirement and moved to Perry County. Did some private investigating for a few years." He paused and lit another cigarette. Grant could hear him inhale and watched the smoke exit his nose and mouth. "Turned sixty-five last year and was planning on staying retired until Walter called."

"Mordiky's the best around," Eaton said.

"How much do you charge?" Grant asked. "Petty has no money. This is pro bono for me. There has to be another lawyer on the case and that will cost the county. I guess I could ask Judge Riley to order the county to pay you."

"Won't be a charge," Mordiky said as he stood. "I got to go. The old lady may think I have a girlfriend."

Grant stood and shook his hand. Mordiky's hand was rough and firm. "By the way, if you see me on the street, introduce yourself because I have no clue what you look like."

"You'll recognize me," Mordiky said as he walked to his pickup.

Eaton waited until the sound of the truck faded. "Mordiky and I go way back. He'll be at the preliminary hearing tomorrow."

"I can use all the help I can get, Judge," Grant said. "But I'm not sure I'll be on the case after tomorrow. Judge Riley told me to show up with co-counsel. The DA suggested George Brewer but he refused."

Eaton stood. "George will be there tomorrow too. I had him out here earlier."

"How did you pull that off?"

"I've been Justice Court judge going on forty years, Counselor. Lots of folks owe me favors. Especially George." Eaton started walking toward his house. "Get some rest."

Grant drove back to town and picked up Jade and the kids from Edwina's and headed to the farm. While Jade was getting Ladd and Ella Reese ready for bed, Grant walked outside and sat on the steps. He wasn't much of a television person and found himself sitting on the porch most nights while Jade and the kids prepared for bed. Some nights, after everyone was asleep, he'd sit on the porch and listen to the sounds of the country. Tonight, he could hear crickets chirping nearby. An owl screeched in the distance. He looked in the direction of the sound and wondered in what kind of tree the wise bird was perched. Probably an oak, he thought. He listened harder. Again, the owl spoke.

Grant's thoughts turned to Ben Petty and tomorrow's hearing. He wondered if Petty was asleep. Or, was Petty awake and listening? And if he was, what was he hearing?

CHAPTER 6

Friday, March 14, 2014

GRANT COULD HEAR the rain dripping off the roof and onto what sounded like metal, or perhaps an aluminum can. He made a mental note to move whatever the object was before the next rainfall. If he didn't he would forget, and then he would remember again the next time it rained and he was lying in bed listening to the annoying sound.

Jade had snuggled close to him and was still asleep. He opened his eyes and watched her. She was so beautiful. Her long eyelashes curled upward and her face was smooth as talcum powder. She had light, almost invisible freckles on her forehead. She'd be forty in a few months, but she looked not a day older than thirty. Her left leg was thrown over his and he reached beneath the covers and felt her skin. He touched her panties, then eased a finger underneath the silk garment. She slowly removed her leg and rolled onto her back. He watched her a few moments before he gently pulled the covers back and removed her panties. She reached for him and pulled him onto her body. He buried his face in her hair, which was spread across the pillow, as he moved with the rhythm of the dripping rain. He loved how she smelled, how she felt. Grant hoped the day would end as well as it had begun.

• • •

After Grant and Ben Petty first met, they began to sneak off and play together. The only rule was that Grant had to be close enough to hear his mama or sister yell if they were looking for him. That rule stayed in place the first couple of times they played. As with most rules, though, they were often bent or broken.

"You ever seen a nekkid woman?" Petty asked.

"Yeah," Grant said. "I've seen my mama by accident one time, and my sister."

"They don't count," Petty said. "They your kin. I mean a real nekkid woman?"

Grant concentrated hard, hoping he could remember a time when he had. "I don't guess I have. We're too young anyway. I don't want to see no naked woman."

"Shoot, boy, you're almost ten and I'm almost eleven. That's plenty old enough. I sure would like to see my teacher, Ms. Martin, nekkid. She's a fox."

Grant looked over his shoulder to see if anyone was near. A sin of this magnitude, even just talked about, carried dire consequences if discovered. They were at their hideout in the woods, a hole they'd dug in the ground about four feet deep and just as wide. They'd covered the top with two pieces of plywood salvaged from the garbage dump. They couldn't go down in the hole today because it was still muddy from the last rainfall. They were sitting on logs chewing rabbit tobacco.

"What about you?" Grant asked. "You ever seen a naked woman?"

Petty stood and reached with his left hand to pull a piece of paper from his back pocket. He handed it to Grant. "Check this out."

Grant unfolded the page and discovered a woman lying on a bed wearing high heel shoes and nothing else. His eyes bulged.

"Wow!" he whispered. "Her jugs are huge! I didn't know they got that big."

Petty took the picture from Grant. "They ain't that big around here. This here woman's from California, probably. All the women out there have boobs like that."

"What you going to do with this?" Grant asked.

"You want it? I found a whole a magazine of nekkid women at the dump."

"No, I'd get in big trouble if I got caught with it."

Petty began to fold the centerfold. Before he could put it back in his pocket, Grant stopped him.

"Can I see it again?"

• • •

Grant walked into the sheriff's office at precisely eight o'clock. Heather Sisco, the dispatcher, saw him and buzzed him through. "You here to see Petty?"

"Yes, ma'am."

She winked at him. "Well this is your lucky day. He just happens to be here." She yelled for a deputy, who appeared a second later from the adjoining office. He led Grant down the hall and pointed at the same room he'd been when he last visited Petty.

Grant walked in and sat down. He heard a loud clanking sound, followed by chains dragging across the painted cement floor. Petty appeared to be wearing the same baggy orange jumpsuit he had on a few days ago. Grant stood as the deputy handcuffed him to a chair that was bolted to the floor before leaving the room.

"Morning, Ben."

Petty nodded.

Frustrated, Grant sighed loudly and leaned closer. "Ben, today is not the day to play the quiet game. I'll say it again: Morning, Ben."

Petty didn't respond at first, but Grant waited him out. Petty shifted in his chair. Then: "Morning."

"In a little while, the deputy will walk you over to the courthouse for your preliminary hearing. You'll get to put your regular clothes on before you go. I'll be there and George Brewer is supposed to be there too. Do you know George?"

Petty nodded no.

"He's helping me on your case," Grant said. "The judge will be there and so will the district attorney. This shouldn't take too long. The DA will have to put on enough evidence to bind you over to the grand jury. Understand that?" Petty looked puzzled so Grant continued. "You'll sit at a table with me and George. You are not to say a word. Understand?"

Petty nodded yes.

"Of course you do." Grant stood and walked to the door to let the deputy know he was finished, then turned to Petty. "I'll see you in a bit."

Grant walked to the courthouse. The parking lot was full, and he saw a car with a Hattiesburg TV station logo on the side. Somebody must have clued them in, he thought, because nobody was here on Monday when the matter was originally scheduled. He stepped into the clerk's office and was told the judge was upstairs in her chambers.

He took the elevator to the second floor where the courtroom was located. He hadn't been in the courtroom since high school and assumed it still looked the same. When he stepped off the elevator he almost ran into Sheriff McInnis.

"Sorry, Sheriff," Grant said.

"No problem. Going in to see Judge Riley?"

"I thought I'd let her know I was here."

The sheriff opened the door and showed Grant in. Riley was sitting behind her desk tossing a tennis ball into the air. Grant looked around the small room and noticed the district attorney along with two others he didn't recognize.

"Mr. Hicks, you know Troy," Riley said without preamble. "The rest of y'all introduce yourselves."

Troy Lee had on a dark gray pinstripe suit with a gold-colored tie. He introduced Grant to his female assistant district attorney, Molly London, and his investigator, Rob Woods. London had dark brown hair, green eyes, and olive skin. She appeared to have a touch of Mediterranean blood and her body seemed perfectly proportioned. Grant decided on the spot that she was the most beautiful woman he had ever seen, before correcting himself mentally for the benefit of Jade (as if she could read his mind from fifteen miles away). Grant was used to taking advantage of jurors with his physical appearance. But he realized that this case would be different—Lee looked like a Ken doll, and London would have male jurors swooning.

"Mr. Hicks, Troy says your man's guilty as hell," Riley said. "The courtroom is packed and a television crew is here. I suggest getting this over quickly."

Grant glanced at the DA before focusing on Riley. "Judge, have y'all been talking about the case without me present?"

She stopped tossing the tennis ball and looked at Grant. "Where's your co-counsel?"

"He's supposed to be here, Your Honor."

She stood, looked at her watch, and pointed at the door. "Y'all get the hell out. See you in two minutes."

Grant opened the door to the courtroom and found Petty already seated at their table. He seemed smaller to Grant. They'd removed the baggy jumpsuit, and he wore jeans and a long sleeve white shirt. His right arm looked tangled in the garment. For the first time since he took the case, Grant felt sorry for Petty. He looked past his client and noticed a large crowd of people watching the proceedings. The television camera in the corner was being operated by a short, stocky man with long sideburns and a pistol mustache. A door behind the bench opened, and the bailiff instructed everyone to rise. Judge Riley entered, sat down, and called court to order.

"Madame Clerk, call the docket."

The clerk stood. "Cause number 2014-10,012, State of Mississippi vs. Benjamin Franklin Petty!"

Grant realized he was perspiring. He pulled a handkerchief from his coat and wiped his forehead, then glanced toward the door. George Brewer was nowhere to be seen. He looked into the crowd for Mordiky Evans but realized he didn't know what the man looked like. Grant began to panic. He'd never been to a preliminary hearing, much less participated in one. He looked at Petty from the corner of his eye and saw that his client seemed more relaxed than he was.

"Call your first witness, Mr. Lee," Riley said.

"Your Honor, the state calls Sheriff Paul McInnis to the stand."

McInnis was sworn in and sat in the witness chair.

"State your name for the record," Lee said.

"Paul McInnis."

"And you're the sheriff here in Greene County?"

"Yes, sir."

"Sheriff, I'll get to the point. Describe to the judge what happened on February twenty-fifth, 2014."

Grant decided George Brewer wasn't going to show and turned his undivided attention to the witness. McInnis, with his cropped hair, reminded Grant of Sergeant Carter from *Gomer Pyle*.

"We got a call that—"

"Objection, Your Honor," Grant said standing. "Hearsay."

Riley had reading glasses on and was thumbing through a court file. She looked over the top of her spectacles at Grant. "Overruled."

"Proceed, Sheriff," Lee said.

"Well, we got a call that some bones had been found. So we responded and discovered the body of Lacy Hanna."

"Objection, Your Honor," Grant said as he jumped from his chair. His knee caught the edge of the table, and a screeching sound echoed through the courtroom. "The sheriff is not a forensic pathologist or an expert, so there's no way that he could have identified the decedent."

Riley leaned up in her chair. "Mr. Hicks, I don't permit—under any circumstances—a speaking objection. You understand me?"

"Yes, Your Honor."

She looked at the district attorney. "Proceed."

Grant hadn't moved. He waited an instant and cleared his throat. Riley looked at him. "Your Honor, you haven't ruled on my objection."

"Overruled."

The sheriff testified that he reached out to the Mississippi Bureau of Investigation, who delivered the bones of the victim to the state's crime lab in Jackson for analysis. Based on a knife found at the scene by investigator Rob Woods—a knife with Ben Petty's initials—a search warrant was obtained and executed by the sheriff. McInnis detailed the search, which included his discovery of a pair of Lacy Hanna's panties and a photo of her at Petty's trailer. Woods then took the stand and authenticated the knife and described the evidence that he believed to be related to Petty. Grant watched in disbelief as the preliminary hearing took on a life of its own. He had no strategy, no defense.

When the district attorney concluded, Judge Riley announced that Petty would be bound over to the grand jury and would remain in custody until his trial, which was set for July 7. Grant stood as Petty was led from the courtroom and back to the jail. He felt his shirt sticking to his back. He didn't turn to look at the crowd. He not only felt embarrassed and defeated, but he was angry at himself for allowing Judge Eaton to get him into this mess. He knew he never should have taken the case.

And, he was certain, every person in the courtroom knew it too.

CHAPTER 7

Friday night, March 14, 2014

GRANT SLID THE spatula underneath the last burger and removed it from the grill. The Hicks family started a Friday night tradition not long after Grant and Jade married, and Ladd looked forward to assisting Grant with grilling duty each week. The father and son used the time together to talk *man to man,* as Ladd often said.

Jade had the buns on the plates along with baked beans and chips when they walked into the kitchen. Grant had taught Ladd to eat his burger just like he did, with ketchup, mustard, and Ruffles potato chips. Ladd would watch Grant stack chips on his bottom bun. Then he'd place the burger on top of the chips before adding the condiments. Grant would smile at Ladd as they both took their first bites and laugh at how much noise they created. Jade thought they were gross.

The front door opened and Edwina stormed into the house. "I'm starving!" she called out. She grabbed a bun and began to prepare a burger.

"Help yourself, Edwina," Jade said.

"She already is, Mama," Ladd said.

Edwina pointed at the child. "You better be quiet, Ladetrus, or I'll eat *your* burger." Edwina sat at the table and looked at Grant. "Heard you pooped and fell back in it today."

"Edwina!" Jade said. "We're eating."

Grant picked up a chip and put it in his mouth. "Oh yeah? What did you hear?"

"That Troy Lee whooped your—" Edwina looked at Jade, who was staring back. She turned to Grant. "I just heard it didn't go so well."

"You heard right," he said.

"Why did you take the case anyway?" Edwina asked. "You need to plead his *tail* guilty and get back to what you know."

There was a knock at the door. Grant pushed back from the table to go see who it was. When he opened up, a slender, middle-aged man wearing an Atlanta Braves cap was on the porch with a dog on a leash.

"Hi," the man said. "My name's Paul Sumner. I'm your new neighbor."

Grant stuck out his hand. "Nice to meet you. I'm Grant Hicks. Whose house did you buy?"

"Just moved into the R.D. Lewis place. I'm renting but hoping to buy."

"That's a pretty one," Grant said. "Want to come in?"

"I can't. This dog strayed up last night, and I was wondering if he was yours."

Grant looked down. "I believe that's the ugliest dog I've ever seen."

Sumner laughed. "He's not the prettiest I've ever seen, either."

Ladd ran to the door the second he heard the word *dog*. He squeezed between Grant's leg and the door to pet the pooch. "Can we keep him, Daddy?" he asked. "Please?"

"No. We have to go back to Atlanta on Sunday."

"But you said I could get another dog since Max died," Ladd begged. "Please?"

By this time, Jade and Edwina were lobbying for the dog, which had wild white hair and orange spots on his back. Grant looked into Jade's eyes, let out a deep breath, and reached for the leash. "Thanks, neighbor."

Sumner appeared relieved to unload the dog. Before he left, Jade insisted that he join them for supper the next time they were in town. He accepted her invitation, then walked to his car and drove away. Ella Reese started crying so Edwina walked back inside to check on her while Jade scurried to fix their new dog a plate of food.

Grant looked at Ladd. "What are you going to name him?"

Ladd smiled. "His name is Wolf."

• • •

Not long after light had given way to darkness and Edwina had departed, Grant's phone rang. He answered it with his usual greeting. "Grant Hicks speaking."

"Mordiky here. Can you talk?"

"Sure. Where are you?"

"I'm at this little store not far from your place."

Grant gave him directions and then informed Jade that company was coming. Ladd was watching television while Ella Reese played with toys on the floor, and a few minutes later Wolf began to bark. Grant eased to the door and watched the approaching lights, which created moving shadows in the yard. He walked outside.

"Howdy, Grant," Mordiky said, as he shut the door to his pickup.

"Hey, Mordiky. Where were you this morning?"

"I was there."

Grant hoped Mordiky couldn't read his expression and

changed the subject. "What's on your mind?"

"Did a little snooping today. I know the DA's investigator, Rob Woods, pretty well. He's a straight shooter but tends to get lazy at times."

"Find out anything?"

"Woods didn't tell me a lot but he seems confident. He was surprised I was working on the case. Said they assumed it would be turned over to the public defender."

Grant watched Wolf sniff the left front tire of Mordiky's truck before he marked his new territory. "As you saw, today didn't go well. And I've visited with my client two times already—he's said less than ten words. Case is going south in a hurry."

Mordiky shifted his weight. When he did, the nightlight in the yard showed his face. His skin was weathered with deep creases in his cheeks. His nose was slender, which made his eyes appear too far apart.

"Woods says they got an eyewitness."

"An eyewitness?" Grant asked. "They didn't say anything about one today. What did he tell you?"

"Apparently, Lacy Hanna's niece was there when she was abducted."

"Really? What's her name? How old is she?"

"Think she's ten now. Don't know her name. But she would've been six or seven at the time, I guess."

"Can I talk to her?" Grant began to pace. "Hell, Mordiky, I don't know all the rules of criminal procedure yet, but I seemed to remember reading that I could talk to the state's witnesses. Do you know if I can?"

"Grant, I ain't no lawyer. Why don't you ask George Brewer?"

"He didn't show today. And if I could find him, I'd kick his fat ass."

Grant heard a clicking sound and turned toward the truck. The passenger's door opened and a man stumbled out. Grant squinted as the breathing got closer. He could see a drink of some sort in the man's left hand. When the light hit his face, Grant recognized Brewer, who was obviously drunk.

"Well here I am, city boy. Come whip my fat ass!"

CHAPTER 8

Saturday, March 15, 2014

SATURDAY MORNING WAS the busiest time of the week in Leakesville, but this particular Saturday the town seemed quiet. Grant had agreed to meet with Mordiky and Brewer at ten. He was early and decided to stop by Ward's for a cup of coffee—the morning regulars would be long gone, but Grant hoped he'd pick up some gossip about the Petty case.

He walked in and noticed a group of men sitting at three tables, with one fellow on his feet and explaining some paperwork. Grant didn't recognize them, but he chose a table close enough to eavesdrop anyway. The man, as it turned out, was going over the rules for visiting a prison. Grant watched him pull a box off the floor and place it on a table before handing out small Bibles to the others. Grant remembered receiving a little red Bible when he was in the fifth grade—these men were Gideons.

Grant pulled his phone from his pocket and opened his Twitter account to catch up on the news. There would be no gossip from these fellows, he thought, so he might as well see what was happening in the wide, wide world beyond Leakesville.

"Excuse me, sir," the man said. "Would you like a Bible?"

Grant looked up. Up close, the leader appeared to be in his early seventies, with slick white hair that was parted deeply on the side. Grant looked at the New Testament extended in his direction.

"No thank you, sir," Grant said. "I have several at home. But I'm sure you can use it at the prison."

"Do you live here?"

"No sir. How about you?"

"I'm from Hattiesburg. We're on our way to distribute Bibles at the correctional institution." The smile vanished from the man's face. The other men had taken their allotment of Bibles and were walking toward their vehicles. "Are you a Christian, young man?"

Grant's first thought was that it wasn't this man's business. But he didn't want to be rude. Grant looked toward the parking lot and was relieved to see Pete Ball walking up Main Street in their direction. Pete was waving at each car that passed. Grant pointed at Pete. "You see that man coming there?"

The man looked toward Pete. "Yes."

"I'm not sure if he's a Christian. You might want to talk to him."

The man set a Bible on Grant's table and caught Pete before he could enter the restaurant. Grant was grateful for the diversion. He left the New Testament and half-empty coffee cup behind and disappeared while the visitor attempted to save Pete's soul.

· · ·

Grant opened the door to Brewer's office and walked inside. He was relieved to see Brewer and Mordiky sitting in the conference room. "Great. Y'all both showed up."

"Don't be a smartass," Brewer said.

"The purpose of this meeting is to make sure we're on the same page," Mordiky said.

Grant nodded. "Sounds good to me."

"What's your schedule?" Mordiky asked. "How often will you be here in Mississippi?"

"I'll go back to Atlanta tomorrow," Grant said. "My son's in school and he doesn't get out until late May. I'll be taking a leave of absence from work. We plan to spend most of the summer here. What about you, Mordiky?"

"I should be able to commit a day a week for now," he answered. "But since our client's life is on the line, I'm not taking on any new projects until this is over. I should be able to commit most of June." Mordiky pulled a calendar from his briefcase and looked at Grant. "What's the trial date?"

"July seventh," Grant said. "Exactly 114 days." He turned to Brewer. "How about you, George? What's your schedule look like?"

"I'm on an as-needed basis," Brewer said. "I agreed to do this as a favor to Judge Eaton so you wouldn't get kicked off the case. I'll be with you at trial and at the place where this thing will be won or lost: the jury selection process."

Mordiky put his calendar away and looked at Grant. "What's your strategy?"

"I'm not sure yet," Grant said. "Ben said he didn't do it and although it looks like he did, I believe him. He seems sincere." Grant paused but neither man spoke. "I'm going to file my discovery motion next week to see what the state has. When I get it, we'll talk to everybody that'll testify."

Brewer had laced his hands behind the back of his head and leaned back in his chair. "Grant, you worry about the technicalities. I haven't tried a case in years, so you try the case." He paused, letting this sink in. "I know the people that live here. The community will talk big and act like Petty's guilty. But once they take that juror's oath, they'll get serious. All we need is one person who believes Petty's innocent, or at least has reasonable doubt as to his guilt, and Petty will live to fight another day."

The men stood. Mordiky reached for a satchel. "Here, Grant, I almost forgot. This is a picture of the Hanna family, which was taken a month before Mrs. Hanna went missing." While Grant was looking at the picture, Mordiky went through his briefcase and dug out another photo. "And this is the niece that Woods claims is the state's eyewitness."

Grant looked at the family portrait. Lacy Hanna was strikingly pretty—he'd never seen eyes as blue. Mr. Hanna seemed plain, he thought, almost vanilla. He wondered how the man attracted such a looker. The two girls in the picture were as pretty as their mother. They appeared close to the same age, maybe ten and twelve years old. They'd be teenagers now.

Grant then focused on the picture Mordiky had in his hand. "Wow," he said quietly. "She has Down Syndrome."

• • •

Grant took Ladd fishing that afternoon. The old pond seemed bigger to Grant when he was a child, but most things did, of course. Growing up, the pond was known more for the water moccasins than the fish. That didn't keep Grant and his friends from fishing in the one-acre body of water, however. He and Ladd had caught a few bream today, but Grant had convinced the boy to release them (the truth was that Grant didn't want to get his hands dirty cleaning fish). They laughed at Wolf, who barked at the corks each time they bobbed. Their new pet had been with them less than twenty-four hours, and Grant saw that the dog already acted like part of the family.

Edwina's Cutlass was in the driveway when they reached the house. She, Jade, and Ella Reese were sitting on the porch.

"Y'all catch anything?" Jade asked.

"Yes!" Ladd yelled. He ran to her. "I caught five and Daddy didn't catch but two. We threw them back, though. Daddy said they needed to grow."

"He just said that because he doesn't know how to clean a fish," Edwina said.

"Yeah, yeah," Grant said as he patted Ladd on the back. "Run and get your bath. We need to leave early tomorrow."

Jade turned to Grant after the screen door snapped shut. "What are we planning to do about Wolf tomorrow?"

"I don't know," Grant said. "He can't go back with us." He turned to Edwina. "How 'bout it, friend?"

"Don't look at me," Edwina said. "I ain't keeping no dog. My auntie would go crazy if I brought that thing home. She has her hands full with my sister's kids anyway. That house ain't big enough for all of us, much less a hyper dog like Wolf."

Jade looked at Grant. "We can't break Ladd's heart."

Grant stood and sighed. "Okay, I guess he'll go with us. I'll fix him a box to ride in." He turned to Edwina. "See you when we come back down."

Later that evening after Jade and the kids went to bed, Grant walked onto the porch and sat on the swing. He used to sit here with his mama and help her shell peas and butterbeans, and he recalled how the rusty chains squeaked with the swing's movement. It wasn't the same swing today, but it felt the same. He thought about his mama. He missed her. Maybe, he thought, he'd see her soon. She hadn't been back to this house since she moved away. He wondered if she'd have the same fond memories that he did. Or maybe it was just too difficult because her husband had taken his life.

Grant thought about Ben Petty. What was he doing at that moment? Was he asleep? His thoughts then turned to the Hanna family. What were they doing tonight? Neely was less than ten miles from where Grant was sitting—Judge Eaton had said they still lived in the same house. Eaton had also told Grant that Mr. Hanna hadn't wanted to move just in case Lacy came back home. Although she'd been gone over three years, had they not ever given up hope? Were they relieved that her remains were found?

Grant knew he was representing the man accused of taking a young wife and mother away from her family. His position wouldn't be a popular one. Grant pondered his own father and once again recalled how disappointed he was when his dad failed to take an unpopular stand. As a teenager, he'd lost respect for his daddy. And although Ladd was too young to understand, Grant had taken Petty's case—partly at least—so his own son would respect him.

And in some small way, to redeem his father's failure.

CHAPTER 9

Thursday, April 17, 2014

G RANT NORMALLY ENJOYED the quarterly partnership meetings at Rimes & Yancey. They'd discuss profits, billable hours, personnel, and other riveting topics. He usually directed the meetings, but today he insisted that another partner run the show. His mind was elsewhere.

He kept looking at the new watch Jade had bought him to celebrate their first kiss. He, of course, had forgotten again. He never forgot their actual wedding anniversary or her birthday. But who celebrated a first kiss? His wife, that's who. The Armani watch had a brown band and buckled together. The timepiece wasn't bad, he thought. It was starting to grow on him.

It had been a month since he'd been to Leakesville, and he was anxious to return. Judge Eaton had been stopping by the jail to check on Petty and make sure that he knew his legal team was working on his case. Grant was leaving at noon to pick Ladd up early from school. Then they'd race home to load the Range Rover before heading back to Greene County with Jade and Ella Reese to spend a long Easter weekend. For Grant, it would be a work-filled weekend, but he found himself looking forward to being at the farm.

He was still considered the managing partner at Rimes & Yancey, but another partner had agreed to handle personnel issues when he took the Petty case. Still another partner ensured the building was maintained, bills were monitored, and that associates were forsaking their private lives for the greater cause of enriching the partners.

After the meeting, one of them followed Grant into his office. "Can we talk?"

"Sure," Grant said. "Have a seat."

"How's the case in Mississippi going?"

"Not the best start, but I think it's going okay," Grant said. "I'm driving down this afternoon, and I'll visit my client again tomorrow morning. I also have an investigator helping out and a local lawyer."

"I respect you for taking the case. I'd be scared to death to handle a murder case. Especially a capital murder case."

"I am nervous, to tell you the truth," Grant said as he looked at his watch. "Anyway, what can I help you with?"

"We need to decide which two new associates to hire. I wanted to get your input."

"You have two that you prefer?"

"Yes, but I'm not sure you'd agree."

Grant stood, walked the man to the door, and patted him on the shoulder. "They're hired. See you next week."

• • •

Jade and the kids had been asleep for an hour. They'd planned on stopping in Mobile for dinner, but Grant didn't want to wake them so he drove on through. He figured they'd stop in Leakesville at the Mexican restaurant and have a drink. One significant change to his hometown had occurred within the last couple of years—Greene County was voted *wet,* meaning alcohol could be sold.

Grant looked out the window and noticed a group of boys fishing on the side of the road in a small creek. Not one of them had a shirt on and Grant could see their ribs as he passed them. He looked in the rearview mirror and watched as they faded away. His thoughts turned to Petty, long ago.

Grant had sneaked away to meet him and two other boys, Brody and Cody Snodgrass, to go fishing in Indian Creek. Grant was the youngest at ten, Petty was eleven, and the Snodgrass brothers were fourteen and fifteen. They had fished for a while, but a cork hadn't as much as bobbed. The boys had become bored.

"Let's go swimming," Petty said.

"We don't have no trunks," Brody said.

"We don't need no damn trunks," Cody said. "We'll go skinny dipping."

"Buck nekkid?" Petty asked.

"Hell yeah," Cody said. "Buck ass naked."

"I can't," Grant said. He felt lightheaded, and sweat began to pool above his top lip. "I'd get into trouble."

"You a candy ass?" Brody asked.

"He ain't chicken," Petty said. "His folks just give him lots of rules. That's all."

Grant appreciated his friend defending his honor. He watched Petty unbutton his shorts with his right hand. Although his arm was bent in an awkward position, Petty had good use of his hand. Grant often wondered how Petty's hand still worked.

Brody Snodgrass had stripped and was in the creek. Petty soon followed. Grant looked over at Cody, who was sitting on a bucket taking off his shoes. The peer pressure rattled and whistled around Grant like the pressure cooker he'd watched on his grandmother's stove. Finally, Grant removed his short pants and walked near the water. When the boys weren't looking, he slipped off his underwear and sat in the creek.

"There you go, boy!" Brody yelled at Grant.

Grant eventually got the nerve to walk deeper into the water. Petty eased over by him and pointed toward Cody Snodgrass. "Look at that sumbitch."

Grant and Petty watched as Cody walked up and down the creek bank, just as naked as the day he was born. Grant whispered to Petty, "Cody sure has a big ding-dong."

Petty didn't take his eyes off Cody's anatomy. "That there's whatcha call a real-life bank-walker."

Grant turned to Petty. "What's a bank-walker?"

"When fellows go skinny dipping," Petty explained, "the one with the biggest pecker don't come in for a while. He walks up and down the bank to let everybody know who's in charge." The boys' eyes were glued to Cody's penis. They scattered as Cody ran toward the water.

"Clear the way, boys," Petty yelled. "Bank-walker's coming in!"

• • •

Grant and Jade had hired Edwina to keep an eye on the farm and to clean it while they were in Atlanta. The house had been scrubbed from ceiling to floor, and Edwina was beaming when the Hicks family walked in the door.

"Wow, Edwina," Jade said. "It looks great!"

"Thanks," she said. "I just appreciate y'all letting me earn some extra cash. And I'm beginning to like it out here."

"Good," Jade said. "We love you being here, too."

"What's the word in town about the Petty trial?" Grant asked.

"Not much talk right now," she said. "Other than I heard at the gas station that he was a Peeping Tom. I told you he was a pervert."

Grant rolled his eyes.

"You know, Yankee, your life would be a lot easier if you'd just listen to me. You think I don't know what goes on in this little town?"

Grant didn't ordinarily mind the kidding, but was sensitive when it came to Petty. He ignored Edwina and unloaded the luggage while the women sat at the kitchen table. In between trips to the SUV, Grant heard Edwina talking about an elderly resident of the nursing home who kept pinching her on the rear. She laughed when she explained to Jade that she'd known the old man for years and how he'd been the biggest racist in the county—but his Alzheimer's had caused him to fall in love with a black woman. Grant chuckled as Edwina told Jade that God had a sense of humor like she did.

"Oh, and I forgot to tell y'all," Edwina said as Grant sat down. "Paul Sumner dropped by a little while ago and invited y'all to Big Creek Baptist Church this Sunday. Said they have an Easter program or something."

"Darn," Grant said. "I was hoping he'd come to take Wolf back."

Jade stuck her tongue out at Grant before turning to Edwina. "That's nice of him to invite us," she said, "but we haven't decided where we'll attend Easter services yet."

After the suitcases were unpacked and the family settled in, Grant called George Brewer and Mordiky to set up a meeting at Brewer's office the next morning. Then he walked outside and sat on the steps and counted the days to the trial—eighty were remaining. He'd spent the last four weeks researching and preparing motions, not to mention asking the assistance of one of Rimes & Yancey's brightest young lawyers. Grant was more confident now, and for the first time since he took the case he believed they had a fighting chance.

He thought of the trial and felt adrenaline race through his veins. He knew that a trial was a war filled with many battles. And starting tomorrow, he thought as he scratched Wolf on the head, the State of Mississippi would begin to feel the sting of warfare.

CHAPTER 10

Friday, April 18, 2014

GRANT WAS WAITING in his Range Rover at Brewer's office when Mordiky pulled his pickup in next to him. Grant stepped out and met him at the rear of his truck.

"George is late as usual," Grant said.

Mordiky lowered the tailgate on the truck and sat down. "He'll be here. Have a seat."

Grant joined him. Mordiky offered a cigar, which Grant declined. Mordiky's cheeks strained under the pressure of lighting the stogie. His eyes flittered as the Havana finally burned red. He squinted. "Damn fine cigar, Grant," he said. "Sure you don't want one?"

"I'm sure," Grant said as he stood. "Enjoy it. I'm going to walk over to the jail and see if our client wants to do more than nod his head. I'll be back in a few."

Grant walked into the sheriff's office and was appreciative that Heather Sisco, without asking, unlocked the door and pointed down the hall. He entered the familiar meeting room and sat down. Moments later McInnis walked in and shut the door.

"Morning, Grant," he said.

"Morning. How's my client?"

"About the same, but I'm afraid I have some bad news."

"What kind of bad news?"

"Seems Petty started talking since the last time you visited," McInnis said. "He's admitted to killing Lacy Hanna."

Grant shot to his feet. "No way. I don't believe you."

"I'm sure he'll deny it to you, but he sure enough did."

"I want to know who the hell's been talking to my client without me present."

"Relax," McInnis said. "It wasn't none of us. It was his cellmate."

"I want to see him."

The sheriff left, and Grant began to pace in the small room like a fenced-in dog trying to attack a postman. A deputy finally walked in, secured Petty, and left them alone.

"Who have you been talking to, Ben?" Grant asked. "And say something or I'm going to pull it out of you." Petty squinted at Grant and adjusted his chair. Grant continued to pace and stared back. "Damn it, man, I've put my reputation on the line for you. I could be in Atlanta billing five hundred dollars per hour, but I'm over here trying to keep the State of Mississippi from shooting your veins full of death. And you won't talk to me but you'll talk to an inmate! For Pete's sake, are you nuts?"

Petty cleared his throat and whispered, "Can we talk outside?"

Grant leaned closer. "What?"

"Can we talk somewhere else?"

Grant stood at full height and frowned. Petty pointed toward the air conditioning vent. Grant looked at the ceiling and nodded before turning back to Petty. "Be right back."

A few minutes later a deputy led Petty outside to the secured recreational area where prisoners went twice a day for exercise and fresh air. Grant took a folding chair and pointed Petty to an empty one across from him. The deputy uncuffed Petty and walked over by the door.

"I didn't talk to nobody," Petty said quietly.

"Who is this cellmate?"

"Name's Jeremiah Shelly, and that son of a bitch is lying. All he's doing is trying to get out of jail."

"I'll worry about him," Grant said as he put on his sunglasses. "Look, Ben, I'm just glad you're talking to me."

"They got that place bugged in there, man," Petty said. "I don't trust nobody."

"That'd be a violation of your constitutional rights. They can't do that."

"To hell they can't."

Grant leaned closer. "Ben, tell me where you were when Lacy Hanna went missing."

"I'd been squirrel hunting," he said. "I told them that a hundred times."

"By yourself?"

"Yeah," he said. "I don't really have no friends. I hunt alone."

Grant pulled a small notepad from his pocket. "Do you know if you were a suspect when she first went missing?"

"I guess I was," Petty said.

"What do you mean?"

"They came and looked in my trailer."

"Who?"

"The other sheriff," Petty said. "Not this one."

"Coaker? When was this?"

"About a year after she went missing," Petty said.

"What about Sheriff McInnis?"

"First time I saw him was the day he hauled me off to jail."

Paul McInnis had defeated Wilson Coaker in the 2011 election, and McInnis had used the unsolved Hanna crime as the centerpiece in his cry for change. It worked, and now, Grant knew, McInnis would be facing reelection next year. He couldn't have the same unsolved crime hanging over his head.

"Look," Grant said as he noticed the deputy looking at his watch. "I know they found a pair of her panties and her picture at your place. But was there anything else?"

Petty leaned in and whispered, "No. I'd done hid it all."

Grant felt his heart skip. He motioned for the deputy to stay where he was while he finished his conversation with Petty.

"Ben," Grant said, "I'm going to ask you one more time, and this is the last time I'm going to ask this question. The evidence doesn't look good at all for you ... did you kill Lacy Hanna? I mean, if you did, I may can work out a plea to keep you from getting the death penalty."

Petty didn't respond.

"Answer me, Ben. Did you kill her?"

"I'm gonna tell you for the last time," Petty said. "I didn't kill her. I wouldn't kill nobody, especially a woman as pretty and nice as Mrs. Hanna. I just liked to look at her, that's all. I may have done something to her in my mind, but I'd never have hurt her."

•••

Brewer's pickup was now parked beside Mordiky's. Grant wasn't ready to walk in the office yet so he sat in his vehicle and started the engine. The vent blew cold air on his face while he gathered his thoughts. What did Ben Petty hide? *Was* he guilty? And what should Grant tell Mordiky and Brewer? *I'd done hid it all!* What did he hide? *Crap, I forgot to ask*, Grant thought to himself. He needed more time with his client. The sheriff's arbitrary limits on his visits with Petty had to stop. He'd file a motion this afternoon and get the judge to increase his access, he decided, and turned off the engine. He started toward Brewer's office, but before he could make it to the door he heard a voice.

"Hey, feller!"

Grant turned to see Pete Ball. This was the last person Grant needed at the moment. "Hey, Pete."

"Need any help on your case?"

"I think we have it under control," he lied. "But thanks."

A car pulled up and a man asked Grant for directions to the town hall. Grant pointed to the building, and the man told him that he was from Chicago and was in town to discuss an economic development proposal. As the man pulled away, Grant noticed Pete shaking his head.

"What's the matter, Pete?"

"I hate a feller who lies," he said.

"How do you know he's lying?"

"You didn't pick up on it?" Pete said, waving his arms. "That man said he was from *Chicargo*. But I saw his tag. He's a lying. He's from *Illanoise*."

Grant smiled but decided not to explain. He told Pete goodbye and walked into the law office. Mordiky was admiring a revolver when Grant stepped into Brewer's office. Brewer was freshly shaven and looked better than Grant had ever seen him. Brewer nodded at Grant and motioned for Mordiky to hand Grant the gun.

"I bought you something," Brewer said.

"A pistol?" Grant asked. "Why do I need a pistol?"

"First of all, it's a revolver," Brewer said. "And second of all, everybody needs a weapon."

Grant hadn't owned a gun since he was young. He'd left his two hunting rifles behind when he went off to college. For the first time, he wondered what happened to the guns.

"Thanks, George."

"Let's get down to business," Mordiky interrupted.

Grant informed them about the jailhouse snitch and the fact that Petty thought the place was bugged. He left out the part about

Petty hiding evidence, though; it had taken weeks to convince Brewer that Petty might be innocent and he wasn't in the mood to start over (especially since Grant, for the first time, wondered himself if his client was guilty). When Grant mentioned filing a motion to increase his time with Petty, Brewer laughed and called the district attorney. Five minutes later, McInnis called and told Brewer they could visit as much as they wanted during the week (as long as enough deputies were on duty for security). Weekends were off limits, though.

Mordiky had again been in contact with the DA's investigator, Woods, and had identified most of the state's witnesses and was gathering information on them. Brewer hadn't done a whole lot, but he seemed optimistic that they could hang the jury. Although Brewer seemed energetic, he didn't appear to be using his newfound exuberance on Petty's case.

On the way to the farm, Grant decided to drive to the Hicks family cemetery and visit his dad's gravesite. The old cemetery wasn't used much anymore, but Grant noticed a relatively new mound of red dirt and walked in that direction. A small metal frame had a slip of paper covered in plastic announcing the occupant, a John Doe—date of birth unknown, date of death on or about January 10, 2014.

Grant walked over and sat at the bench at the foot of his dad's resting spot and read the inscription on the headstone for the hundredth time. He missed his father, and he could sure use his advice now. The gray stone was actually a double; Grant's mother's name and date of birth was on one side, but Grant knew she would never occupy the spot. She'd been married to his stepfather for almost as long as she was married to his dad. Besides, North Carolina was her home now.

Grant closed his eyes and listened. The wind was high in the trees but seemed too busy to dip down into the cemetery. He listened for a bird, but they weren't singing. His thoughts drifted to his childhood. He knew that growing up in this town was special. But, like most kids, he didn't know it at the time. There were two places that held precious memories for him. The first was the time spent with his dad at the baseball field.

The second was the time he'd spent with Ben Petty.

CHAPTER 11

Saturday, April 19, 2014.

GRANT ARRIVED AT Petty's mobile home half an hour before he was scheduled to meet Judge Eaton there. The trailer was hidden behind a rotting, brown house which was sitting a few feet from the dirt road. The west side of the house had stumbled off its blocks, as if the old structure tried to get away or seek help for the condition in which it was left. No windows remained. The house reminded Grant of an unburied corpse or skull.

Petty's trailer wasn't much better. The yellow and white tin box was a seventy-foot-long piece of rusting metal. The front door was locked so Grant walked around back. He noticed that several panels were missing and exposed wet insulation and PVC pipes. Blue tarps were draped across the roof and were stained by the rotting leaves from the tired old trees hanging over the structure. Grant checked the back door and found it locked, too. A cream-colored Gran Torino was parked under an oak beside a rotting shed; limbs dotted the hood and roof of the automobile. Grant peeked inside and saw that the front seat cushions were torn and the back seat was missing.

He decided to walk around the place to see what he could find. He spotted a trail and walked slowly along, pushing limbs and briars out of the way. He found an artesian well with a steady stream of water. A white five-gallon bucket had been placed beneath the pipe and was overflowing. Grant followed the path of water to a hill which fell into a small creek. He then saw something hanging on the side of a tree. He walked in that direction and saw small clumps of white paper strewn sporadically across the leaves. He leaned around the tree and found a wet, half-used roll of toilet paper hanging on a broken limb. He grimaced when he realized he was standing where Petty used the bathroom. He could feel himself getting sick and was grateful to hear a horn blow. He hurried back up the hill.

"I see you found it," Eaton said.

"I can't believe he lives here," Grant said. He spotted an electric wire running from a service pole to the trailer, and an empty hole where the power meter once rested. "How long has he been without power?"

"I don't know," Eaton said as he pulled a key from his shirt pocket. Eaton pushed the door open and the odor hit them before they could enter.

"Damn," Grant said. "What is that *smell*?"

Eaton pulled a handkerchief from his pocket and handed it to Grant. Eaton then placed a piece of paper over his nose. Grant followed him inside. Eaton aimed a flashlight, which provided the only light in the place. The windows, Grant saw, were covered with aluminum foil or cardboard. There was very little furniture, which made the search more bearable.

Grant managed to activate the flashlight app on his phone and walked toward the back. The foul smell burned his nostrils through the thin cloth. He found the source of the odor just before he gagged.

"Judge," he hissed. "Come look at this."

Eaton's beam of light landed on a dead rat that had to be ten inches long. A stream of ants were cleaning up the remains. Eaton went outside and came back with a shovel. He scooped up the dead rodent and tossed it out the front door.

"I knew he was living poor," Eaton said as he walked back toward Grant, "but not this poor."

"I've never asked, but what's your connection to Ben Petty?"

"He appeared before me once. I gave him community service, and he took a liking to me. After that, he'd show up at court occasionally. I took him to lunch a time or two. He has no family as far as I know. I think he was just lonely."

"What was the crime?"

"Killed a turkey out of season," Eaton said. "He trusted me, I guess. I'd drop by occasionally and bring him a few things. When they arrested him and explained that he had the right to an attorney, he asked for me."

"But you're not an attorney," Grant said.

"He thought I was. When I explained to him that I wasn't, I promised I'd find him one. So I did."

With the smell not quite as bad, the men combed the place for any clues or personal belongings. The only items of value were a rifle and a collection of pocket knives which the judge took to make sure they weren't stolen. Grant was surprised to find Petty's clothes neatly folded in boxes in his bedroom. He picked up a cell phone, which was dead. He looked for a charger but remembered the electricity was off. He went into the kitchen and twisted the faucet, but no water came. Then he joined Eaton on the front porch.

"Judge, did you know Sheriff Coaker searched this place before he left office?"

"I suspected that," he said. "They came to me to sign a warrant and I wouldn't do it."

"Why?"

"No probable cause. They were on a fishing expedition. Petty had done some work for the Hannas a few days before she went missing."

Grant frowned. "Well, who signed it?"

"Nobody, as far as I know. The thing I couldn't figure out then was why Coaker was so eager. Paul McInnis was the sheriff-elect and Coaker only had a few days left in office."

Grant stared at the old judge. "Maybe he wanted to solve the crime before Paul McInnis took office. I mean, that was the central issue in the campaign, wasn't it?"

Eaton walked back to the trailer and locked the door. He then took a pouch of tobacco out of his pocket and placed a small handful in his mouth. Grant waited in silence as Eaton adjusted the chaw, spitting out small strands of tobacco like he was expelling a bug from his mouth.

"Yeah, it was," Eaton said. "But Coaker was too lazy for that." Eaton got into his pickup and rolled the window down. "Who knows, Counselor. Maybe Coaker will tell you. Anyway, why did you want to inspect Petty's trailer? What were you looking for?"

Grant glanced at the rundown trailer, then back at the judge. "I honestly don't know."

When Eaton's truck had disappeared and the dust had settled, Grant decided to tour the abandoned house. Most of the floors had collapsed, and he could smell the dark black dirt as he picked his way across the rotted wood. He could see sunlight beaming through where the front door once stood, so he headed that way. A spider web enveloped him, and he almost gave himself a black eye wiping the web from his face and hair. He hurried toward the opening but stopped when he saw dust swirling in front of him, dancing in a stream of light which had made its way into the darkness. The light seemed to be pointing to an old closet door.

He walked to the door and pulled, but it was jammed. He

grabbed the knob with both hands and pulled—still stuck. He placed his foot on the door facing and pulled harder. The door gave way, and Grant fell back onto an old block that once held the wooden floor. He got to his feet, pulled out his cell, and turned on the flashlight app. He saw pieces of wood stacked in a neat pile, which struck him as odd. He began to remove the lumber and noticed a wooden box hidden behind another exposed block. He pulled it out, wiped the dust off, and walked outside with the box.

The top was nailed shut. He tucked it under his arm and walked around the yard looking for a tool of some sort. Underneath the trailer he found a rusted screwdriver with the grip of its handle missing. He stopped in his tracks and ducked as he heard the caw of a crow.

"Son of a bitch," Grant muttered, glad no one had seen him startle as he watched the bird flee from a nearby oak. He placed the metal tool in a crack near one of the box's hinges and pried off the lid. The box was full of magazines, including *Playboy* and *Hustler*. There were *Sports Illustrated* swimsuit editions.

At the bottom of the box Grant discovered a brown envelope which had been taped shut with gray masking tape. He opened it and pulled out several pictures. He recognized the lady in the photographs.

"My god," Grant said to himself. "He did kill her."

CHAPTER 12

Sunday, April 20, 2014

LADD BOLTED INTO his parents' room before daylight and shouted, "The Easter Bunny came, the Easter Bunny came!" Jade and Grant sat up in the bed and watched him sit on the floor and open his basket. Grant was always amazed at the thoughtfulness of his wife. She had started a special Hicks family tradition for each holiday: special pajamas at Christmas, feeding (anonymously) a needy family at Thanksgiving, and the Hicks clan dressing up for Halloween (even Grant). But Easter was Jade's favorite.

Grant recalled their first Easter together. They had to pack breakfast and find a secluded place outside Atlanta to watch the sunrise. She told Grant that Easter represented the victory of good over evil—a happy ending. Many parents today were buying expensive gifts for their children on Easter, but not Jade. Grant could tell she wasn't comfortable with the whole Easter Bunny idea, but she compromised to make her kids happy.

She stepped to the window and pulled back the curtain. "Let's get Ella Reese and walk outside. The sun will be up soon."

"Okay," Grant said. "I'll get the food out of the fridge and warm it in the microwave."

Ella Reese was asleep in Jade's arms as the family sat on a blanket in their backyard. The pasture behind their house rolled down a slow hill toward the woods. The sun was beginning to warm the morning dampness. Grant looked across the field and saw at least a hundred small spider webs sprinkled across the dewy bahia grass.

Jade took Grant's hand. "I love this place."

Grant smiled. "I do too."

"What was your favorite memory of childhood here?"

"Oh, gosh. There are so many." Grant pointed toward a grass-covered mound. "Pitching to my dad was my favorite, I guess."

Ladd looked up from the stash of candy in his basket. "Daddy, can I pitch as good as you?"

"Man, you're better than I was," Grant said. "Next time we come, we'll bring our gloves and I'll catch for you."

After breakfast they dressed for church. Jade had prepared the children's outfits last night and got herself ready first (the kids would be dressed last to decrease the chance of Ella Reese spilling juice on her pink dress and to prevent Ladd from getting his pants dirty). Grant was sitting in the den reading the *Atlanta Journal-Constitution* online when Jade walked into the room. He did a double-take—she had on a red and white dress that fit her body perfectly and wore white flats without hose. Grant was amazed at how she could make such a simple outfit look so elegant. He was proud she was his wife.

"God, you're beautiful," he said, pulling her close.

She pecked him on his lips and straightened his tie. "You look pretty good yourself. Now let's get the kids ready. Church is in half an hour."

Grant hadn't been to Big Creek Baptist Church since he left after high school. He'd once vowed never to come back to Greene County, or to the church he attended as a child. But the death of Brandon Smallwood had changed his destiny and, as with a lot of youthful declarations, time had caused him to eat his words.

He hadn't told Jade that he now thought Ben Petty was guilty. In fact, he hadn't discussed it with anyone. He trusted her and had occasionally violated client confidences with her, but not this time. What if she accidentally let it slip to Edwina? The whole world would know then. And Grant could be disbarred.

He'd read the rules of professional conduct over and over and knew he couldn't disclose his secret to anyone. Well, technically, he could share it with George Brewer. But not yet. He was afraid Brewer would withdraw or not lend his help. And the truth was that he needed Brewer.

The small church was packed, which was no surprise. The Hickses walked toward the entrance and were met by an overly friendly greeter. He introduced himself, but Grant wasn't listening. He held Ella Reese as Jade and Ladd followed to a pew in the middle of the church. Jade was her usual friendly self, smiling and saying hello to the folks who sat near them. Grant wasn't in the mood to socialize, though, so he busied himself with his daughter. When she got bored with him, he read the church bulletin. He smiled as he realized the bulletin was in practically the same format as it was when he sat here over twenty years ago. He felt a hand on his shoulder and looked up. It was Paul Sumner, their neighbor.

"Howdy, Grant," Sumner said. "Glad you got my invitation."

Grant shook his hand. "Hello, Paul."

"Happy y'all could join us. By the way, how's that *pretty* dog?"

"He's not any better looking, but he's fitting in quite well."

Sumner returned to his pew when the pianist began to play. After the first congregational hymn, an old man stood in the pulpit and made announcements for what seemed to Grant to be an eternity. He looked discreetly around the church and, on the opposite side of the sanctuary near the front, spotted them. Grant shifted in his pew. He couldn't see the girls' faces, but there was no mistaking Ronnie Hanna's profile. Grant felt himself perspire. What were the Hannas doing here? He was so preoccupied that he didn't notice the announcements were over and that the congregation was singing again. Jade, sensing a problem, squeezed his hand.

"You okay?" she whispered.

Grant nodded yes and looked back at the door. As soon as the service ended and the invitation started, he'd ask Jade to leave. They'd skip the traditional fellowship afterwards, too. He'd explain to Jade when they got home, but he just couldn't face the Hannas.

Time seemed to stand still. Grant watched the preacher (who was sitting in an oversized chair) and hoped he wouldn't be long-winded. But Grant knew better. Today was Easter, and the preacher wouldn't see a crowd this big for another year. Grant figured he best get comfortable, but it got worse when the preacher stepped to the podium.

"Friends, we have a special treat today," he said. "These girls have endured an awful lot over their short lives but they've kept their faith. They've walked the Christian walk and been an example to all of us. They can sing like angels, too. Marly and Jenna, y'all come on up."

Grant wanted to dive under the pew and low-crawl out of the sanctuary. He glanced at Jade, who was smiling in the girls' direction. She obviously had no idea who they were. The oldest girl nodded toward the ceiling and Grant looked behind him and saw a small window, which must have housed the sound room. Music began to play and the song was unmistakable. The Hanna girls delivered a rendition of "He's Alive" that was nearly as good as Dolly Parton's version.

Almost an hour later the sermon mercifully ended, capped off with what Grant believed to be the longest prayer in church history. The reverend walked to the back of the church during his closing prayer in order to greet the congregants as they left. Grant wanted to leave in the worst way but noticed that Ella Reese had spilled her bag onto the floor. Crackers and toys were scattered under the pew in front of them, and he and Jade tidied up. Then Grant led Jade and the kids toward the side door, which he remembered being located behind the choir loft.

Jade frowned at Grant's insistence on leaving without greeting folks and shaking the preacher's hand, but she followed him past the pulpit. A few people stopped them and thanked them for visiting. Grant had lost eye contact with the Hannas and hoped that they'd exited at the front. The Hickses were almost there when a door opened to the ladies' restroom and Marly Hanna almost walked into Grant.

"Oh, I'm sorry, sir."

"No problem," Grant said. "Have a good day."

Jade smiled. "That was the most beautiful version of that song I've ever heard."

"Thank you, ma'am."

Keep quiet, Jade ... just keep moving ...

"I'm Jade. This is my husband, Grant, and this is Ladd and Ella Reese."

"Nice to meet y'all," she said. "My name's Marly Hanna."

Grant, knowing he was busted, watched Jade's eyes narrow. He knew that look. He'd seen it many times when she'd figured out a riddle or puzzle. "Nice to meet you, too," she said. "Happy Easter."

Grant got them outside and into the vehicle. At the very least, he thought, they'd managed to avoid Ronnie Hanna. Jade finally broke the silence when Grant pulled away from the church and drove toward the farm.

"Were those Lacy Hanna's children?"

Grant looked at her and didn't answer. He didn't have to. His eyes told her that they were.

Jade turned to gaze out of the passenger window. Grant watched as she wiped a tear from her cheek. He knew the trial would be difficult on the Hanna family. And he also figured, to a lesser extent, that it would be difficult on his family too. He glanced back at Jade. At that moment, he couldn't imagine loving another person more than he loved his wife.

CHAPTER 13

Sunday night, April 20, 2014

THE RIDE BACK to Atlanta, Jade thought, seemed to take longer and longer. She'd admitted to herself that she wanted to move home and turned slightly to watch Grant as he drove. He had a habit of talking to himself and, like he did when he spoke verbally, used his hands. He'd catch himself sometimes and pretend he was trying to scratch his hand or reach for something on the dash. But she knew better.

Jade also knew the Petty case weighed heavy on him. He wasn't sleeping well, and she watched him get out of bed each night and sit at his desk, making notes or researching. They would celebrate four years of marriage on October 10. She didn't think it would have been possible to love him more than she did the day they were married, but she did. He was a wonderful father to their children and had always loved Ladd as much as he did Ella Reese.

She was shocked when he showed her their income tax return the first year they'd filed together. She knew he was making a good living, but she had no idea he was earning as much as he did. He had expensive automobiles, dressed well, and looked a bit spoiled (but in a good way). He was confident but not cocky. Grant was her soul mate and her very own knight in shining armor. Would he give up his position and ownership interest in the firm to move home? Would he give up the income he'd never replace in Greene County? Maybe one day, she thought. Maybe one day.

Jade had a Facebook account to keep up with friends in Greene County and the few she still had from her days in Hollywood after high school. She and Grant were still a hundred miles from home and both kids were asleep, so she pulled out her phone and scrolled through the news feed. Spotting a friend request, she clicked on the red notification. Her heart skipped a beat when she read the name *Marly Hanna.* She looked at Grant but turned away when he caught her staring.

"We'll be home by eleven, baby," he said.

She patted him on the hand. "Ladd will be a bear getting him up for school tomorrow."

Grant smiled and turned back to the road. The screen on Jade's phone had darkened so she unlocked it and stared at the friend request. She knew Grant would tell her not to accept it, but she was curious. Grant didn't fool much with social media and never asked Jade about her Facebook account. So he'd never find out if she and Marly were Facebook friends, she knew. She paused, then pressed confirm. Tomorrow, Jade thought, she would look at Marly's profile when Grant was at work and she was at her computer.

Jade continued to scroll down her page. One of her friends had a bad day and needed prayer. Jade left a comment that she would. Edwina was complaining about men, which had become her favorite pastime. Then a bubble popped up on the right side of her screen—she had received a message. She opened it to find the beautiful profile picture of Marly Hanna.

It was nice meeting you and your family today. I hope y'all come back to church soon. If you ever need a babysitter, let me know. And I hope you don't mind me saying that you remind me a lot of my mother. She was beautiful, just like you. Anyway, thanks for accepting my friend request—Marly

Jade decided to wait until they got home to respond. But after they put the kids to bed and unloaded the Range Rover, she changed her mind. She didn't want Grant looking over her shoulder. She lay in bed and kept looking at her phone and reading the message from Marly. For the first time, she wondered what Lacy Hanna had looked like. Up till now, she'd only focused on Petty, and Grant's ability to represent the man.

Jade looked again at Marly's profile picture. She was wearing a high school cheerleader uniform and had a cute white bow in her hair. Jade thought of growing up without her own mom and living with her grandmother. Jade's mother was alive, but she might as well have been dead because Jade rarely saw her. Then she mentally corrected herself—Jade carried a tiny hope that one day her mother would want to be a part of her life. Marly and her sister didn't have that hope, because Lacy Hanna was not coming back.

Jade looked at the clock on the nightstand. It was 3:33 a.m. She put her phone down and closed her eyes. But all she could see was Marly Hanna.

• • •

Three days had passed since Jade had received Marly's message. Ella Reese was taking her afternoon nap and Ladd wouldn't be home from school for another two hours. She walked to the computer and opened her Facebook page. She clicked on Marly's message and decided to respond.

Marly, thanks for your message. I'm sorry I'm so late in responding. I enjoyed so much meeting you and listening to you and Jenna sing. Both of you are beautiful and talented. Your compliment was probably the sweetest I've ever received. I can tell your mom was a gorgeous lady just by looking at you. And thanks for the babysitting offer! Perhaps one day we can take you up on it. Take care and study hard! All the best, Jade Hicks

She pressed send and instantly felt her stomach tumble. She knew in a small way she'd betrayed her husband but rationalized it by thinking of Marly. After all, Marly contacted her, not the other way around. Surely Grant would understand.

Jade logged out and walked into the bathroom to wash her face. Maybe, she hoped as she stared at herself in the mirror, Marly wouldn't respond.

CHAPTER 14

Friday, May 16, 2014

THE STATE OF Mississippi vs. Benjamin Franklin Petty was proceeding on schedule. Petty had been indicted three weeks ago, and Grant had flown to Mobile, rented a car, and drove to Leakesville to explain the formality to his client. Grant then hurried back to Atlanta, where he squeezed in a week-long civil trial, multiple depositions, and two summary judgment motion hearings. He was tired but hadn't slowed down enough to notice, and he was relieved to be back in Leakesville until the trial was over.

The deputy walked Petty outside and stood next to the door. Petty shuffled toward Grant with his eyes squinted. The skies were overcast, but the sun was on the verge of punching through.

"Hey, Ben," Grant said, pointing at the rusty metal folding chair. "Have a seat."

"Can we stand over yonder by the fence?"

Grant stood and followed him to the corner of the secured area. "Sheriff McInnis told me we could visit an hour, so let's talk. How are they treating you?"

"Pretty good, I reckon," Petty said. "Ain't got much I can compare it to since I ain't never been in no jail."

"You eating?"

"Enough, I reckon."

"Well," Grant said, "you're losing weight."

Petty didn't answer, his eyes on a car driving by.

"Ben, why did you have a scrapbook with me in it?"

Petty turned. "Don't rightly know. Saw your picture in the paper a long time ago, so I cut it out. Just kept doing it." He smiled at Grant. "You're the closest person I know to being famous."

"You know what they say, Ben: Everybody's famous in a small town."

Petty glanced at another passing vehicle. "Guess I'm famous now."

Grant nodded at Heather Sisco as she walked toward the courthouse. A construction crew was roofing a building nearby and the men predictably began their catcalls. Sisco never looked their way, and Grant smiled at her resolve. He looked at Petty.

"Let me give you an update on your case, Ben."

"Can we talk about something else?"

Grant had decided not to mention to Petty—at least not yet—that he'd found Lacy Hanna's pictures amid his stash of magazines. "Okay, what do you want to talk about?"

"We had fun when we were little, didn't we?"

Grant smiled. "We did. I was thinking a few weeks ago about us skinny dipping with the Snodgrass boys. You taught me what a bank-walker was."

"That Cody was hung like a mule, wasn't he?"

"Wonder whatever happened to them."

"Last I heard, they were living in Buzzard Roost, down in George County," Petty said. "But that was a good while ago."

"You remember old Mr. Sawyer, used to drive our bus?"

Petty laughed. "Yeah. That sucker looked like the tin man

from *The Wizard of Oz.*"

"He did," Grant said, laughing now. "And he kept his head leaning to the right, like one side weighed more than the other."

They chatted and laughed for the next forty minutes. The deputy watching from a distance, Grant figured, had to be as confused as a man could be; Petty was about to be tried for capital murder, and he and his lawyer were having a big old time. Grant finally looked at his watch.

"Ben, before I go, I want you to know I'm going to defend you to the best of my ability. You believe me, don't you?"

Petty went to the dull, expressionless gaze that Grant first saw over two months ago. "They're going to convict me, ain't they?"

Grant stepped close. "Look, man, I need to know what you hid when Sheriff Coaker searched your trailer."

Ben didn't answer.

"I won't tell a soul. I can't. I'd be disbarred if I did."

Petty looked away, but Grant chose to wait him out. If he didn't want to speak, Grant would let the clock run out on their visit. If Petty wanted to be stubborn, he could, too. The deputy announced that they had two minutes. Grant started away.

"Grant?"

He stopped, took a breath, and walked back to where Petty was standing. "Yeah?"

"Remember that time you almost drowned in Big Creek?"

Grant took his sunglasses off. "How could I forget? You saved my life. I wouldn't be here if it wasn't for you."

The deputy started in their direction. Petty leaned in close. "I need you to save mine."

Grant drove to the farm thinking of Petty. This latest conversation reminded him that Ben was the same person he'd played with as a child. But how could he have killed someone? It didn't seem possible. Like most boys in Mississippi, Petty liked to hunt. But he never just *killed* animals. The Ben Petty he remembered respected life too much.

Grant already missed Jade and the kids. Ladd would be out of school in two weeks and they would join him then. He decided to spend some time working around the place today. He'd bought a used Massey Ferguson tractor and hoped he remembered how to use it. Later tonight he'd join Mordiky and Brewer at Judge Eaton's place to start developing their trial strategy. In the meantime, he thought, he'd spend as much time as he could recreating the place he still called home. The place where Ben Petty walked into his life.

• • •

Judge Eaton suggested that Petty's legal team meet at his house at 8:30, and Grant had spent the afternoon on his tractor and was sitting on the front steps drinking iced tea when he heard gravel crunching beneath approaching tires. He used a hand towel to wipe his face and peered at an unfamiliar silver Maxima. He recognized the driver, though, when she stepped out and shut the door. Heather Sisco wore tight jeans, flip-flops, and a plain white t-shirt. He stood.

"What brings you here?"

She smiled and walked closer. "You have any more of that iced tea?" She brushed past him and sat on the swing. Her smell ignited Grant's senses.

"Sure, I'll be right back."

He hurried inside and looked at the clock. It was a few minutes past seven and although he wasn't pressed for time, he needed to shower and get to Eaton's. He figured he had until 7:30 to find out what she wanted. On his way back out he saw the family portrait and knew Jade wouldn't care one bit for this attractive young female being here. An internal voice told him to get her out as he handed her the glass.

"Now, Miss Sisco, how can I help you?"

She sipped tea before responding. "Please call me Heather," she said. "My mom is Miss Sisco." She slid over in the swing. "Sit down."

Grant looked over his shoulder. The chair which normally was on the porch was not there; he remembered moving it to the back porch the last time they were here. He couldn't be rude, he thought, so he joined her.

"How old are you, Grant?"

"Forty-one," he answered. "Almost old enough to be your daddy."

She grinned. When she did, he noticed wrinkles that appeared on her nose when she smiled. She had green eyes, light brown hair, and high cheekbones. She was not fair-complected, but Grant figured she had to work to keep a tan. The one thing that was clear was how stunning she was. He thought of Jade again and knew he needed to get Sisco on the road.

"Don't worry, Grant," she said. "I'm not here to get in bed with you."

Grant was caught off guard and managed a smile. "Oh, I know that. How did you find my place?"

"This is Greene County. And you're kind of famous. Most people know where you live."

Hmm. "How long have you been a dispatcher?"

"Started when Sheriff McInnis took office just over two years ago. I actually have a degree in criminal justice. Planned to go to law school but I chickened out."

"Why?"

"I don't know. I may eventually go. I'll be twenty-eight in a few days so I'm not getting any younger."

"Well, if I can help, let me know," he said. "Law school isn't as hard as people think. You can handle it."

She reached over and gently turned his wrist in her direction to check the time. "Guess I better go."

"You still haven't said why you drove out here."

She stood and handed him the glass, saying nothing. She started for the Maxima and Grant walked behind her and fought the urge to watch her jeans. She opened the door and placed her right foot on the edge of the floorboard.

"Grant, you need to be careful who you trust," she said after a long moment.

"Do you know something I don't?"

She sat in the front seat and lowered her window as Grant shut the door and looked down at her. She wore red lipstick and Grant noticed the fullness of her lips.

"The district attorney for one. Watch him with both eyes. He's a tricky S.O.B."

"Fair enough." Wouldn't hurt to learn what he could from this woman, he thought. "Anything else?"

She started the car. "Yeah, there *is* something else. I hope your wife knows how lucky she is."

Grant watched her drive away. Was she flirting? If Jade were here, he knew what she'd say. *Hell yeah she was flirting!* Maybe she was just flattering an older guy, Grant thought. Or ... maybe she was sincerely passing along advice. Grant would never betray Jade, though, and he didn't like what he'd felt just now. He went inside to shower and knew he couldn't let his guard down. He couldn't let pride cause him to fall.

On his way to Judge Eaton's house, he called Jade and told her how much he loved her.

CHAPTER 15

Friday, May 16, 2014

THE MEN WERE inside when Grant arrived at Eaton's house. They had just finished eating and Mordiky was writing on a white board that had been set up for the meeting. Eaton's house was as plain on the inside as it was outside. The floors were hardwood and, Grant noticed, in need of refinishing. A bar covered with cheap, lime-green Formica separated the den from the small kitchen.

"It's about time you got here, Hicks," Brewer said as he looked at his watch.

"Get you a bowl of chili, Counselor," Eaton said. "Drinks are in the fridge."

"Thanks, Judge," Grant said. He slapped Brewer's wingtips, which were propped up on a coffee table. "And, George, you're one to talk about being late."

Grant noticed that the old judge kept his kitchen spotless. There was no dishwasher, meaning he washed the dishes the old-fashioned way. The aroma made Grant's mouth water when Eaton lifted the lid off the pot. He filled his bowl and crumbled some crackers into the chili, then grabbed a can of Barq's root beer and sat near Mordiky.

"What you got there?" he asked.

Mordiky finished writing and turned to Grant. "This is what we know. Lacy Hanna was abducted on December 13, 2010. The 911 call came in at 7:24 that morning. The school bus picked up the Hanna girls at approximately seven o'clock, which tells me the killer was hiding nearby and most likely knew what time the bus would come. And that Ronnie Hanna would be at work."

Grant looked at Brewer. "Did we get our discovery?"

"Yes. But I don't trust that damn DA. He has the reputation of sandbagging lawyers. And his ambition makes him dangerous."

Grant almost blurted that Heather Sisco had just left his house and told him not to trust Troy Lee, but he thought he'd better keep that a secret, too. "Did we get the 911 recording?"

Mordiky tapped a computer sitting on the coffee table. It took several seconds before the recording played. After the 911 operator answered, no words could be heard—they heard breathing and the whimpering of a child. The operator dispatched a deputy and the child stayed on the line until the officer arrived. The recording ended.

"That's it?" Grant asked.

"Yep," Brewer said.

Grant looked at Mordiky. "Tell me about the girl that made the call. Has she made a statement?"

"Nope. Woods said they tried but she wouldn't talk."

"They don't have her listed as a witness to testify at trial," Brewer said.

"I thought you said she was an eyewitness," Grant said, staring at Mordiky.

"Apparently she wasn't, exactly," Mordiky replied. "Rob Woods told me she was, but she's not talking. All we know is, she saw something in that house and it caused her to call 911."

"She has Down Syndrome," Brewer said. "Don't know if she's capable of giving a statement."

Grant had been researching Down Syndrome and believed otherwise. "Down Syndrome kids can be very perceptive. I'd like to talk to her. She still around here?"

"Well," Mordiky said, "she never lived here. She lived in Pascagoula but not anymore. Her parents moved to Austin, Texas, two years ago. There's apparently friction between the girl's mother, who is Lacy Hanna's sister, and Ronnie."

"If she doesn't testify, they have no eyewitness and this becomes a circumstantial evidence case," Grant said. "The state will have to provide proof to exclude every other reasonable hypothesis."

"Not so fast, Johnnie Cochran," Brewer said, with a little smirk. "You're forgetting the jailhouse snitch. They apparently have a confession."

Grant stopped eating and leaned back. "Can we get him excluded as a witness?"

"I don't know. Let me do some research on the criminal."

Eaton had fixed coffee and poured each of them a cup. He hadn't said a word, and Grant watched the old man settle in his recliner. For the first time, he noticed a gray-haired dachshund stretched out between the chair and the fireplace's hearth. The dog looked as old as its owner and hadn't moved the entire time Grant had been in the house. He broke his stare when the dog blinked and turned back to Mordiky.

"What circumstantial evidence do they have?" he asked.

Mordiky pointed at the white board. "They found Petty's pocket knife near the location of the body. They found some of Hanna's lingerie and her picture at Petty's trailer. Petty worked at their house the week before, and Petty has no corroborated alibi."

"Plus," Brewer said, "folks around here think Petty is some

kind of deviant. This ain't looking good, men. If I'm on that jury, that bastard is getting convicted."

Mordiky looked at Eaton. "Walter, you know him better than anybody here. You think he killed her?"

Eaton pushed the footrest down on the recliner and sat up. "I do not. The man's right arm is messed up. Mrs. Hanna was small, but I believe she would have put up a fight. You fellows don't focus on whether he did it, just focus on creating reasonable doubt."

"Grant, how much use does he have of his right arm?" Mordiky asked.

"He can use his hand okay. He just can't straighten his arm out."

"So theoretically he was capable of pulling it off?" Brewer asked.

"Theoretically?" Grant thought a few seconds. "Yes."

The men met for another hour before dispersing. Grant was caught up in what they discussed and didn't remember making the drive home. He felt bad about not disclosing that Petty said he'd hidden evidence when his house was first searched by Sheriff Coaker. Hell, Grant thought, he didn't even know what Petty had hidden. Could it have been the pictures he'd found in the old house? He thought about the pictures, the panties, the knife ... and guilt. Grant decided that he'd treat Petty's case like a moot court competition in law school. He'd do the best he could, fight till the end, and return to Atlanta after the jury returned its verdict. He had a life apart from this case. A good life.

Grant had been reading Hemingway's *For Whom the Bell Tolls* for over a month. It was slow reading, but he was determined to finish. His eyes felt heavy, so he turned off the lamp and rolled onto his stomach to fall asleep. The burdensome facts of the Petty case kept creeping into his mind, though. The only thing that pushed the upcoming trial from his mind was to picture

Heather Sisco walking toward the front porch. Pride goeth before destruction, he kept thinking, until his slumber caused him to think no more.

•••

At some point in the night, Grant realized someone *was* knocking at his front door, that what he was hearing *wasn't* a dream. He fumbled for his phone and saw 4:23 a.m. on the screen. He pulled on his pajama bottoms and t-shirt and walked toward the sound. His faculties alert now, he decided to pause in the hallway and listen for another knock. Was someone looking for trouble? He thought about the revolver George Brewer had given him, but it was in his Jeep out in the barn. Jade wouldn't let him keep it in the house because of the kids.

Now the sound was gone. Grant, his heart beating fast, crept into Ladd's bedroom, which faced the front of the house. He eased the curtain back and thought about the old saying, *it's always darkest before dawn.* That old adage was spot on—it was so dark he couldn't see where the yard gave way to the woods. He squinted hard but could see nothing. Grant wondered if he was just being paranoid, but he'd sure heard the knocking. He went to the utility room and found a claw hammer. He gripped the tool firmly and, after taking a deep breath, strode to the front door and flipped on the porch light.

It didn't come on. He didn't remember the light being out before. Now he was angry. Who the hell was it? He retreated to the kitchen and found a flashlight. Should he call someone? And why was he scared? He hadn't heard a car engine, so whoever knocked still might be out there. He sat on the floor and stared at the door handle. It'd be daylight soon, he thought, and he would wait for another knock.

•••

An hour went by. Grant was still on the floor and no less concerned about the knock he was certain he'd heard. He was glad Jade wasn't here to witness his bravery (or lack thereof, he thought with a grim smile). He pulled back the curtain of the front door and noticed nothing strange. He then eased the door open and stepped outside. The sun was coming up, and the air was thick. He walked out to the gravel driveway and looked for evidence of a visitor and didn't find a thing. Frustrated, he decided to shower and ride to town for breakfast. He paused and looked toward the barn, thinking about the revolver. He'd keep it in the house tonight.

He stepped back onto the porch and froze. A light bulb was lying on the swing. His eyes shot to the socket, which was empty. He peered over his shoulder and looked around the yard as he walked to the swing. Below the bulb was a roll of masking tape. His heart beating fast again, he reached for the bulb and knocked it off the swing, where it broke and scattered small shards of glass at his feet. The soft thud made Grant imagine his skull being crushed against cement. The tape fell to the porch and began to roll toward the edge. Grant grabbed it and hurried inside, slamming the front door shut. He made sure all windows and doors were locked and peered again out the front door.

The more he thought about it, the madder he became. Someone was screwing with him, and the fear that had earlier paralyzed him was gone. He dialed Sheriff McInnis's cell.

"Sheriff, it's Grant Hicks. You need to ride out here," he said without preamble. "Somebody's screwing with the wrong man."

CHAPTER 16

Monday, May 19, 2014

THREE CIRCUIT COURT judges covered the judicial district in which Greene County was situated. These judges each reserved the courtroom a week at a time to try cases and accept guilty pleas, and Judge Riley held court in Greene County one week every other month. This morning, Riley was on the bench when Grant walked in and sat on the front row.

He looked around the room. Other than District Attorney Troy Lee and Assistant District Attorney Molly London, he didn't know any of the lawyers. One by one, attorneys stood beside their clients, and Judge Riley laboriously walked each defendant through the plea colloquy. Grant made eye contact with Sheriff McInnis, who was standing beside investigator Rob Woods. McInnis nodded, but Grant didn't return the gesture.

After the last defendant was cuffed and marched to the county jail, Judge Riley asked if anyone else had business before the court.

Grant stood. "I do, Your Honor."

"Are you on the docket?" Riley asked.

"No, ma'am."

"Court's adjourned." She slammed down the gavel and walked out the side door.

Grant hurried out of the courtroom and approached her chambers. Her bailiff stopped him. "You can't go in there."

"I need to see the judge."

The bailiff told Grant to wait while he went to check with Riley. Grant began to pace but stopped when he heard laughter from inside the chambers. Before he thought better of it, he barged in and found Riley on the phone. She gave him a cross look. The bailiff was standing in front of Riley's desk and pointed at the door. Grant's face reddened. He'd become insecure and assumed others were there and laughing at him. He backed out and started to walk to the stairs.

"Hicks!" Riley yelled.

Grant stopped and turned around. He figured he was about to get an earful.

"Hungry?" she asked. "Want to grab some lunch?"

He wasn't, but he couldn't turn down the opportunity to spend time alone with the judge. "I assume that's okay? Under the rules, I mean. Can I eat with you?"

She rolled her eyes. "Of course you can. Meet me at the Mexican restaurant."

• • •

Grant felt sad that the White Oak Restaurant was no longer in business and missed eating breakfast there. The newly remodeled venue was colorful and packed with locals, though, and business appeared good. Grant couldn't have imagined a successful Mexican restaurant in Leakesville when he grew up here, but times had changed.

He followed Riley into the back seating area of the restaurant and was surprised to see the DA and his staff sitting at the end of two tables which had been shoved together for the occasion. Sheriff McInnis and another deputy were there too. Pain shot through Grant's stomach, and for a moment he thought he'd have to find a restroom. He waited for the judge to take the seat at the end of the table, then sat to her right—directly across from Troy Lee.

Judge Riley waved the waiter to the table and asked everyone what they wanted to drink. The waiter obviously knew who she was because he seemed to be aware of who would be paying for the food. Riley then turned to Grant and suggested what he should have for lunch (Grant felt it was an order). After the waiter returned with their drinks and took their orders, the judge resumed control.

"Okay, Mr. Hicks," she said, "what were you doing in my courtroom without being on the docket?"

Grant glanced around the table before turning his attention to her. This was how court proceedings took place in a small town?

"I wanted a conference with you and Mr. Lee."

"Go," she said, resting her chin on her balled-up right fist.

"I'd prefer just the three of us."

"Grant, if this is about the Petty case," Lee interrupted, "everyone here is involved. So go for it. What's on your mind?"

Grant turned to him. "I need to fly to Austin, Texas, to interview the little girl who was in the house when Lacy Hanna was abducted."

"She can't help you," Lee said. "Rob interviewed her extensively after the kidnapping. And he spoke to her mother last week. The girl is not a competent witness."

Grant was trying to decide how to respond when the food came out—delivered, he figured, in record time. After the waiter left, Judge Riley spoke.

"We're not going to talk about the case while we eat," she said. "You can go talk to her. Nobody's stopping you."

"I need the county to pay for it," Grant said. "And I'd like to take someone with me who has experience with a child with Down Syndrome. To help with the interview."

"I'll sign an order reimbursing you for your travel expenses, but nobody else. If you insist on someone else tagging along, you figure out how to pay for it." Riley picked up her fork. "Conference over. Let's eat."

Fair enough, Grant thought to himself. He noticed the obvious effort by Sheriff McInnis to avoid him. The sheriff had blown off his request to investigate the identity of his early-morning visitor on Saturday; McInnis didn't even send a deputy until Sunday afternoon. And Grant didn't hide the fact that he was angry with McInnis. Sure enough, the sheriff looked at his phone and said he had an emergency, which Grant figured was a lie. McInnis excused himself and headed for the door.

After the meal, Grant dropped by Brewer's office. It was locked. He drove toward the farm and looked forward to working outside. Jade and the kids would be here at the end of next week, and he wanted to surprise Jade by having the place looking better than ever. Plus, he thought, working outside cleared his mind and helped him think. He needed to do both.

CHAPTER 17

Thursday, May 22, 2014

THE CALENDAR INDICATED it was spring, but the thermometer said otherwise. Grant was grateful to lose the wingtips, starched shirts, and ties—all a necessity at Rimes & Yancey. He was growing accustomed to the dress of a small town lawyer. Unless a court appearance was required, khakis and a polo worked fine. Several firms in Atlanta had casual Friday, although Rimes & Yancey would never allow such foolishness. They wanted their attorneys looking like they were worth $500 an hour at all times.

Grant was on his way to George Brewer's house and had already made three wrong turns. The house was located five miles northeast of Leakesville on a red clay and gravel road that the county had stopped servicing years ago. Grant had been trying to contact his co-counsel for a week; Judge Eaton had stopped by to let him know that Brewer had fallen off the wagon again. Eaton had suggested that he give Brewer a few more days to sober up, but Grant couldn't wait. The trial was in forty-six days.

Brewer answered the door in baggy, light blue shorts and a red Ole Miss t-shirt at least two sizes too small. He wore an orange cap with the word *Destin* printed across the top. He hadn't shaved in a while and Grant noticed he was wearing two different socks. They were both white, but one was much longer than the other.

Brewer let him in, then fell back in an oversized blue recliner and lit a cigarette. Grant took the couch. "Smoke?"

"No thanks," Grant said. "You okay, George?"

Brewer placed the lit cigarette in a freshly emptied ashtray. "Yeah, I'm fine," he said. "How's the case coming along?"

"Pretty good."

Brewer lifted the cigarette to his lips and inhaled. Grant looked at the walls and recognized the light brown paneling that was popular a generation ago. The house was at least 3,000 square feet, and the interior didn't appear to have been updated since it was built. Grant noticed a painting above the television of a woman and two children.

"Who is that?" he asked, pointing.

Brewer stared. It took him a second. "That's my wife ... and our children."

"It's beautiful. When was it painted?"

Brewer sipped from an Alabama Crimson Tide stadium cup. "Back in seventy-three." He turned to Grant. "It's going to be a while before I can help you. But I'll be there at trial."

Brewer seemed sober but was clearly drinking again. Grant prided himself in not having an addictive personality and didn't understand addiction of any kind—why didn't Brewer just quit the sauce?

"Can I do anything to help you, George?"

"Will Petty testify?" Brewer asked.

"Haven't decided. But I don't think he will do well under cross examination."

"Who are our witnesses?"

"I'm thinking of not calling a single one," Grant replied.

"Thought we'd shoot holes in their case and maybe cause enough reasonable doubt to avoid a conviction."

"Mordiky been any help?"

"Yes. He and I have planned our attack on the state's witnesses. But they don't have many. They got Rob Woods, the DA's investigator, Sheriff McInnis, former sheriff Wilson Coaker, Mr. Hanna, the forensic pathologist, the dental expert, and a lady who claims she saw Petty walking near the Hanna's the morning of the kidnapping. But they can't find her. Apparently an anonymous tip." Grant leaned back. "The bottom line is that this is a circumstantial case—but for the jailhouse snitch, of course. And I think we can discredit him."

Brewer took a deep drag from the cigarette before grinding it into the tray. He turned to Grant. "You need to call a witness or two. If Petty doesn't testify and you don't call any witnesses, the jury will think you're hiding something."

"But who would I call?"

"Find a way to get Walter Eaton on the stand," Brewer said. "He's a legend here. If folks believe he's vouching for Petty, that'll carry a lot of weight."

"Any ideas on how to make that happen?"

"I'll talk to Walter." Brewer reached for the bottle of Scotch that was tucked beside his chair. He refilled his cup and looked at Grant. "Drink?"

Grant shook his head no and decided to attack the elephant in the room. "George, you need to put that bottle down. For good."

Brewer screwed the lid back on and ignored him.

"It can't be that hard, man. There are people willing to help you."

"What else you come here for?" Brewer snapped.

Grant knew he'd gone too far. He stood. "Let me know if you need me."

Brewer said nothing.

Grant looked back at the portrait. Brewer was clearly living alone, and Grant assumed the former Mrs. Brewer couldn't live with a drunk. He decided not to ask about her.

"By the way, where are your sons now?"

"In my backyard," Brewer answered, pointing toward the wall.

Grant walked to a window and pulled back the curtain. Tucked away in the corner of the yard were three headstones. Grant swallowed hard and turned to Brewer. He was so ashamed he was afraid he might cry.

"I'm sorry, George," he whispered. "I had no idea."

"That's okay," Brewer said as he stood with a slight wobble. "I lost them all in seventy-four. Car wreck."

Grant walked in front of Brewer as they stepped onto the brick front porch, which was lined with black, cast-iron columns. He noticed tiny lines of green moss running along the cement which joined the bricks together. He could tell the house and yard were once immaculate. He had a feeling that the last time the house looked lived-in was 1974. He told Brewer goodbye and walked to his SUV. Pulling out of the driveway, he peered back at Brewer, who was walking up the steps and onto the porch. A feeling swept across Grant that he hadn't felt in a while—he knew he'd bonded with Brewer in a way he couldn't explain.

Grant thought about Jade and the kids. They'd be driving to Mississippi in a little over a week. What would he do if he lost them? Would he bury them in his backyard? Would he continue to bury them with a bottle? Conviction swept through Grant's body as he realized, once more, that a person never really knew what battles another faced. And what demons were at his door.

CHAPTER 18

Thursday, May 29, 2014

JADE LAUGHED WHEN Grant had called and shared his idea. He wanted Edwina to fly with him to Austin, Texas, to visit the little girl who was in the Hanna home when Lacy went missing. When he didn't laugh with her, she stopped and asked if he was serious. "As a heart attack," he'd said. Edwina's niece had Down Syndrome, and Edwina was the only person Grant knew who could help him communicate with the child.

Jade wasn't amused, however, when he finally told her about his early morning visitor a few days ago. He knew she'd worry, so he waited until the alarm system and sensored lights were installed before he told her. He also had deadbolts placed on all the doors. Like Grant, Jade was upset that Sheriff McInnis had waited more than a day to send a deputy to the farm to investigate. They both agreed that Paul McInnis was not like McInnis's dad, who'd served twenty years as Greene County's highest law enforcement officer.

The flight with Edwina was scheduled to leave from Mobile. She initially refused to go unless they drove; she'd never flown before and she'd told Grant she wasn't about to start now. Grant, though, offered to pay her $1,000, which quickly changed her mind. He pulled into Edwina's driveway at six that morning, stepped onto the dirt, and walked toward the front door to help her with her bag. She must have heard him because the door flew open.

"Come get my bags, Yankee," Edwina said. When Grant had first met Edwina she nicknamed him Yankee, but she now called him by his real name in front of Jade.

"Bags?" he asked. "We're only going to be gone two days."

She pointed at a worn blue suitcase that was bulging at the top. "I'm going prepared," she said. "No telling what'll happen."

Grant strained to lift the suitcase. Edwina's aunt, standing alongside, insisted that he eat breakfast—when he declined she fixed him a bacon biscuit and put it in a bag. She also handed him a plastic glass filled with milk. He thanked her and finally made it out the door. He looked behind him and saw Edwina and her aunt hugging and crying on the porch. Grant chuckled to himself. They were acting like Edwina was moving overseas and wouldn't be home for years.

When Grant reached the airport he glanced at Edwina. She was praying. A plane roared overhead and she opened her eyes and ducked. He laughed. "Edwina, why are you so jumpy?"

"Cause, Yankee," she said, "if the good Lord intended me to fly, he'd put wings on my back."

Grant stopped the SUV underneath the airline sign. He noticed Edwina hadn't opened her door so he walked to her side and opened it for her. She stepped out and watched other travelers as if they deserved to be looked upon with suspicion. He rolled her suitcase to a bench and left Edwina there while he parked the vehicle. When he returned, Edwina was praying again. He nudged her and they walked inside the terminal with Edwina holding her stomach.

"I need to go to the bathroom," she said.

Grant noticed that Edwina's usual bubbly personality had been replaced with fear and nervousness. He pointed at the ticket counter. "I'll wait for you over there."

Edwina was wearing an outfit that looked like a cross between pajamas and a sweat suit—she'd told Grant that if the plane crashed she was at least going to die comfortable. He turned his attention to the airport terminal screen to see if their flight to Austin was on schedule, and it was. A moment later he heard a commotion and watched as Edwina jogged toward him with a paper towel over her nose. Grant hurried toward her.

"What happened?" Grant asked. "Are you okay?"

She removed the paper from her nose. "No, I'm not okay!" she said. "That's one of them unisex bathrooms. And some big dude came walking out of that bathroom all prim and proper but I swear," she said as she looked toward heaven, "that man, Dear Jesus, just shit the devil."

Grant noticed people trying to hide their laughter. He couldn't hide his.

• • •

The unlikely pair boarded the plane and found their seats. Grant helped Edwina buckle and tighten her belt. He'd begun to feel real pity for her. Before they boarded the plane, she had to go to the bathroom three different times, once to vomit. Grant offered her a sleeping pill for the flight but she refused. She told him she wanted to be awake when they died.

Grant took the middle seat and put Edwina by the window. He adjusted the air vent to cool them as the other passengers found their seats. She leaned toward Grant.

"Yankee, what if a terrorist sits by us?" she whispered. "What the hell you gonna do then?"

Grant chuckled. "There won't be any terrorists on this flight.

Settle down, Edwina."

Grant watched her stretch her neck to look over the row of seats in front of them. A large white man with a ponytail glanced at his boarding pass, then at the letter and numbers above their row. He stuffed a book bag in the compartment above them and backed into the seat next to Grant. Grant turned to Edwina and noticed she had her eyes closed and was praying again. He smiled and shook his head. The man ignored them, opened a magazine, and started to read. Grant put a hand on Edwina's shoulder and smiled to assure her that there was nothing to worry about.

The plane landed in Austin a few minutes ahead of schedule. Grant turned his phone on and watched it vibrate as text messages arrived. Jade had texted to ask about Edwina, and his law office needed him to call a client. One message read CALL ME ASAP. He didn't recognize the number, but the prefix indicated that it was someone from Leakesville. He dialed while Edwina ducked into a restroom to regain her composure.

"It's about time you called," Heather Sisco whispered, answering without any sort of greeting.

"Heather?"

"Yes. Where are you?"

Grant frowned. He wanted to tell her it was none of her business. "I'm out of town. What's up?"

"When will you be back?"

"Day after tomorrow," he said as he saw Edwina walking in his direction. "You mind telling me what you need?"

Sisco paused. "I could get fired for this, but I overheard a conversation this morning between the sheriff and Rob Woods the investigator," she said. "They were talking about the Petty case."

"And?"

Grant heard what sounded like Sisco covering the phone. She finally whispered, "Call me when you get back. I gotta go."

The call ended. Something about this didn't feel right. And why in the hell, Grant thought, did crap like this happen when he was out of town? He knew he'd worry until he got home and was able to finish the conversation with Sisco. He saw Edwina standing beneath the sign that pointed to the baggage claim area. She motioned for him to hurry, and he broke into a smile. The Edwina he knew was back. His break was over.

• • •

The Driskill was Grant's favorite Austin hotel. He'd discovered it several years ago when he was stuck three weeks in the Texas capital city for a trial. He looked forward to bringing Jade here in the future to enjoy the city and a few nights on Sixth Street. At the moment, though, he wondered why Edwina had not joined him for breakfast. He'd called her room earlier to make sure she was awake. He was getting nervous and looked at his watch. The Pentecosts were due any minute.

The waitress refilled his coffee cup for the third time. He kept looking toward the hotel entrance, sipping at every glance. He checked the time again and looked up to discover Paula and Calvin Pentecost walking into the hotel lobby. Their daughter Caroline was with them.

He dialed Edwina's cell phone, but the call went directly to her voice mail. Grant began to perspire. The Pentecosts were early and Edwina was late! He asked the waitress to charge his breakfast to his room and walked toward the family. Caroline was standing next to her mother, holding her hand. Calvin had found the coffee station and was pouring himself a cup when Grant reached him.

"Mr. Pentecost?"

Calvin was shorter than Grant and looked fifty. His hair was bunched in the middle, as if he was trying to hold on to his youth with the latest style. He turned to Grant and smiled.

"Call me Calvin," he said as he extended his hand. "You must be Grant."

"I am," he said. "Thanks for meeting me."

Calvin turned to his wife. "Honey?"

Paula and Caroline walked toward them. As she got closer, Grant noticed the striking similarities between Paula and her sister, Lacy. Paula's hair was darker but the resemblance was unmistakable. Paula looked at least ten years younger than Calvin, Grant noticed. Caroline wore her brown hair bobbed and looked curiously around the hotel lobby. Grant couldn't decide whether to extend his hand to Paula or wait for her to go first. He'd been told many years ago by a retired member of the military to allow a lady to offer her hand. As if on cue, she reached to shake his hand.

"I'm Paula," she said. "And this is Caroline."

Grant smiled and spoke to the little girl. "Hey, Caroline. I'm happy to meet you."

Caroline barely made eye contact. Other guests were busy checking out of the hotel and Caroline seemed distracted. The elevator opened then, and Grant did a double-take as Edwina stepped off, still in her pajamas. She had an oversized book in her hand as she approached them.

Grant pointed toward her. "This is Edwina," he said. "She obviously just got out of bed."

Caroline was staring at Edwina. The pajamas were pink and the shirt was white with a teddy bear on the front. Grant knew he'd turned red—he could feel the blood in his face. He glanced at Calvin, who was smiling. So was Caroline.

Edwina ignored the adults and spoke to Caroline. "You like my pajamas?" Caroline smiled and shook her head yes. "Do you have any pajamas?" Caroline didn't take her eyes off Edwina as she shook her head yes once again. Grant thought a small bomb had gone off in Edwina's hair; it was unruly and frizzy. He watched Caroline look at Edwina's slippers. They were fluffy and gold with a dog's smiling face at the toe. "You like my slippers, don't you?"

Caroline smiled. "Yeah."

Edwina looked at Grant for the first time. "Caroline and I want to go look at that cow up there." Edwina turned to Paula. "That okay, Mrs. Pentecost?"

The Pentecosts were smiling, and Grant felt himself relax. Edwina took Caroline's hand and led her up the steps to the next floor, where the hotel had a colorful bull on display which appeared to be made from ceramic material.

"She's quite the character," Calvin said.

"You have no idea," Grant replied. He pointed them to a table out of earshot of Edwina and Caroline. The Pentecosts seemed to be comfortable.

"So what can we do for you, Grant?" Calvin asked.

"First," Grant said as he turned to Paula, "thanks for not hanging up on me."

"I must say I was surprised when you explained who you were and why you called," she said. "And I'll be blunt. I'm not interested in helping defend the man accused of murdering my sister."

Grant glanced at Calvin before concentrating on Paula. "I understand. I really do," he said. "And please know that I'm not here to convince you he is innocent. I'm just trying to do my duty as his lawyer and cover all the bases."

"Have you talked to Ronnie?" Calvin asked.

"No," Grant said. "I've never met him. To be honest, I'm not a criminal defense lawyer. I don't think it's acceptable practice for the defense lawyer to speak to the victim's family."

"Well, you called us, didn't you?" Paula asked. Grant looked at her. She seemed angry now.

"That's a good point," he said. "And I'm sorry if I'm out of line."

"What do you want from us? What do you want from Caroline?"

Grant looked at Edwina and Caroline. They were sitting at a piano and flipping the pages of Edwina's book. "Has Caroline been able to describe what she saw?"

"We had to move, Mr. Hicks," Paula said. "Ronnie wouldn't move because he thought Lacy would walk in one night like nothing had ever happened. When we'd visit, Caroline would have nightmares after we left. She's too afraid that the bad man may show back up. So to make the visits inconvenient, we left."

"Does she ever talk about it?"

"Never," Calvin said. "She never has."

"To be honest," Grant said, "I've never been around a Down Syndrome child."

Paula nodded toward Caroline. "Well, you've missed a blessing."

Grant turned to Edwina and Caroline. "Edwina's my wife's best friend. Her niece has Down Syndrome, so I brought her along."

Paula sighed. "That wasn't necessary. Caroline is a bright, loving child. She doesn't need an interpreter." Grant grimaced at this. "But it looks like ... she's made a new friend."

"When was the last time y'all spoke to Rob Woods?"

Calvin looked at his wife. "He called a few weeks ago. Wanted to know if I thought Caroline had anything else to offer. I told him I didn't think so."

"We talked to the investigator the day it happened, the day after, a week or two after that, and that was it," Paula said. "Until he called Calvin a few weeks ago."

"Did you talk to anybody in the sheriff's office?"

"Sheriff Coaker a few times," Calvin said. "We've never met the new sheriff."

"Was there ever a recording or transcript made from the

interviews of Caroline?"

"I think so," Calvin said. "But we never signed anything. Mainly because she didn't say anything."

"Has she ever told y'all what happened?"

Calvin stared at Paula and nodded his head just a bit. She turned to Grant. "Caroline said a bad man came in the house and took Aunt Lacy."

Grant waited and hoped there was more.

"But she can't describe the man. And sadly, Mr. Hicks, she's been looking for him ever since."

Grant took his time. "Do you think she would recognize him? If she saw him again, would she recognize him?"

Paula looked off at Caroline and Edwina. "I believe she would. And it scares me."

Grant hesitated before asking his next question. "Can I show her a picture?"

Calvin eased to the edge of his seat and placed his hand on top of Paula's. She didn't break her stare with Grant. "Is the picture of your client?" Paula asked.

"It is."

"When was the picture taken?" Calvin asked.

"About a year before the kidnapping," Grant said. "He still looks about the same."

The moment seemed to hang in the air. Grant wondered if the couple was going to get up and leave. Then Paula stood and walked to the piano. She spoke to Caroline and took her hand and they walked toward Grant. Edwina followed close behind. Grant glanced at Calvin, who was watching his wife and daughter. Paula looked at Caroline when they made it to the table.

"Caroline, Mr. Hicks wants to show you a picture," she said, her voice calm but brittle to Grant's ears.

He reached inside his jacket and removed a five-by-seven of Petty and placed it on the table. He watched Caroline look at the picture. Edwina stood a few feet away. Silence filled the room like hay bursting from thin strings which kept the dead grass at bay.

"Can I look at the book?" Caroline asked quietly.

Edwina took her hand. "Of course you can. Let's walk over there."

Paula picked up the picture and stared at it. Then she wiped a tear and handed the photo back to Grant. Seconds passed as Grant waited. "I believe your client is innocent," she said.

Grant searched for ways to process this revelation. He wanted to talk more, but he could sense that the Pentecosts were emotionally drained. He thanked them for meeting him, and the family said goodbye. Edwina gave the book to Caroline and promised to send her another one when she returned home.

Edwina's nerves were a bit frayed on the flight back to Mississippi, but she handled the trip with grace. Grant was impressed at the way she'd interacted with Caroline. He watched her sleep and smiled as he pictured her stepping off the elevator in her pajamas. He'd tried to compliment her after the Pentecosts had departed, but she waved it away and said Caroline was a sweet child. He'd always thought of Edwina as Jade's friend.

Now, he realized, Edwina was his friend too.

CHAPTER 19

Saturday, May 31, 2014

For at least the tenth time in the past five minutes, Grant looked out the front window. He'd called Heather Sisco as soon as he dropped Edwina at her house. He'd become energized by his visit with the Pentecosts and was eager to meet with Sisco to learn her secret. Grant was also looking forward to Jade and the kids' arrival tomorrow. Jade had wanted to drive down today, but Grant insisted that they wait until he was at the farm. He was still shaken by his mystery visitor a few days ago, and he didn't want Jade and Ladd and Ella Reese spending the night here alone in the event his flight from Austin was cancelled or delayed.

Grant grabbed a bottle of water and walked onto the porch. He looked at his watch. It was 8:33, and Sisco was late. He wondered if she'd changed her mind. He looked at his phone to be sure he hadn't missed her call. He hadn't. Then he heard what sounded like a scream echo deep in the woods. He listened harder, turning his ear in the direction of the sound. He felt for the revolver he now kept nearby, touched the cold metal in his hand.

The Peter Bay

He heard the sound again, but this time it sounded like a bird. It reminded him of Ben Petty.

He remembered the last time he'd seen Petty as a child. It was a cold February morning. Thin flakes of ice had caked the ground and crunched as they walked in the grass. They'd agreed to sneak out of their houses and meet at the end of Grant's dirt road. The day before, they'd developed a plan to scare old Grover Broome. Broome was a grouchy old cuss who'd used every opportunity to humiliate the boys, especially Petty. Broome worked at the shipyard and, without fail, left for work at four each morning.

The community was on high alert amid rumors of an alleged black panther sighting. Broome was at the neighborhood store when Grant and Petty had walked up a few days before. The boys bought themselves Cokes and bags of peanuts and were sitting on a bench in front of the store. They listened to the men debate the possible existence of such an animal. For no apparent reason, Broome looked at Petty and told the other men that they ought to tie up the *cripple* boy in the middle of the woods and use him for bait. Then Broome walked over to Petty and asked him what he thought about that idea.

Petty had looked at him and said, "Screw you, old bastard."

Broome backhanded him, knocking Petty's cap onto the ground. Petty then spit in Broome's face and ran. The men ignored Grant as he slowly walked away. He still wondered why the other men didn't stand up for Petty.

On the day they got even, Grant and Petty met at three in the morning. Grant remembered walking toward Broome's house; there was no moon and he could barely make out Petty's silhouette in front of him. They hid behind Broome's propane gas tank in the backyard and Petty screamed—a loud screeching sound. The boys giggled as dogs began barking in the front yard and lights flew on throughout the house. Petty led Grant into the woods and stopped a few feet from Broome's front yard. He screamed again. The dogs had circled the house and were barking, hair raised on their backs. Broome stepped out on the front porch holding his shotgun. The boys lay flat and still, watching the old man. Grant still remembered the coldness of the hard ground against his chest. The dogs must have heard something around back and ran in that direction. When they did, Broome reached for the corner post of the porch to lean out and get a better look, but he missed the pole and fell face-first into the yard. There he was, wailing in pain and screaming for his wife. The dogs were standing over the old fool as the boys sneaked away from their hiding place. When they were out of view of the house, they ran as fast as they could.

Word spread quickly that old man Broome was in the hospital. He'd busted some ribs and dislocated his shoulder. The guilt was eating at Grant so he confessed to his mother. She made him apologize to Broome, and Grant's father paid his medical bills and for the time he lost at work. Grant was grounded for weeks and forbidden from playing with Petty. Petty's great-grandparents didn't make him apologize, but they *did* turn him over to social services. They claimed they couldn't handle him, and Grant had lost his friend.

He wouldn't see him again until he walked into the Greene County jail almost three months ago.

Grant gave up on Sisco and went inside the house and locked the door. Now it was nine-thirty and he assumed she had changed her mind, but his heart skipped when his phone rang—until he realized it was Jade. She'd called to make sure he didn't need anything from Atlanta and said they'd be staying at the farm until the Petty trial was over. Grant could tell from Jade's voice that she was excited. He talked briefly to Ladd and reminded him to bring his baseball glove. They were finally going to clean off the old pitcher's mound.

He was in the bathroom brushing his teeth when he heard a knock at the door. He wiped his mouth and looked in the mirror, then at his watch. Now it was 10:15. Sisco was almost two hours late.

"You finally made it," he said, opening the door.

"I'm sorry."

"I'd given up and was getting ready for bed."

"Can I come in?" she asked.

He paused briefly then stepped back. "Okay."

Sisco wore jeans, an oversized t-shirt, and tennis shoes. Her hair was pinned at the top and she wore no makeup. Grant still thought she was pretty but not in the sensual way he'd grown accustomed. She looked younger than twenty-seven, and he instantly felt guilty for the thoughts he'd had before.

"Why so late?"

"I couldn't leave," she said. "I had company."

Grant pointed her to the couch. He sat in the chair next to it. "What were you trying to tell me over the phone?"

"I could lose my job," she said.

"If it will make you feel any better, I don't plan on telling anyone."

"I've applied for law school."

"That's good," he answered impatiently. "I'm sure you'll get in."

"I talked to the dean at Mississippi College and he thinks I may can start this fall. Ole Miss put me on a waiting list."

"Both are great schools." Grant glanced at the clock. "But that's not why you called me. Is it?"

"Do you promise not to get me in trouble?"

"I do," he said. "As long as you promise not to get me in trouble."

She looked confused. "How could I get you in trouble?"

"I'm married," he said. "It's after ten and you're in my house.

People talk."

She smiled. "Yeah, I guess they would. But we're not ... you know ..." She paused and Grant sensed she was attempting to read him. "I'm sorry if I've put you in a tough spot, but I figured this was the place we could be alone."

"So," Grant said. "Spill it."

"The jailhouse snitch was a set-up."

"I figured he was, but we have no proof. George Brewer told me he was transferred out of Greene County on Thursday." Grant frowned as he watched Sisco. "How do you know he was a plant?"

"The sheriff has a private bathroom in his office. The one the officers use at the office can be dirty at times. Sheriff McInnis was gone last Wednesday, so I was in his bathroom when he and Rob Woods walked in. Before I could walk out, I overheard Woods tell the sheriff that they'd be moving the prisoner. And that he'd served his purpose."

Grant stood and began to pace. He stopped and looked at Sisco. "I need you to testify."

"I'll get fired."

"Does Sheriff McInnis know you were in the bathroom?"

"No," she said. "When he walked Woods out of his office, I snuck out." She stood and walked up to Grant. "Can I work for you?"

This sounded sincere enough, he thought. And she'd just mentioned law school.

"I promise not to hurt you," he said. "Let me figure this out. You just keep doing your job and listening."

She embraced him. Excitement and guilt shot through his veins. He pulled away and stared into her eyes.

"You also have to make me a promise," he said.

She held his hand. "Sure."

"We can't touch. Ever."

She released his hand and kissed him on the cheek. "Okay, that's the last time I'll touch you."

She walked past him, out the door, and to her car. He stood on the porch and watched as she pulled away. He had no idea if she waved back. Before he closed the door he heard the screeching sound again from the woods. He thought of Petty once more. He was anxious to visit his client to tell him the news.

Assuming Sisco could be trusted.

CHAPTER 20

Sunday, June 1, 2014

G RANT HEARD A car door shut and pulled back the curtain. He watched Ladd open the Volvo's back door and Wolf leap to the ground. Jade had taken Ella Reese from her car seat and was walking toward the house. Jade, he saw, had a new hair style. Her bangs were now cut above her eyes and her hair barely touched her neck. She looked smaller. Younger. More beautiful.

He opened the door and kissed her. A wet kiss, a long kiss. He'd missed her more than he realized. Jade was still holding Ella Reese as he held his bride's cheeks in the palms of his hands. Ladd noticed and ran to separate them, squeezing in between his parents. Grant backed away and tickled him until he fell to the floor, giggling. Grant looked up and saw Ella Reese laughing. He reached for her and hugged her tightly. His family was home.

After the kids were settled in and the clothes were unpacked, Jade joined Grant by the grill as he prepared dinner. She laughed as Grant gave her a somewhat exaggerated spin on Edwina's first flight. Her smile faded, though, when Grant gave her the details of his early morning visitor. After dinner, he walked her through the instructions for activating and deactivating the alarm system. Then he asked her to look out the back window.

She opened the blind. "What is that?"

"It's a camper."

"Duh," she said. "I know it's a camper. Why is it in our backyard? Are we going camping?"

"No," he said. "Not anytime soon, anyway. Let's go look at it."

Grant held Ella Reese as Jade, Ladd, and Wolf inspected the camper. Jade sat on the small couch and stared at Grant. "Okay. What's up?"

"The trial starts five weeks from tomorrow," he said. "There will be some long days of preparation. I need the peace of mind that you and the kids are okay."

"So someone is moving in?"

"Yes, but just until all this is over."

"Who?"

"Pete Ball."

Jade laughed. "Are you serious?"

"As a heart attack."

"You'll feel safe with Pete Ball protecting the kids and me?"

"He has the eyes of a hawk," Grant said. "And Pete won't let a cricket chirp without investigating. He's not as simpleminded as folks think."

"He's cross-eyed, Grant." Jade said. "Cross-eyed!"

Grant smiled. "Yeah, but whichever eye he's looking through is powerful. He doesn't miss a thing. Plus, he's loyal. I'd have him with me in a foxhole."

"Guess I'm okay with it if you are," Jade said. "But don't plan on staying out too late at night."

"I won't. There may not be a need for Pete, but I'd feel better with somebody here during the day while I'm working."

"When will he be here?"

"In the morning."

"I hope he understands that we have rules," Jade said, raising an eyebrow. "I don't want him to teach Ladd any bad habits."

"I've told him," Grant said. "And if he has company, there can't be any alcohol or smoking in front of the kids. But I believe he and Ladd will hit it off."

They stepped out of the camper. Jade stopped Grant. "Do you believe the person that was here the other morning has anything to do with the Lacy Hanna case?"

Grant saw the worry on her face. He kissed her and gazed into her eyes. "Probably not, but I'm not taking any chances."

• • •

When Grant walked into the sheriff's office the next morning, Heather Sisco waved him through the door. She was on the telephone but appeared to be in a good mood. He stood and waited in front of her work station. A deputy walked in and poured himself a cup of coffee.

"Want some?" the deputy asked.

"Sure," Grant said.

"Here to see Petty?"

"I am."

The deputy handed Grant a small Styrofoam cup filled with dark black coffee. Then: "How do you attorneys do it?"

"How do we do what?"

"Represent people you know are guilty."

Sisco was now off the phone and listening. Grant smiled at her and sipped from the cup, trying not to grimace at the strength of the java. "My client is innocent," he said, as if it were a proven fact.

The deputy laughed as he walked toward the door. "That's what they all say."

Grant turned his attention to Sisco. "Morning."

"Morning," she said in a whisper. "I'm thinking about quitting."

Grant noticed a patrol car pull into the parking lot. He knew his private time with Sisco was short. "What would you do?"

"I'll figure that out."

She stood and walked out the side door of the building and called for two deputies, who she instructed to make sure Grant and Petty were able to visit. One led him to the recreation area while the other retrieved Petty and escorted him to a chair across from Grant.

"How are you, Ben?" he asked when they were close.

"Okay, I guess," he said. "Where have you been?"

"Texas."

"I'm starting to get nervous. I've been having bad dreams."

"What kind of dreams?"

"Last night I dreamed I was on death row," Petty said.

Grant glanced to the west. Black clouds were moving in their direction. "Ben, we're working hard on your case. Our investigator has been looking into the background of all their witnesses. George Brewer knows everyone in Greene County, and he'll make sure the jury that hears your case is a fair one. I'll try the case and I'm ready. I could try it tomorrow," he added. That wasn't the truth, but he felt his old friend needed reassurance.

"Who will be my witnesses?" Petty asked.

"At this point, we're not planning to call any."

Petty frowned. "People 'round here will think I done it for sure. I want to testify."

"We don't think that's a good idea," Grant said.

"Why? I got nothing to hide."

Grant looked around. The wind had picked up. He leaned closer to Petty. "But you *do* have something to hide." Petty stared at Grant and didn't respond. Large drops of rain began to patter around them. "I found your stash of Lacy Hanna pictures."

Petty showed no expression and didn't flinch. "Where are they?"

"Where did you get those pictures?"

"I don't remember. Where are they?"

Grant gave him a smirk. "Oh, come on, Ben. They're boudoir pictures. You expect me to believe that you don't remember?" The deputy standing guard yelled for them to wrap it up. Petty stood and walked toward him. Grant stopped him with a firm grip on his arm. "Ben, I'm going to ask you one more time: Where did you get the pictures?"

"I stole them," he said and pulled his arm away.

"When?"

"The summer before she was murdered. I was doing some work around their place and I saw them. So I took them."

"Shit, Ben," Grant said. "Why in the hell did you do that?"

"I ain't killed nobody. I wouldn't hurt her."

The clouds opened and heavy rain pelted them as they walked toward the building. Grant had planned on keeping the fact that he'd found the pictures a secret, even from Petty. Now, he thought, he *had* to tell Brewer. And was there a duty to disclose the pictures to the district attorney? He hurried past Sisco, who was on the phone with her back to him. He thought about the jailhouse snitch and what Sisco had revealed.

To hell with the DA, he thought. He wouldn't tell Lee a damn thing.

CHAPTER 21

Tuesday, June 3, 2014

GRANT HAD SET up bi-weekly meetings at Brewer's office for them to plan and adjust strategy if necessary. Brewer still didn't seem fully engaged, but Mordiky was committed. Grant was impressed with the old investigator. The purpose of today's meeting was to prepare for Friday's motion hearing before Judge Riley.

The circuit clerk had called yesterday and let Grant know that Judge Riley requested a conference with the attorneys before she'd hear the motions Petty's team had filed. Grant had filed a *Motion in Limine* asking the judge to preclude the testimony of the jailhouse snitch. It was a motion, Brewer had told Grant, that had a snowball's chance in hell. Grant had also filed a motion for additional discovery. He felt the district attorney was sandbagging and hadn't disclosed relevant materials. Brewer told Grant not to hold his breath on that one either.

Jade and the kids had settled in for the summer and Grant had, too. He secretly pondered moving back home to Leakesville, but there was no money to be made here. He'd called Judge Eaton last night to talk, and the judge invited him over for coffee.

Grant needed his old friend's advice.

"Morning, Counselor," Eaton said as Grant joined him on his porch.

"Morning, Judge."

"Trial's getting closer. How's Ben doing?"

"Seems to be holding up pretty well."

"Mordiky came by yesterday," Eaton said. "He said y'all decided against Petty testifying?"

"That's right. We believe the best strategy is to create reasonable doubt. The prosecution's case has some holes."

"I wouldn't be so sure about that if I were you," Eaton said. "Let me summarize: First, Petty has no supported alibi. Second, they found some of Hanna's lingerie in his trailer. Third, his pocket knife was found at the location of the body. That about cover it?"

Grant thought for a moment before answering. He decided against telling the judge about the pictures he'd found at Petty's place. Right now, he thought Eaton still believed Petty was innocent. For his part, Grant had gone back and forth between believing he was guilty or innocent. Then he thought about the Pentecosts.

"I do have one possible witness," Grant said.

"Who?" Eaton asked.

"You knew I flew to Austin last week to visit Lacy Hanna's niece, didn't you?"

"Was it worth the trip?"

"I showed her Petty's picture," Grant said. "She had no reaction."

"Did she see the perpetrator the morning Hanna was taken?"

"According to her parents she did."

"Do her parents believe she would recognize the killer?" Eaton asked.

"They do," Grant said. "In fact, after the little girl walked off, her mother told me that she believed Petty was innocent."

"Then you have to call her as a witness," Eaton said.

"I'm meeting with George and Mordiky later today. I'll discuss that with them." A large cat had walked up and was purring while it moved between Grant's legs. "I wish you could testify, Judge."

"If they find him guilty, call me in mitigation. That's all I can do."

"Yes sir. Thank you."

The cat climbed into Eaton's lap. "Have you spoken to Wilson Coaker?"

Coaker's name was on the prosecution's witness list, but Grant hadn't given him much thought. He was still upset the defeated sheriff searched Petty's trailer without a warrant.

"No, sir. Where does he live?"

"In Leaf. He's in the phone book."

"Judge, how well do you know Heather Sisco?"

"The little dispatcher?"

"Yes."

"Not well," Eaton said. "I knew her grandfather. He was a good man." Eaton leaned over and put the cat on the porch floor. "Why do you ask?"

"She came to see me."

"At your house?" Eaton asked, squinting. "Was your wife there?"

"Yes sir, at the house," Grant said, feeling a bit uncomfortable. "She came the first time and warned me not to trust the district attorney, Troy Lee. Then, when I was in Austin, she called and said she needed to meet again. I met her at the house when I got back. She told me the jailhouse snitch was a plant, said she'd overheard Sheriff McInnis and Troy Lee's investigator discussing it."

"You think she's telling the truth?"

Up to this point Grant hadn't questioned her veracity. He looked at the old judge. "Why would she lie?"

Eaton reached for a can of bug spray that was on a small table beside his chair. He shook the can and sprayed it in a half circle.

"Damn mosquitos," he said, looking back at Grant. "I'm not saying she's lying. But she may not can be trusted either."

Grant wondered if Eaton thought him naive. And this was a big deal: was Sisco lying to him? Or, did she know what she was talking about? He instantly became angry at himself and then at Sisco. The judge stood, indicating the meeting was over. Grant stood too.

"Thanks for the advice, Judge."

"I've got one more tip for you," Eaton said. "I assume by the fact that you dodged my question, your wife wasn't there when Sisco came to see you." Eaton stepped closer to make his point. "You never *ever* meet that young lady by yourself again, especially at your house. Understood?"

Grant swallowed, feeling a bit like he'd disappointed his own father. "Yes, sir. It won't happen again."

• • •

When Grant walked into Brewer's building he noticed a change. The dusty water fountain was clean and in working condition. New blinds had been installed on the windows, and the hole at the bottom of the front door was gone; in fact, the whole door had been replaced. Grant opened it and walked inside. The law office was clean and organized, with an older lady at the receptionist's desk. Grant introduced himself, and she sent him to see Brewer.

"Wow, George," Grant said. "What happened?"

"After you left the other day," Brewer said, "I poured the whiskey out and decided I wanted to finish my career strong. So I got my ass to work."

"I'm impressed."

"Mordiky is in Jackson. He's backtracking Petty's life for the sentencing phase."

Grant's brow furrowed. "You think we're going to lose?"

"If the trial was today? Yes I do. We have to be ready to mitigate if he's found guilty. With his family background, we may can at least save his life."

"Did Petty live in Jackson?"

"Mordiky talked to the school superintendent here who pulled his records," Brewer said. "Apparently he transferred to a school in Jackson after he left here. I think he was living up there before he moved down here. That's all I know." Brewer leaned up in his chair. "Tell me about the interview with the little girl."

Grant told Brewer about his meeting with the Pentecosts. The more Grant talked, the more excited Brewer became—he scribbled notes on a yellow legal pad. Grant began to feel guilty about not disclosing to Brewer the pictures he'd found at Petty's.

"Finally," Brewer said, "a breakthrough. We'll call ... what's the girl's mother's name?"

"Her name's Paula Pentecost, and her daughter's name is Caroline."

"We'll call the mother first and then put the little girl on the stand and ask Petty to stand up. It'll be like Tom Robinson catching that glass with his one good hand. And Petty has a screwed-up arm, too. We'll make it as dramatic as possible."

"What about the other evidence?" Grant asked. "The picture? The pocket knife? The lingerie?"

"What's Petty's explanation?"

"He says he stole the picture. We haven't discussed the panties and knife."

"You haven't asked him about the knife and panties?" Brewer sighed. "What in the hell have y'all been doing over there?"

"I've been getting him to trust me," Grant said. "I'll ask

during my next visit."

Brewer thumbed through Petty's file, which was open on his desk. "We need an explanation for those items. You work on that. I'm going to make some calls. We need an expert on children with Down Syndrome to testify too."

Grant spent another hour with Brewer. They'd meet again first thing Friday morning before their conference and motions hearing at nine-thirty. On the ride back to the farm Grant thought about the case. They were ready for the state's witnesses (except for Sheriff Coaker, who Grant would visit soon). So far, Grant thought, there weren't any surprises in the information they'd received in discovery. He hoped it stayed that way.

Grant pulled up and saw Ladd and Wolf playing ball in the yard. Ladd would throw the tennis ball to the mutt, and the dog hadn't learned to bring it back; Ladd would catch him and take the ball away and throw it again. Jade and Ella Reese sat on a blanket in the shade underneath the pecan tree. Grant nodded at Pete, who stood in the distance trying to blend into the background. Grant walked over and sat next to Jade and kissed her. He was a lucky man, he thought. A damn lucky man.

CHAPTER 22

Friday, June 6, 2014

GRANT NOTICED MORDIKY'S pickup next to Brewer's in front of the law office. He pulled into a parking spot a few spaces down and looked in the rearview mirror to straighten his tie. He wasn't as nervous about his appearances before Judge Riley these days. He didn't expect to accomplish a whole lot today, but he wanted to keep the DA busy. Grant walked into Brewer's office and found Brewer, Mordiky, and a man he'd never met before drinking coffee.

"Grant Hicks," Brewer said, "this is John Miles."

Grant shook the man's hand. Miles's grip folded Grant's fingers together. Grant cringed and wanted a do-over on the handshake for fear that Miles would think he was soft but decided to let it go. The receptionist walked in and handed Grant a cup of black coffee, and Brewer resumed control.

"Good news, man. We have an alibi."

"Really?" Grant looked at Brewer, then at Miles.

"I saw Ben Petty the morning of the kidnapping," Miles said.

"Where? What time?"

"As the crow flies, I live about three miles from Petty," Miles said. "I'd played hooky from work and went deer hunting. I climbed a tree using my tree climber. Not long after I got situated, I heard a limb or two break. I threw off my safety and was waiting. That's when I saw him."

"You sure it was Petty?" Grant asked.

"Damn right. Almost shot his ass."

Grant stood and wanted to pace, but there was no room. Mordiky was looking at the floor. Brewer was reading the *Mississippi Rules of Court*, a leather-bound volume that was open on his desk.

"Do you recall the exact time it was? Did he see you?" Grant asked.

"No, he didn't see me," Miles said. "And it was no later than eight that morning."

Grant shook Miles's hand again, gripping it hard to reclaim part of his manhood. "Mr. Miles, we're going to need you to testify."

Miles didn't respond, looking instead at Brewer. Grant watched Brewer put his finger on a rule. "Here it is. Rule 9.05." He looked at Grant. "Has Troy Lee given us a written demand for our alibi defense?"

"Yes, and I responded."

"Good, if we call John, we'll need to supplement our answer."

"There's no *if* to it," Grant said. "We're calling him."

Mordiky finally spoke. "Mr. Miles, you weren't supposed to be hunting that day, were you?"

Miles looked down. "No, sir."

"Why?" Grant asked.

Brewer interrupted. "Because he's a convicted felon. He ain't supposed to have a firearm."

"Shit!" Grant said, throwing his hands in the air.

"Relax, Counselor. John will testify. The statute of limitations has run on that crime." The men laughed, Miles included. "We're just messing with you."

Grant was so relieved he didn't care. "I'll supplement our discovery response after today's hearing."

"Not so fast," Brewer said. "We'll supplement the week before trial."

"We can't run the risk of him being excluded as a witness."

"You let me worry about that."

Grant turned to Miles. "Why did you come forward?"

"I've been keeping up with things," Miles said. "George represented me the first time I went to prison. I was guilty that time. But the second time I was innocent. I just don't want another fellow having to go through what I did."

After Miles left, Grant looked at his watch—they'd appear in front of Riley soon. Mordiky went for another cup of coffee, then sat in the chair Miles had just vacated.

"Boys," he said. "If the DA finds what I've found, it's not gonna look good for our client."

"What do you mean?" Grant felt his excitement ebb and thought of helium-filled balloons bouncing off the ceiling tiles.

"This is what I know so far. Petty dropped out of school in the tenth grade and has no GED." Mordiky sighed. "His dad killed himself after shooting his mother when Petty was eleven months old. Apparently his father had flung him against a wall by his arm. When they found him he was alive but just barely."

Brewer interrupted. "We need to finish this when we get back. It's nine o'clock and Riley wanted to see us before her docket call."

Grant ignored Brewer and stared at Mordiky. "Where did he live before he moved here? I think he was nine when he got to town."

"In DHS custody after he left," Mordiky said. "Before he got here, he lived mainly with an aunt."

"Well, what's so bad about that?" Grant asked. "I mean, related to his trial. His past should help if he's convicted. At least during the sentencing phase."

"He has a youth court history," Mordiky said.

"Where?"

"Hinds County."

"Those records are confidential," Grant said weakly, peering in Brewer's direction. "Aren't they?"

"I think the DA knows already and is pretending he don't." Brewer stood. "I'm walking to the courthouse. Y'all better follow me."

Grant ignored Brewer and focused on Mordiky. "What was his charge or delinquent act?"

Brewer had stopped at the door. He was holding his briefcase and looking at his watch. Mordiky sighed again.

"Voyeurism."

"Who was he watching?"

"He'd crawled into the ceiling of the school he was attending and was watching the ladies in the teacher's lounge bathroom."

"Really?" Grant asked. "How did you find out?"

"I have my ways," Mordiky said.

"We don't need to worry about that," Brewer said as they headed for the door. "If we're late for Judge Riley's conference, we'll have bigger fish to fry than our client being a pervert."

• • •

For the first time as a group, the Petty legal team climbed the steps of the Greene County courthouse. Grant carried his leather briefcase and was dressed in a tailored suit, crisp white dress shirt, light blue silk tie with matching pocket square, and polished black wingtips. Mordiky wore tan khakis, brown cowboy boots, a white shirt with two pockets on the front, and a navy blue sport coat. Brewer had donned a light gray pair of slacks that appeared a tad worn, white short sleeve shirt, brown penny loafers, and a maroon patterned tie. His gray sport coat was too big, but Brewer didn't seem to mind.

They walked into the courtroom and found the bailiff sitting in the jury box talking to the court reporter—he informed them that the judge was running late. The courtroom was otherwise empty. Mordiky took a seat on the front row while Grant and Brewer sat at Counselor's table.

Brewer leaned over and whispered. "Let me handle the motions today."

Grant frowned. "Are you sure?"

"Yes. It's been awhile. And if I'm going to help try this case, I need practice."

"I thought you were only going to help with jury selection and ride shotgun at the trial."

"I did say that," Brewer said as Judge Riley walked into the courtroom, "but I can't let you have all the fun." He patted Grant on the leg before they stood to welcome the judge.

Judge Riley was in slacks with a pullover shirt. Grant again noticed the lack of jewelry (other than her wedding ring). She sat in a chair at their table and instructed them to sit down. She turned to the bailiff, who was now standing behind her.

"Where the hell is everybody?"

The bailiff hurried toward the door but was met by District Attorney Troy Lee along with his assistant, Molly London. The court reporter assumed her position and the circuit clerk walked in with files in her arms.

Riley stood and walked to the judges' bench. "Just because I'm late doesn't mean y'all can be." The clerk handed Riley two files and retreated to the clerk's table, which was to the right of the judge. Riley put on her reading glasses and thumbed through one of the files. She looked over her glasses at Grant and Brewer. "Which one of you will argue the motions?"

Brewer stood. "I will, Your Honor."

Grant thought he spotted a smile from Riley. "Welcome back to my courtroom, George."

"Thank you, Judge."

"And for the state?" Riley asked as she looked at the prosecutors.

London stood. "I will, Your Honor."

Riley turned back to Brewer. "Which motions are you arguing today?"

Brewer stood and walked to a wooden podium in the center of the room about twenty feet from the judge. He was holding a stack of disheveled papers in his left hand. "Judge, we've noticed two motions for argument today. The first one asks for more definitive answers from the state on its responses to our discovery. The second deals with the jailhouse snitch."

Riley looked at London. "Respond to his motion on discovery."

London stood. Her hair was in a ponytail and she wore black slacks with a white top. Her sleeves were rolled up, which showed off her Michael Kors watch. A bracelet dangled loosely on her right wrist. "Judge, we have provided everything the rules require." She pointed at Grant. "I think the problem, Your Honor, is that Mr. Hicks thinks this is a civil matter. Several of the requests made by him are not applicable."

Grant stood to respond but Brewer waved him off. "Judge," Brewer said, "All we need is for you to instruct them, on the record, to comply with the Uniform Circuit and County Court discovery rules. Contrary to what Ms. London says, the discovery answers are not complete."

"Ms. London," Riley said. "You know what the rules require. If y'all don't provide everything, I'm not allowing it at trial. Understood?"

"Yes, Your Honor," London said, and sat back down.

"Next motion, George." Riley said.

"Judge, we believe the jailhouse snitch should be excluded. He's unreliable and his testimony, if allowed, would be too prejudicial. He's a frequent flyer in your court and everybody knows he's fishing for leniency from the district attorney's office."

Riley turned to London, who was already standing. "Your Honor, despite the fact Mr. Shelly has a criminal record, that doesn't mean he can't testify. If that were the test, there would never be a jailhouse informant who *could* testify. Furthermore, Mr. Shelly couldn't help being put in the same cell with a murderer—"

"Objection!" Grant snarled as he jumped from his chair. "Ben Petty's *not* a murderer. I ask that Ms. London's statement be stricken from the record."

Brewer turned and gave Grant an admonishing look just before Riley leaned up in her chair. "Sit down, Mr. Hicks," she said with an edge in her voice. "Only one lawyer is allowed to speak at a time. Right now, that's not you. If you do it again, I'll have my bailiff escort you from the courtroom." She turned back to London. "Continue."

London frowned at Grant before turning back to Riley. "As I was saying, Judge, Mr. Shelly fits the description of every other jailhouse snitch in the history of criminal jurisprudence. The jury will receive the usual instruction cautioning them, but the state has every right—and I dare say *duty*—to call Jeremiah Shelly as a witness."

Riley turned to Brewer, who had rolled up the papers in his hand and was twisting them as he spoke. "Judge," he said looking at London before turning back to Riley, "we have reasonable suspicion to believe that Jeremiah Shelly was planted in the Greene County jail for the sole purpose of concocting this story so this isn't a circumstantial evidence case."

Troy Lee sprang from his chair. "Your Honor, I want to respond to Mr. Brewer's baseless allegation."

Grant turned to Lee. "It's not your turn."

Riley slapped her hand on the bench. "Mr. Bailiff, get Mr. Lee and Mr. Hicks out of my courtroom. Now!" The bailiff walked toward the two well-dressed lawyers. Grant was furious but knew not to shoot his mouth off and make this worse. "And both of you are fined $100. Pay the clerk's office or spend a night in jail. Got it?!?"

Both men nodded and walked with the bailiff toward the door. Grant looked at Mordiky on his way past and glared when the investigator winked at him. He didn't think it was a tad bit funny. He paid his fine and stomped back to Brewer's building. He hurried past the receptionist and was pacing in Brewer's office when Brewer and Mordiky joined him fifteen minutes later. Grant brushed past them and shut the door.

"Okay, George," he said angrily. "When did you speak to Heather Sisco?"

"Heather Sisco?" Brewer asked. "Why would I talk to her?"

"Don't play coy with me. Did she come to you?"

Brewer pointed at the vacant chair next to Mordiky. "Sit down, Grant. And what in the hell are you talking about?"

"She came to see me," Grant said.

"Who is Heather Sisco?" Mordiky asked.

"That hot little dispatcher at the sheriff's office," Brewer said. He gave Grant a long, cool look. "Apparently, she and Grant are getting to know each other. Talk, Counselor."

"You really haven't spoken to her?"

"No," Brewer said. "I was just trying to piss off the DA."

Grant sighed. "Heather Sisco came to see me and said that she overheard the sheriff and Rob Woods discussing Jeremiah Shelly. She said they all but admitted Shelly was a plant."

Brewer leaned back in his chair. "Will she testify to that?"

"I think so," Grant said. "She wanted to quit working over there, but I told her to stay and keep her ears open."

Mordiky crossed his legs and looked at Grant. "Where did she meet you?"

Grant hesitated. Mordiky and Brewer made eye contact, and he felt himself turn red. "She came to my place."

"Don't tell me you're screwing her," Brewer said.

"Of course not," Grant snapped. "I'm not crazy. I wouldn't risk my marriage."

"What if she's lying?" Mordiky asked. "What if they sent her to get information from you? I've been around a long time and know two things that make men do crazy things: money and shaky pudding."

Brewer looked at Mordiky. "Do a little background check on Sisco." He turned to Grant. "Why didn't you tell me Sisco told you that?"

"I was planning to this morning, but when I walked in and Miles was here, I forgot."

"Anything else you're hiding from us?" Brewer asked.

Grant looked away. "Well ... there are some pictures we need to discuss."

CHAPTER 23

Friday, June 13, 2014

GRANT HAD MOVED from his makeshift office at the farm to the space Brewer cleaned out for him. The office had become Brewer's personal storage unit and Grant was amazed at the antique oak desk that was buried beneath Brewer's collection of junk. For his part, Grant had the entire office technologically modernized. He was surprised that Brewer still used books to research. He showed Brewer that the legal world was at his fingertips. He tried to get Brewer to put a computer on his desk, but the old-fashioned lawyer refused. He told Grant that he was too old to learn new tricks.

The trial was only twenty-four days away and the Petty legal team was in high gear. Brewer had been sifting through updated discovery and preparing questions and strategy for each witness. As far as they could tell, the district attorney had not picked up on the fact that they'd be calling the Pentecosts as witnesses (they'd update their witness list a week before trial). They'd also found an expert at the University of Southern Mississippi who would testify that Caroline's behavior (not identifying Petty as the perpetrator) was a reliable indicator that Petty was *not* the person she saw in the Hanna house on December 13, 2010.

As usual, Grant had arrived hours before Brewer, who liked to begin his day between nine and ten o'clock. He heard the door open and was waiting for Brewer to walk in.

"Hello?" a man asked. "Anybody here?"

Brewer's receptionist had gone to the post office. Grant pushed away from his desk and walked into the lobby. There was a man at Brewer's office door. Grant did a double-take when he realized it was Ronnie Hanna.

"Mr. Hanna?"

Hanna looked up. He wore a pair of jeans and a striped, button-down shirt. "Mr. Hicks," he said. "Can we talk?"

Grant took him back to his office and pointed to a chair. "Would you like some coffee?"

"No, thank you."

Grant sat behind his desk and focused on his visitor. "What can I do for you, Mr. Hanna?"

"I just need to get something off my chest," Hanna said. "The past three and a half years have been a nightmare. I wouldn't wish what my girls and I have been through on my worst enemy."

"I understand."

"With all due respect, Mr. Hicks, you don't understand. I know you have a job to do, and I don't hold anything personal against you for representing the man that killed my wife and the mother of my kids."

Grant felt his heart sink. The brief hope that Hanna had come to offer information helpful to Petty's case had vanished. Hanna stood, and Grant did, too.

"Mr. Hicks, my daughters have had a hell of a time dealing with this," Hanna continued. "I just wanted to come tell you to ask your wife not to contact my daughter Marly anymore."

What? Grant wondered if Hanna could see the bewilderment

on his face. He was confused, surprised, and angry all at once. Jade was communicating with one of the Hanna girls? Since when, and how? He was ready to confront his wife right then, but made himself calm down.

"My goodness. Are you sure?"

"Marly left her Facebook page open a few days ago," Hanna said. "I read their emails."

Grant felt his jaw tighten. "I can assure you it won't happen again."

"I appreciate it," Hanna said. "Marly has had the toughest time. I didn't say anything to her. Both my girls are getting nervous with the trial coming up and I didn't want to add to her stress. I figured I'd talk to you and ask you to discuss it with your wife."

"I promise I'll handle it," Grant said.

Hanna thanked him and left. Grant eased to the window and watched Hanna walk to his pickup. As soon as Hanna's truck was out of sight, Grant hurried to his Range Rover and sped toward the farm. Jade had some explaining to do.

• • •

Jade smiled when Grant walked in the front door. He didn't return the gesture. "Where are the kids?" he asked.

"What's wrong, Grant?" she asked, frowning now. "Has something happened?"

Grant stared at her. "The kids?"

"Ella Reese is napping, and Ladd is outside with Pete."

"Why are you communicating with Marly Hanna?"

Jade sat on a bar stool and wiped the bangs from her forehead. "Grant, don't jump to conclusions."

He moved to a foot from her. She'd never seen him this angry with her. "What the hell do you mean, 'Don't jump to conclusions?' Damn it, Jade, please tell me you're not that stupid!"

Jade stood and faced him. "Do *not* raise your voice at me, and there will be no cussing in this house. And if you ever call me stupid again I will leave this house and never come back."

She marched into the kitchen. Grant followed right behind.

"Don't you realize that I'm defending the man accused of killing that girl's mother? And that he could be put to death?"

"Of course I do. I'm not *stupid*."

Grant sat at the breakfast table. "I want to see your Facebook page. *Now.*"

She left the kitchen and returned with her laptop. She slid it across the table. "There," she said. "Knock yourself out."

"I don't know how to get into it."

She pulled the computer toward her and opened the page. She clicked on the messages she'd exchanged with Marly, then left him there and walked outside. A few minutes later Grant walked out the front door.

"I'm sorry I lost my temper," he said softly. Jade was staring out into the yard. His use of *stupid* hurt deeply—it made her wonder if, deep down, he thought she was just as much of an idiot as her wayward sister. "But what were you thinking? Ben's life is at stake, honey."

She finally turned to him. They'd been married three years and this was the first serious argument they'd had. He'd never raised his voice at her or cursed.

"Did you even bother to read the emails?" Jade asked.

"Yes."

"Then as you can see, there's nothing in them about your precious case. She's a sweet child who happens to miss her dead mother. I thought I'd be a friend."

Grant said nothing and started for the Range Rover.

"Who told you, anyway?"

"Her dad. And he asked me to tell you to quit emailing his daughter."

• • •

Despite Grant's rocky start to the day, he felt that the Petty legal team had a productive one. Grant had to admit that he was impressed with George Brewer. He imagined him in his prime and the powerful lawyer Brewer must have been.

They agreed to call Paula and possibly Calvin Pentecost as witnesses. They'd follow the Pentecosts' testimony with their expert on the cognitive ability of children with Down Syndrome. Then they'd roll the dice and call Caroline. Grant knew tension would be high at that moment in the trial. It was risky, but they agreed that Petty needed to put on a defense. Even if a gamble was required.

They were split on whether Petty himself should testify. Brewer emphatically opposed it. Grant supported it, though not as emphatically. Brewer was afraid Petty wouldn't be able to explain how a pocket knife with his initials was at the scene of the crime. Grant agreed that there was no explanation—at least not yet. Worse, in Brewer's opinion, Petty would look guilty trying to explain how Lacy Hanna's panties ended up in his trailer.

Grant looked at his watch and decided it was time to call it a day. He was still mad at Jade but his anger had dulled. The emails he read were innocuous. Of all people who would befriend a scared teenager, Jade would be that person. But Jade *had* to know he'd be upset at her for not running it by him first. He was getting angry all over again when Mordiky walked in.

"Hey, Grant," Mordiky said as he took off his cowboy hat and sat down. "Surprised you're still here."

"I was about to leave," he said. "Making any progress?"

"I still have some gaps in Petty's earlier years. But I think with his background we may can save his life."

"Found any family members that could testify about his childhood?"

"I've tried to locate his DHS caseworkers and found one. Most have left the agency. I also found a half-sister in Columbus. I'm going up there Monday." Mordiky paused. "Want to ride with me?"

"Sure," Grant said. "I'd like to meet her."

Mordiky shifted in his chair. "I sense you've grown fond of the dispatcher."

"Heather Sisco?" Grant asked, watching his tone. This, too, hit a nerve, but he didn't need to get mad at Mordiky. "She flirted some, and I shouldn't have let that happen. But she wants to go to law school. I told her I'd help her if I could."

"I've been tracking her with my GPS."

This made Grant's heart speed up. He knew he hadn't been alone with Sisco or heard from her since he told Brewer and Mordiky about her visit. "And ...?"

"I trailed her last night," Mordiky said. "She met a man in a white GMC pickup at Walmart in Waynesboro and followed him to a hotel in Meridian."

Grant felt a surprising tinge of jealousy. "Any idea who she met?"

"Sheriff Paul McInnis."

CHAPTER 24

Monday, June 16, 2014

JADE HAD BEEN nervous before, but nothing like this. Grant was her life and she loved him more than anything. She'd never planned to alienate him. But for the first time in their marriage, she felt like she had. She knew he was still upset about her emails to Marly Hanna. She also knew that if he found out she was meeting Marly this morning, he'd blow a gasket.

Jade turned onto the road leading to the Hicks Family Cemetery. She had emailed Marly a final time to let her know that she needed to *unfriend* her on Facebook until the trial was over. Jade didn't reveal to Marly that her father had gone to see Grant. She told the teenager that she needed to do this temporarily for her husband. Marly responded that she understood … and immediately requested Jade's cell number. Jade hesitated at first, but trusted the girl and gave it to her.

Jade loved so many things about Grant, including the fact that he annoyed her. She smiled as she thought about the way he had to have every little thing in order. His socks, his shoes, his shirts, his ties, his underwear. He had a unique organization system for everything—it was one of his quirks.

Jade cut the engine, stepped out of her car, and breathed in the crisp air. Then she walked toward the bench at the foot of Grant's father's grave. The overcast sky had cooled the temperature, but no rain was in the forecast.

Grant's investigator, Mordiky, had picked him up early this morning. They were on their way to Columbus to meet Ben Petty's sister and it would be late this evening before he returned. Otherwise, she thought, she would not have agreed to meet Marly after she'd received the girl's text message two hours ago. Jade crossed her legs and looked toward Edwina's Cutlass, which had just entered the clearing. Jade had arranged for Edwina to pick Marly up in town and drive her to the cemetery.

Jade stood and watched Marly and Edwina walk toward them. "Hello, ladies," she said.

Marly had fallen a half step behind Edwina. "Girl, why in the hell did you pick a graveyard?" Edwina asked, wide-eyed.

Jade laughed. "Because these folks out here can keep a secret." She walked to Marly and hugged her.

"Hey, Mrs. Hicks," Marly said.

"Oh, please call me Jade. I'm not that old yet."

"Huh," Edwina snorted. "You are too! Do the math, girl. If you hadn't been gallivanting around Hollywood, you'd have a daughter her age by now."

Jade frowned at Edwina. "Don't remind me of my age, girl."

"Ladies, I'm going to sit in my car while y'all visit," Edwina said, and criss-crossed through the cemetery, avoiding headstones and burial plots.

"Sit down, Marly," Jade said, patting the bench. "You okay? How's summer so far?"

Jade immediately regretted asking the question. The alleged murderer of Marly's mother would be tried in a few days. How *could* her summer be going?

"It's fine," she said. "I'm just worried about Daddy."

Jade thought the way Marly pronounced "Daddy" was cute. She always imagined that if she'd ever known her father, she'd have called him *Deddy,* too.

She put her hand on Marly's arm. "It'll all be over soon."

"I know," Marly said. "I just want to move out of that house. But Daddy won't. Jenna and I asked him the other night if we could move when the trial was over, but he said he was planning to die in that house. I think he still believes Momma's coming home."

Jade frowned. "Has he talked to anyone about it?"

"I don't think so," she said. "Our pastor visits occasionally, but that's all I know of."

"Does your dad have any brothers or sisters? What about his parents?"

"He has a brother, but he lives in California and we rarely see him. My grandfather passed away when I was little and my grandmother is in a nursing home in Pascagoula. My mom's parents were older when she was born. They've been gone a while."

"Marly, have you talked to your pastor about your concerns?"

"No, ma'am." Marly's eyes filled with tears. "I just want my old daddy back."

Jade hugged her. "It's going to be alright," she whispered. "I promise."

Jade looked toward Edwina's car and saw her friend looking in their direction. Jade pulled back and wiped the tears from Marly's face. "I'm going to make you a promise," she said. Marly didn't speak so Jade continued. "We're going meet every Monday till this is over."

"I'd like that. My Aunt Paula and I talk some, but she lives in Texas. I wish she were closer."

Jade thought about Austin, Texas, and Marly's young cousin who was in the Hanna house when Marly's mother was abducted.

"Is she your mother's sister?"

"Yes, ma'am," Marly said. "But she and Daddy don't talk anymore."

"Why?" Jade asked.

"Daddy got mad because Aunt Paula and Uncle Calvin moved. He felt like they abandoned us and Momma. But I know they didn't. They were just trying to help my cousin, Caroline. She was in the house when Momma was kidnapped. She can't even come back to the house, it upsets her so much."

Jade spent half an hour with Marly. She was finally able to get the hurting teenager to smile. Then she walked her to Edwina's car. Before Marly got in, she hugged Jade and thanked her for being there for her. As the Cutlass drove away, Jade had a feeling that Marly Hanna would always be a part of her life.

She hoped Grant would eventually understand.

CHAPTER 25

Monday, June 16, 2014

L IGHT POLES WERE flashing past. Grant tried to count them but couldn't. There were too many. He recalled the one time (the only time) that he and Petty rode in the same car together. He and his friend had been playing in the barn when Petty stepped on a long, rusty nail. Petty didn't want Grant to tell his mother, but there was too much blood. He told her anyway.

They sat in the back seat together as she rushed Petty to town to see the doctor. Looking back, Grant now realized that his mother was uncomfortable around Petty. Was it because he was poor? Or was she afraid that he'd be a bad influence on her son? Either way, Grant thought to himself, he'd be less judgmental of his children's friends. At least he hoped he would.

Grant returned to the present and glanced at Mordiky. He had been on his phone most of the drive from Leakesville to Columbus as Mordiky drove. Even though he was focused on Petty's case and had taken a leave of absence from his firm in Atlanta, he still needed to maintain contact with some of his clients. Mordiky didn't seem to mind; he'd been chain smoking and left a trail of cigarette butts in his wake as he tossed them out the window. Grant started to point out to his investigator that he was littering but decided against it. After all, Mordiky was driving, and he was working for free. Grant dropped his phone on the seat between them.

"Ever been to Columbus, Grant?" Mordiky asked.

"I've been to Columbus, Georgia, and Columbus, Ohio," Grant replied. "But ironically, I'm from Mississippi, and I've never been to Columbus, Mississippi."

A large sign welcomed visitors to Columbus: *The Friendly City*. He hoped that Petty's sister would live up to the sign. He looked at Mordiky. "Wow. I didn't know Tennessee Williams was from here."

"Yep," Mordiky replied. "Mississippi is short on some things, but talent ain't one of them."

They took the first downtown exit, which took them past the historic district and several square blocks of merchants and eventually past Mississippi University for Women. Soon the street narrowed to two lanes. They crossed a railroad track and parked in a grocery store lot where they could view a row of small wooden houses across the street.

"According to my source," Mordiky said, "she lives in the second house from the tracks."

Grant looked that way. "Neat little place. How'd you find her?"

"When I was at the elementary school Ben Petty attended, a teacher remembered the kids. She had Petty in her classroom the first year she taught. I was lucky to find her; she's actually retired but volunteers as a tutor a couple days a week. She showed me their pictures in an old annual. His sister had a different last name than Petty."

"Which is what?"

"It's Elaine Doss now," Mordiky said. "Maiden name was

Fox. I believe she's currently divorced."

"How'd you find her up here?"

"Facebook." Mordiky smiled at Grant. "Seems everybody but you, me, George, and Petty has one of those pages. My wife found her for me."

Grant chuckled. "Hell," he said, "I'm too busy for social media."

Mordiky turned the key and his pickup came to life. "There she is."

Mordiky pointed at a skinny lady walking into the yard. Two cats come out from underneath the porch and began to dance at her feet. She reached down and rubbed the felines. Mordiky eased his truck out of the lot and parked along the curb in front of the house. The structure was yellow with light blue trim. Two white plastic chairs sat empty on the front porch. Grant got out and looked at the roof and saw worn shingles that needed to be replaced. He walked past the mailbox and smiled—she had a standard black box affixed to a four-by-four pole. The pole was anchored in a base of concrete which appeared to be formed by a flower pot of some sort. Grant wondered why she hadn't just dug a hole like the other homeowners on the narrow street had.

Mordiky removed his cowboy hat and knocked on the door. They heard footsteps and a blind opened from inside.

"Who is it?" the woman asked, staring through the glass.

"Ma'am," Mordiky said. "My name is Mordiky Evans." He pointed at Grant. "This is Grant Hicks. We'd like to talk to you about your brother Ben."

The blind closed and she opened the door. "He in some kind of trouble?"

"Yes, ma'am," Mordiky said. "We're trying to help him."

She backed inside. "Come in, I reckon." The cats were sitting on the couch. She walked over and picked them up and set them outside on the porch. "Have a seat."

Mordiky nodded at Grant and sat on the couch. Grant got the message. Mordiky's job was done, and he had to take over.

"Ms. Doss, I'm Ben's attorney."

"What's he in trouble for?"

"He's been charged with capital murder."

Elaine Doss stared impassively. Grant searched her wrinkled face for surprise. He knew she was four years older than Petty, but her face made her look sixty or more. She coughed, and he recognized the hack of a smoker.

"I ain't seen him since he was nine," she said. "I'm afraid I can't help you."

"We don't need help with the actual case itself. But if he's convicted, the state's asking that he be put to death."

Doss didn't so much as blink.

"The way his trial will work is that if he's found guilty of the crime, then there is a second phase," Grant continued. "It's called the sentencing phase. The state will put on proof of aggravating factors and ask the jury to give him the death penalty. After which, we can put on what are called mitigating factors."

She looked at Mordiky. "Are you a lawyer too?"

"No, ma'am," he said. "I'm an investigator."

"Good," she said. "I'm not a fan of lawyers." She turned back to Grant. "The reason I'm not fond of you people is y'all claim you're explaining something but all you do is confuse people. What the hell is *miligating* factors?"

Grant thought about correcting her wording but knew better. "We are looking for information about his childhood that may cause the jury to stop short of giving him the death penalty."

Doss looked at Mordiky. "Can *you* explain all this to me? I ain't following him."

Mordiky sat straighter. "We know that Ben's—I'm sorry; *y'all's*—mother was murdered by Ben's daddy. We know that you and Ben lived in Jackson for a spell. Then y'all were split up in foster care. Ben moved in with your great-grandparents in Greene County for a couple years before he was turned back over to DHS. He bounced around until he ran away at sixteen."

"Sounds like you got it figured out," she said. "Why do you need me?"

"We're looking for any information that may cause the jury to feel sympathy for Ben," Mordiky said. "Do you remember what happened to his arm?"

Doss stared blankly for a moment, as if in a trance. Mordiky looked at Grant. Neither said a word. Finally she spoke. "How is he?"

Grant decided to risk getting tossed from the house. "He's doing pretty good." He noticed the stern look she gave him. "Mordiky hasn't actually met him. I have."

"Is he married?"

"No, ma'am," Grant said. "He's single. I don't think he's ever been married."

"Are they going to fry him?" she asked.

The State of Mississippi no longer used the electric chair. Like other states, lethal injection was used to carry out a sentence of death, but Grant skipped the explanation.

"Not if we can help it. Can you tell us what happened to his arm?"

Doss wrung her hands, then clasped them in her lap. Grant saw a tear roll down her cheek, then another. Mordiky pulled a handkerchief from his pocket and handed it to her. She wiped her eyes.

"I'm sorry," she said. "It's been years since I've talked about any of this."

"Take your time, Ms. Doss," Mordiky said.

"We just had it so hard," she said. "It's hard to talk about."

"Do you want us to leave and come back later?" Grant asked.

"No," she said. "I'll be fine. I just need a second." She got up and walked off toward the back. Grant heard a drawer being opened, and she returned and handed him an old snapshot. It was of Ben asleep, in a hospital bed. He was extremely small and appeared malnourished. He was obviously in intensive care, with tubes taped all over his little body. His arm was in an odd-shaped miniature cast.

"How old was he here?" Grant asked.

"Eleven months," she said. "They tried to fix his arm. Is it still messed up?"

"It is," he said. "But he can use his hand and arm a good bit. It's just crooked." He held the picture and watched her take her seat. "Can you tell us what happened? Do you remember?"

"I wish I could forget," she said. "Ben's no-good daddy had been drinking and was *mean* when he drank whiskey. He and Momma had another fight. I ran into the room where the crib was and hid. Ben woke up and got to crying. I was almost five and couldn't make him stop. That's when Momma came in the room and picked him up." Doss wiped her eyes and continued. "Ben's daddy followed her in there and tried to take Ben from her. When Momma wouldn't let go, Ben got louder. I was peeking from the crack in the closet door when I saw Ben's daddy jerk him away from Momma and hit her with Ben holding him by his arm. Like he was a hammer or something."

"What happened next?" Mordiky asked.

Doss picked up a pack of Virginia Slims from an end table and lit a cigarette. She took a deep drag, then sent a mouthful of smoke into the air. "I sat in the closet and covered myself with a blanket," she said. "That's when I heard the gunshot. Not long after, like a few seconds, I heard another shot. Ben's daddy had done shot Momma, then shot hisself."

"Did you find Ben?" Grant asked.

"No," she said. "The neighbors heard the shooting and called the cops. Nobody knew I was in there till the neighbors told them I was missing. That's when they found my hiding place."

Grant and Mordiky spent over an hour with Elaine Doss. She went on to tell them that after the shooting, the Department of Human Services took them into custody. They were eventually placed in the care of their mother's sister. Grant got the impression that Doss didn't care for her aunt a whole lot.

Seeing them out, Doss took Mordiky's business card and promised to call if she thought of anything that might help her brother. Grant, as they turned to go, asked if she'd be willing to testify at Petty's sentencing hearing if one was necessary.

"Maybe next time," Doss said. Then she closed the door.

CHAPTER 26

Friday, June 20, 2014

JADE WAS THRILLED (and relieved) when Grant asked her out on a date, as the atmosphere around the farm had been a bit tense lately. In the three and a half years that she and Grant had been married, she knew how uptight he became before a trial. On the bright side, she thought, he appeared to have forgiven her for the emails to Marly Hanna (she prayed that he not find out about their secret meetings). Deep down she knew she shouldn't meet Marly again, but she couldn't turn her back on her. The teenager missed her mother and needed a friend, an adult friend.

Jade still loved the way Grant approached married life. He wasn't by anybody's definition a romantic. He was serious ninety-nine percent of the time, but when she least expected it, he'd surprise her with a weekend getaway or dinner date. Tonight was one of those times.

Edwina had agreed to keep the kids and spend the night at the farm since they would be out past her bedtime. Normally, Edwina never would have accepted Jade's offer to stay because she was a bit scared to be alone that far out of town after dark. But with Pete Ball on duty in the camper, she felt safer. She and Pete had actually grown to like each other in a strange way (they still pretended to despise one another, but Jade knew the truth). Jade recalled the day a few years ago when she, Edwina, and Grant had driven to Lucedale. Grant had agreed to give Pete—who walked most places—a ride back to Leakesville. Pete had used a racial slur and Grant had to chastise him, and get him out of the vehicle before Edwina choked him to death.

"Where are we going?" Jade asked.

"I thought we'd go to Brownstone's in Hattiesburg," Grant said, "since our first date was there."

Jade reached for his hand. "Sweetheart, that wasn't our first date. The way I remember it, we were going together as *friends*."

He smiled. "I guess you're right."

Jade admired his profile as he drove. She loved the strong jaw and the high cheekbones. The summer sun had tanned him, and his dark hair and brown eyes still caused Jade's heart to skip when he walked into a room. She still thought he was the best-looking man she'd ever met.

"Do you remember the game we played on the way to Hattiesburg that night?" she asked.

"I do. Want to play again?"

She smiled. "Yes, we haven't done that in a while. I love the question game."

"Okay, I'll go first," he said. "This game gets harder to play the more we know each other. I feel like we've been together forever." He gave her a look of concentration. "Favorite football player?"

"Ugh," she sighed. "You know I don't watch football." She placed her finger to her lip. "Eli Manning. He played at Ole Miss." She thought a moment. "My turn. Favorite Mississippi author?"

"That's easy. Larry Brown, by a long shot. If you could pick anyone alive today to meet, who would you choose?"

"That's hard," she said. "Hmm. This may sound juvenile, but I'd love to meet Taylor Swift. She seems so genuine. What about you? Who would you like to meet?"

Jade noticed that the look on Grant's face had changed. He appeared to be daydreaming. She waited him out. He finally turned to her. "I'd like to meet Lacy Hanna's killer."

Jade looked ahead and watched a dog dart across the highway. They hadn't discussed the Hanna case much. Grant rarely discussed his work, which normally was okay with Jade. But she'd grown curious about the Hanna case, and this had opened the door.

"You nervous about the trial, Grant?"

"Not really," he said. "Don't misunderstand. I was at first. But the more I've worked on it, the more confident I've become. We still have an uphill battle, though."

"So you don't think Ben Petty killed her?"

He hit his blinker as they neared the restaurant. "I do not. I'll be honest, though. I did for a little while and I've gone back and forth. But the more I work on the case, the more I believe he's innocent."

"Well, who would have done it? Have y'all found any other leads or suspects?"

He found a parking spot and turned off the engine. "I don't know who killed her," he said. "The state's case is circumstantial. The hardest thing for us to overcome is the fact that Ben's pocket knife was found near the body." He stared ahead a moment. "And the body was dumped twenty miles from Hanna's house and fifteen miles from Ben's." He looked at Jade. "Whoever killed her dropped that knife there. And that's a huge problem for us."

"What connection was there between the Hannas and Ben Petty?" Jade asked carefully. She'd wanted to ask Marly the question but purposely avoided the subject with the teenager.

"Not totally sure," Grant said. "Petty hasn't told me how they met."

They held hands as they walked toward the restaurant. Jade's phone rang when they reached the front doors. She pulled it from her purse and saw Edwina's name on the screen.

"Hey, girl. What's up?"

"Jade, y'all got to come home," Edwina said urgently. "There's been a shooting."

"A shooting? Where?"

"Here," she said. "Outside the house."

Grant, aware something was wrong, pointed back at the SUV. Jade nodded firmly. "At our house?"

"Yes. Somebody just started shooting outside," Edwina replied. "Three times. I called 911."

"The kids are inside, right?" Jade asked, as they climbed into the Range Rover and Grant cranked the engine. "Tell me they're okay, Edwina."

"They're fine. Ladd thought it was firecrackers. Pete's outside looking for whoever was shooting."

"We're coming," she said. "Be there as fast as we can."

Two squad cars were parked in front of the house when they arrived. Edwina and the kids must have still been inside. Pete was leaning against the sheriff's cruiser when Grant jumped out of the Range Rover.

"Did y'all find who did this?" Grant asked.

"Hey, Grant," Sheriff McInnis said, more casually than Jade cared for. "We think it was just some kids goofing off."

"Oh, come on, Sheriff," Grant snapped. "There aren't any kids in the middle of summer randomly shooting a gun." Grant turned to Pete. "What did you hear?"

Pete stood straight. "I was in the camper watching TV and heard them shooting. I'd just walked around the house like you told me to. I hadn't seen nothing. I ran and checked on Edwina and the younguns first, then walked up the road. Whoever it was, wasn't in no car."

"Grant, I'll send a deputy out in the morning when it's daylight," McInnis said. "We'll look and see if we can find anything."

"Sheriff, if something happens to my family, I'm holding you personally responsible," Grant said. "You hear me?"

McInnis's face tightened. "What are you implying?"

"I'm not implying anything," Grant said. "I'm being as direct as I know how. I may have spent my adult life in the big city, Sheriff, but I'm not naive. This is the second thing that's happened here and this is the second time you acted like you don't give a crap."

The sheriff glanced at Jade, then gave Grant a long, cool look. Sensing trouble, maybe, Pete walked up and stood by Grant's side.

"Let me tell you something, Mr. Hicks," McInnis said. His eyes were slits. "Nobody, I mean *nobody*, tells me how to run my office. I know my daddy thought a lot of your daddy, and he thinks a lot of you and your wife. But you will *not* talk to me in that tone." He brushed past Grant on his way to his cruiser. "Somebody will be out here in the morning."

"Sheriff," Grant said as he followed, "somebody *else* killed Lacy Hanna. Not Ben Petty. And there's somebody trying to scare me and my family. Doesn't that concern you?"

The sheriff climbed into his cruiser, closed his door, and lowered his window. "Mr. Hicks, I investigated the incident you called about a few weeks ago. I'll investigate tonight's shooting, too. For all I know, somebody's doing this to make your client look innocent." He pointed at Pete. "Old cross-eyed Pete may have shot that gun tonight."

"You go to hell!" Grant said, pointing at the sheriff. "You're not a fraction of the man your daddy is. Get the hell off my property."

The sheriff roared out of the driveway with his deputy following close behind. Jade, having watched this play out, was proud of Grant's willingness to confront the sheriff—she, too, didn't like what she picked up. She hugged Grant and walked inside to check on the kids. She looked out the window in time to see Grant shake Pete's hand before Pete disappeared around the corner of the house.

Grant walked to the Range Rover and opened the door. Jade was surprised to see him emerge with a firearm, and she jumped when she felt Edwina's hand on her shoulder. Circumstances had changed, she knew, as she turned and hugged her friend.

For the first time, she felt afraid.

CHAPTER 27

Monday, June 23, 2014

GRANT HAD NOTICED the smell the first time he entered George Brewer's office, a smell that took him way back. When he was a kid, he'd sometimes accompany his dad to the courthouse. They'd walk down to the basement below the chancery clerk's office where the older records were stored, and Grant recalled watching his dad open the large books and read handwritten notes that were decades old. The smell of those old books and records made Grant think of his dad. Brewer's office smelled like that, to a degree.

Grant updated Brewer on his weekend, specifically the stern words he'd used with the sheriff. Brewer listened but said nothing, and Grant knew he was monopolizing the conversation and decided to change the subject.

"So. How was your weekend, sir?"

"Not worth a damn," Brewer said. "I'm heartbroken."

"Why? What happened?" Grant asked.

"The only other woman that I would have considered for my second wife got married this weekend. I guess I'll die alone."

Grant leaned up in his chair. "I'm sorry, George. A local woman?"

"No," Brewer said. "She lives in New York."

"New York? Who is she?"

"Katie Couric. She married some rich-ass financier."

Grant laughed. "You are one crazy man."

Brewer looked at his watch. "Two weeks from right now, Counselor, and we'll be picking a jury."

Grant looked at his watch, too. "I guess we will." He looked up. "When did Mordiky say he'd be here?"

"Half hour ago," Brewer said. "He got a call from Petty's sister yesterday morning, so he drove back to Columbus. Said he had something real important to tell us." Grant moved to another chair and got Brewer's attention with his movements. "You okay, Grant?"

He sighed. "I just can't figure the sheriff out. You think he's dirty?"

"Hell, I hope not," Brewer said. "I donated to his campaign."

"He just seems so apathetic. I've had two suspicious incidents at the farm and he just blew them off."

"Not to mention he's screwing his dispatcher."

"Speaking of her," Grant said. "She texted this morning. Said she needed to talk."

Before Brewer could respond, the door opened and the cigarette smell appeared before Mordiky did.

"Morning, fellas," the old investigator said. He tossed his cowboy hat on Brewer's 1970s model couch. Grant wondered why Brewer had a couch in his office but was afraid to ask.

"What did you find out?" Brewer asked.

"What?" Mordiky asked. "No coffee?"

"I'm out," Brewer said. He yelled for his secretary and sent her to Ward's for three cups of coffee. "Now, what you got?"

Mordiky faced them. "Bet my life that a Greene County jury

will not send Ben Petty to death row. I spent six hours with Elaine Doss yesterday. She's coming to testify."

"Really?" Grant asked in surprise. "When I meet with Petty tomorrow, I'll let him know."

"No," Mordiky said. "Don't tell him. She doesn't want him to know. Not yet, anyway."

"Why?" Brewer asked. "Think she'll back out?"

"No, I don't think so," Mordiky said. "She's just nervous. She and Petty had a tough time as kids. In my entire career, I've never heard of a sadder case. It's pitiful."

A client of Brewer's had interrupted them. While Brewer disposed of the man, Grant and Mordiky chatted wastefully, but they eventually stopped and sat in silence. The secretary had returned with coffee. Grant heard Brewer tell her to hold all calls and only interrupt if a dead body was found on his property. He handed the men the coffee and sat down. It was Mordiky's time to talk.

"When Petty's dad shot his mom and killed himself, Petty almost died," Mordiky said. "He stayed in the hospital three months with all sorts of injuries. By the way, Grant, have you subpoenaed those medical records?"

"Yes," he said. "I should have them soon. Taking them a while to get them."

"Anyway," Mordiky continued, "Elaine and Petty bounced around in DHS custody a year or so till their aunt took them in. The aunt's name is Rachel Spence. She's the sister to Petty's mother. Elaine thinks the aunt is still alive and living in Alabama somewhere. I'm looking for her now."

"How long did Petty and Elaine live together?" Grant asked.

"They moved in with the aunt when Petty was three and Elaine was seven. They were split up just before Petty moved here to live with his great-grandparents."

"Get to the part that's going to keep the needle out of our

boy's arm," Brewer said.

"The aunt was married to a guy named George Spence. He was an alcoholic and a child abuser ... a pedophile."

"Don't tell me he abused Elaine," Brewer said.

"She said for the first couple of years, he'd slip into her room and fondle her while he masturbated," Mordiky said, looking at the floor. "She pretended she was asleep, hoping he'd quit. But he kept doing it."

"Did Petty know?" Grant asked.

Mordiky lit a cigarette. "He knew later. Spence started having sex with Elaine when she was eleven. She tried to tell her aunt, but the aunt accused her of lying." Mordiky blew smoke toward the ceiling. "So one night Elaine asked Petty to stay in her room to keep Spence from messing with her. Petty was asleep on the floor when Spence came into the room and stumbled over Petty. He kicked the kid unmercifully, broke several ribs."

"Did he go to hospital?" Brewer asked.

"No. According to Elaine, they didn't give him so much as an aspirin. Anyway, the uncle left for another woman, but a year or so later he returned drunker and meaner. By this time, Petty had decided he would protect his sister. And sure enough, he got the chance."

"What happened?" Grant whispered.

"Elaine had started having a menstrual cycle," Mordiky said. "Petty had been watching from his room to see if Spence went into Elaine's room, and he did one night and Elaine told him she was on her period. He was tanked up on whiskey and turned her over on her belly in order to sodomize her. His underwear was at his feet when Petty ran into the room and jumped on his back. Petty wasn't a match for Spence." Mordiky stood and walked to the door to make sure the secretary wasn't eavesdropping. He turned to Grant and Brewer. "He threw Petty on the bed, turned him over, and sodomized him in front of Elaine. She said she still can see Petty's face straining from the pain, the tears rolling down his face. The aunt eventually walked in and pulled him off Petty."

"Oh my god," Grant said as he stood. He felt like he'd been punched in the stomach. "I had no idea."

"A few days later, Petty was sent down here and Elaine was sent to a group home for girls. She stayed there till she turned eighteen. She and Petty haven't seen each other since."

"I wonder why they haven't looked for each other," Brewer wondered aloud.

"Elaine said she's wanted to, but thought she'd try to forget the past, and the only way was to avoid seeing Petty."

"Whatever happened to George Spence?" Brewer asked.

"Don't know," Mordiky said.

"Well," Brewer said, "After this trial is over, I'm paying you to find him. If he's alive, I'm going to beat the shit out of him."

"Why didn't she tell us this last Monday?" Grant asked.

Mordiky grinned and pointed at the two attorneys. "She don't trust you tricky bastards."

• • •

Marly Hanna had sent Jade a text and let her know she'd be a few minutes late. Jade straightened the flowers on Grant's father's headstone before strolling through the small cemetery and randomly straightening up flowers on other headstones. She made a mental note to suggest to Grant that they spend a day here cleaning the grounds.

Jade was relieved to see Marly's car pull up next to her Volvo. They decided it was best not to involve Edwina any more than they had already. She watched Marly walk toward her in shorts and a t-shirt, sidestepping the graves of Grant's ancestors.

Jade hugged Marly. "Hey, baby. How are you?"

"I'm good," Marly said. "Are you sure it's okay for us to talk?"

"Of course," Jade said. "The trial is in two weeks, so this will all be over soon."

Marly nodded. "How are your children?"

"They're doing well. I think they like being at the farm better than our home in Atlanta."

"What are their names again? I feel terrible that I haven't asked about your children."

Jade smiled. "That's okay. Their names are Ladd and Ella Reese. They're with Edwina's aunt. They love staying there. She spoils them a little too much, though."

"They are so cute," she said. "Maybe I'll get to see them soon."

"You will," Jade said. She noticed Marly seemed more relaxed today than last week. "How's your dad?"

"He's okay, I guess," she said. "He's been spending a lot of time with us lately."

"Have y'all talked about the trial?"

"A little. Daddy has a tough time talking to us about things sometimes. He had to ask a lady from church to talk to us when Jenna and I started having our periods."

Jade put her hand on Marly's. "That's so sweet. Your daddy loves you and your sister very much."

Marly smiled. "He does. I just hope he gets over what happened to Momma. Maybe when this is all over he can find a girlfriend. Jenna and I will be gone in a few years. And I don't want him to be alone."

"He will," Jade said. "He just needs closure."

"Mrs. Jade, I think Daddy is afraid that Petty didn't do it."

"Why?" Jade asked. "What makes you say that?"

"Ben Petty worked for Momma and Daddy some," she said. "A man from our church was at the house the other night, and I heard Daddy tell him he hoped that they had the right man."

"Well, let's pray that God's will be done."

"I just want this over," Marly said. "What if Ben Petty is found guilty but Daddy still wonders if he did it? I'm worried he'll never have peace."

"Then that's what we will pray for. Okay?"

Marly hugged Jade. Jade held her and stroked her hair. "Anything you need me to do for you and Jenna?"

Marly laughed. "Maybe you can fix Daddy up with a date after this is over."

Jade laughed. "Well, us girls will scheme to do that."

They discussed places Marly wanted to visit, colleges she might attend and, of course, boys. Jade encouraged her to date but not get serious. Marly told Jade she was more concerned about Jenna; her sister had been boy-crazy since kindergarten. Jade eventually walked Marly to her car and watched her drive away.

Jade then looked skyward and closed her eyes. She prayed for Marly and Jenna. She prayed for Ronnie Hanna. She prayed for Grant. She prayed for Ben Petty. And she prayed that God would protect them all and somehow relieve the pain that linked them together.

CHAPTER 28

Tuesday, June 24, 2014

GRANT HAD ALWAYS heard the line *there's a reason for everything*. But was there? He never quite understood that simplistic (at least in his mind) application of life's events. He walked outside and sat on the steps. Daylight was at least an hour away, maybe two. He sat and listened. He could hear nothing but a lone cricket whose chirp seemed hoarse and old. Grant wondered if the insect was trying to wake the others.

Grant's high school days flashed before him in the morning darkness. His mind drifted to his friend Brandon Smallwood, who was convicted because of fear and bigotry by the same people who'd subscribed to the theory that *there's a time and place for everything*. Grant, for the thousandth time it seemed, recalled the day that he begged his dad to represent Smallwood. But Michael Hicks refused. Grant lost respect for the only hero he'd ever known, only to recapture it long after the funeral of his dad that he didn't attend.

Grant's mind had drifted so far that he didn't hear Pete walk up. "Hey, feller."

Grant jumped. "Crap, Pete. You scared me."

"Sorry 'bout that," he said. "What you doing out here?"

"Couldn't sleep," he said. "What about you?"

"I walk around during the night to make sure nobody's sniffing around."

Grant slid over and motioned for Pete to sit. "I really appreciate you staying out here, man."

Pete sighed. "I felt bad I couldn't catch who shot that gun the other night."

"If I'd have been here, I wouldn't have caught them either."

A second passed. Then: "You hear that?"

Grant felt his heart speed up and tilted his head. "Hear what? I don't hear a thing."

"Me neither," Pete said. "That's good, ain't it?"

Grant grunted, then patted him on the shoulder and stood. "Yeah, I guess it is good. Going to lay back down a few minutes. Get some rest, Pete."

Pete looked up. "Reckon who killed Mrs. Hanna?"

"Do you believe Petty's innocent, Pete?"

"Don't you?" Pete asked.

"Yeah, I do," Grant said. "I do believe he's innocent."

• • •

Grant had gotten back to sleep and his dreams were overlapping one another. He'd climbed a tree and was looking for a person; he thought it was a man, but it could have been a woman, or perhaps even a thing or place. He wedged himself between two huge limbs and fell asleep. Then he heard voices. He was trying to wake up but couldn't open his eyes. He then heard a distinct voice and looked up. Jade was shaking him, trying to wrestle him from his slumber.

"Grant. Hey Grant, wake up," she said.

He blinked and looked around. "Oh man," he said. "What

time is it?"

"It's seven o'clock," she said. "Somebody's outside. I hear voices."

Grant jumped to his feet and ran to the window. "For crying out loud. Pete has Mordiky."

They walked outside, where Mordiky was walking toward the house with his hands behind his head while Pete held him at gunpoint.

"I caught the rascal," Pete said proudly.

"Put your gun down, Pete. That man works for me."

Pete looked down and lowered his weapon. Mordiky turned and gave him a sad smile. "I tried to tell you." Then Mordiky turned to Grant. "I'm going to be out of town for a couple of days and wanted to speak to you before I left."

"Where's your truck?" Grant asked.

"About a mile up the road," he said. "She just quit on me."

"You fellows come on in," Jade said. "I'll put on some coffee."

Grant introduced Mordiky to Jade and Pete. He invited Pete in for coffee too, but Pete seemed to be pouting and declined. Grant sensed Pete was embarrassed for mistaking Mordiky for a bad guy, and he would make sure he thanked Pete before he left for work. Mordiky lumbered in and sat at the kitchen table.

"I thought that cross-eyed fellow was gonna shoot me," Mordiky said. "I tried to explain who I was, but he wouldn't have none of it."

"Pete's just trying to help. He means well."

Jade handed Mordiky a cup of coffee. "Here you go. This'll calm your nerves."

"Thank you, ma'am," he said. "I'm sorry to cause such a commotion."

"Where you headed?" Grant asked.

"Lake, Mississippi."

"Lake?" Jade asked. "Where's that?"

"Small town between Jackson and Meridian," Mordiky said. He turned to Grant. "I'll be back by Friday. You and George have everything under control?"

"I hope so. He and I are going to meet with Ben tomorrow. We need to discuss the pocket knife with him."

"What about the lingerie?"

"That too," Grant said. "We're ready for the prosecutor's witnesses. There's enough circumstantial evidence to convict, but I also believe we can create reasonable doubt. If the jury finds him guilty, we'll switch to mitigation mode and try to save his life. Thanks to your excellent work, I believe we can keep him off death row."

Jade had joined them at the table and was listening. "Mr. Mordiky, if Ben Petty's innocent, who do you think killed Lacy Hanna?"

"Good question, which brings me to why I'm going out of town." Mordiky looked at Grant. "I spent this weekend calling my friends who are still investigating for the state. Two of them told me that they had unsolved kidnappings in their parts of the world."

Grant frowned. "Are there any similar facts?"

"Yes. Two women. Both under forty and attractive. That's all I know at this point. One's in Scott County, other in Coahoma County. I'll be back Friday."

Grant glanced at his watch. "Be careful. Let me know if anything pans out."

"I will," he said. "It's a long shot, but at this point we don't have much to lose. I'll also drive through Jackson and serve a summons on Petty's former teacher to testify at mitigation if we need her."

Grant stood when Mordiky did. Jade stopped Mordiky before he left the kitchen. "Before you go," she said, "we're having a cookout here on the Fourth." She handed him an invitation.

"Love for you and your wife to come."

"Thanks," Mordiky said, smiling. "We'll be here."

"Great. We're going to invite a few folks over. Nothing real big, but Grant and I were talking the other night and we want to do something for you and the others helping on Ben's case."

Mordiky nodded at Jade. "That's mighty nice." He turned to Grant. "I hate to ask you this, but can we swap vehicles till I get back?"

"Sure," Grant said. He handed the Range Rover's keys to Mordiky. "I'll call a wrecker to pull your truck to the shop."

"That won't be necessary," he said. "I called Judge Eaton. He's on his way to fix it now." Wolf had walked up to smell Mordiky's leg. He reached to pet the friendly dog. "No offense, but this is one homely dog."

Grant laughed. "Good thing he doesn't have a mirror."

They watched the SUV pull away. Jade playfully pushed Grant before petting the dog and walking inside. Grant went to check on his security guard and found Pete in his camper still pouting. After Grant convinced Pete that he would have done exactly the same thing, Pete lightened up. He threw his gun over his shoulder and resumed post.

There were thirteen days until the trial. Grant expected it to last a week to ten days, two weeks at the most. Then he'd prepare his post-trial motions. He figured he'd be back at his desk at Rimes & Yancey by August 1. He had to admit that he was looking forward to returning to what he knew. He also admitted that he wasn't looking forward to leaving the farm. He couldn't have it all, he thought to himself as he walked up the steps. Nobody could.

CHAPTER 29

Wednesday, June 25, 2014

"HEARD FROM MORDIKY?" Brewer asked as they walked toward the sheriff's office.

"Not yet," Grant said. "Maybe he'll pull a rabbit out of the hat."

"I hope he doesn't waste too much time. By the way, Judge Riley's office faxed orders on all our pending motions. Denied them all."

"Are you surprised?" Grant asked.

"Not really," Brewer said. "The case is ready to be tried. She's a good judge and doesn't care who wins. She doesn't like to get reversed so we'll get a fair shake."

"Good," Grant said. He held the door open for Brewer and followed him inside. Heather Sisco was reading a law school admissions test preparatory book—Grant saw her wearing glasses for the first time. Her hair was longer than he remembered. Then it hit him that she'd always worn it in a ponytail or pinned. He tapped on the window, and she removed the glasses and looked his way and smiled. Grant felt an unwelcome jolt go through him and wondered if Brewer sensed it.

"Y'all ready to see Ben Petty?" she asked.

"Yes we are," Brewer answered. "How are you today, young lady?"

Sisco didn't respond to Brewer. She looked at Grant and let her stare linger. Grant felt himself turn red. Brewer certainly picked up on the vibe and would probably mention it later.

"Oh," she said, breaking her stare and turning to Brewer. "I'm well."

Sheriff McInnis walked toward them but avoided eye contact with Grant. "Morning, Counselors. George, I have y'all set up like you asked." He called over a deputy, and the man led them to the courthouse.

"Where are we going?" Grant asked Brewer.

"Since Petty is too paranoid to talk inside the jail, I called the sheriff and made arrangements to have our meeting in the jury room," he said. "I ain't sitting outside in this hot weather."

Two deputies were standing guard at the entrance. When they walked in, the first thing Grant noticed was the chairs. They were mismatched and looked uncomfortable. The walls needed painting, and he saw cobwebs hanging in the corners of the ceiling. Metal pipes were exposed and a door was open that led to a bathroom which doubled as a storage closet. Grant shook his head at the thin white string hanging from the light fixture and wondered if he'd stepped back in time. A large roach even scurried across the wall when they sat down. Grant figured that a jury wouldn't deliberate long in this place, that they'd want to get the hell out of this drab room as soon as possible. Maybe that was the idea behind keeping it in such poor condition.

"How are you, Ben?" Grant asked, bringing himself to the present.

"Okay, I reckon," Petty said.

The way Petty said *I reckon* reminded Grant of Petty's sister

Elaine. They did favor, he thought. They were both skinny, had bad skin, and their hair was thin and dirty brown.

"We need to ask you some questions, Ben," Brewer said. He clicked his pen and looked at a legal pad. "Grant wants you to testify and I don't. What's your pleasure?"

Petty squinted at Brewer. "I don't pleasure none of this." He turned to Grant. "Can I trust him?"

"Of course," Grant said. "He's on our side."

Petty turned back to Brewer. "I want to testify, then."

"Okay," Grant said. "Are you sure?"

"Yes. A fellow that won't defend himself is either Jesus Christ or guilty as hell. I can't walk on water and I sure enough didn't kill nobody."

"Do you know John Miles?" Brewer asked.

"I don't think so. I may know him if I see him."

"You're in luck. Miles said he saw you squirrel hunting the morning Lacy Hanna went missing."

"I told you I wasn't lying," Petty said to Grant.

"Well, it's not all good news," Grant replied. "John Miles is a convicted felon. I'm sure the DA will try to impeach his testimony. But it's better than nothing."

"Look, Ben," Brewer said. "Let's talk about the three major problems we have. First, your pocket knife was at the scene where the body was found. Can you explain that?"

Petty shifted in his seat and took his time. "Was it a Barlow?"

"No, an Old Timer. Has your initials on it."

"I ain't never had a knife with my initials on it," Petty said immediately. "Never even heard of one with initials."

"What are your initials?" Brewer asked.

"B.F.P."

"You sure that's not your knife?" Grant asked.

"Ain't mine," he said. "I like Barlows. I have several at my place."

Brewer was scribbling on his notepad. He stopped writing, tossed down his pen, and gazed at Petty. "What about her lingerie? Explain how her panties ended up between the mattresses at your trailer."

Petty turned to Grant. "I thought I'd hid everything. I promise."

"That doesn't matter now, Ben." Grant saw that Brewer had folded his arms and rolled his eyes. "We just need the truth so we can be ready when these items are introduced into evidence."

Petty pointed at Brewer with his eyes on Grant. "Will he tell anybody?"

"I can't," Brewer said. "And even if I could, I wouldn't."

"You know I worked at the Hanna place some, right?"

"Yes," Grant said. "What type of work?"

"Odds and ends. I'd help Mr. Hanna put up fence or haul hay. Small repair jobs around the place."

"Were you screwing Lacy Hanna?" Brewer asked. Grant whirled and gave Brewer a stern look. "Hell, Grant, let's just get it out on the table."

"No, siree, she wouldn't do such a thing as that," Petty said calmly. "She was a nice lady."

"Well, what in the hell were you doing with her panties?" Brewer asked impatiently.

Petty turned to Grant to answer. "One day I was working for Mr. Hanna, back months before she went missing. I was helping him replace a commode and I saw her panties in a hamper. So I stuck them in my pocket."

"Why?" Grant asked.

"I don't know," Petty said. He spread his arms. "I just did."

Grant opened his briefcase and placed a file folder in front of Petty. He opened it and spread out several pictures of Lacy Hanna in lingerie. Grant looked at Brewer, both men having caught Petty's keen reaction to the pictures; he was clearly infatuated with the woman. Grant put them back in the folder and slid the folder in his briefcase. Petty watched until it disappeared.

"Now," Grant said. "Explain where you got the pictures."

"That ain't all of them, one's a missing."

"You damn right one's missing," Brewer said. He leaned close to Petty. "The DA has it. Now, where did you get the damn pictures?"

Petty glared at Brewer. Then he looked into the distance. "I stole them."

...

Brewer walked faster than Grant thought possible on their way back to the office. He stormed past the secretary and ignored her effort to hand him a stack of phone messages. He waited for Grant to walk in and shut the door.

"That son of a bitch is lying, Grant."

"I don't believe he is, George."

"Well I got some oceanfront property in Tennessee to sell your gullible ass."

"Hear me out," Grant said. "He may be lying, but we can't focus on that now. He had a crush on the woman and stole a pair of her panties and her French boudoir pictures. That's the narrative. All we need is one juror."

"Are you hallucinating?" Brewer asked, his voice rising. "A knife with Ben Petty's initials was within twenty feet of the dead body, the sheriff found Lacy Hanna's panties and her—what are those pictures called?"

"French boudoir," Grant said.

"A picture of her in black panties and a red bra laying across a piano bench. And you know every juror there is gonna assume he was wacking off using her for inspiration." Brewer opened the top drawer to his desk, grabbed a cigarette, and put it between his lips. He couldn't get the Marlboro lit so he wadded it up and threw it and the lighter in the garbage. He pointed at Grant. "That son of a bitch is guilty. I can't believe I got my ass into this shit."

"Calm down, George. Let's take a couple days off. We both need it."

Brewer slumped slightly. "I'm sorry to take it out on you, Grant. I've represented guilty folks before and I'll do it again." He stood and picked up his truck keys. "I'll be back here Friday and we'll regroup. Just wish I hadn't poured all my whiskey out."

On his way to the farm, Grant found Jade's soundtrack to *The Lord of the Rings.* He slid it into the CD player and turned the volume up loud as he sped through the countryside. There was no way Brewer could believe Petty was innocent again, and Grant admitted he was doubting Petty too. He'd lost his confidence again and wondered how he could reclaim it before the trial, which started in twelve short days.

CHAPTER 30

Saturday, June 28, 2014

JADE ENJOYED THE convenience of their Keurig, but this morning she preferred the smell of coffee brewing. She rose early to prepare a full breakfast for her family ... and Pete Ball. Jade had grown attached to Pete. She noticed how he blushed with pride when she thanked him for being there for her and the kids. Grant was right, she thought. Pete would take a bullet for any of them.

She heard footsteps approaching the kitchen. She'd hoped the smell of fried bacon would wake her crew. Her plan worked.

"Good morning, baby," Grant said as he walked into the kitchen. "Smells delicious."

She smiled. "I wanted to fix y'all an old-fashioned breakfast this morning. Can you go get Pete?"

Grant walked over and embraced his wife. "God, you're beautiful." He kissed her, then pulled her body into his. "Want to go back to bed a few minutes?"

She grinned. "Maybe tonight, buster. Look behind you."

Grant turned to see Ladd standing with his hands on his hips. "Unhand my momma!"

The boys tussled a bit before Ella Reese entered the room laughing. She jumped on her dad and brother. Jade smiled at the pile of love on her kitchen floor. She walked out the back door and a minute later Pete followed her inside. They sat at the dining room table and held hands while Ladd returned thanks.

Today was Leakesville's Fourth of July celebration. The small town celebrated on the last Saturday in June each year, and Jade secretly looked forward to the Hanna girls singing tonight.

"Pete, you going to town with us today?" Grant asked.

"Don't you think I should watch the place?"

"You're going with us," Jade said. "We'll all be in town and there's no use in you staying out here by yourself."

Pete appeared relieved. "Thank you, ma'am. I'd be much obliged to go with y'all. Can we stay for the street dance?"

"Of course," Jade said. "The kids want to watch the fireworks show."

"What time does it all get started?" Grant asked.

"According to the paper," Jade said, "the parade is at six o'clock. Speaking and singing start right after that. Fireworks are at nine and the street dance is last."

Wolf started barking. Pete walked to the front door. "That fellow that looks like *The Rifleman* is here."

Grant chuckled. "Mordiky? Tell him to come in."

Pete opened the door and Mordiky walked in, hat in hand. "Morning, folks."

"Come join us for breakfast," Jade said.

"I believe I will," he said. He handed the Range Rover's keys back to Grant. "Thanks for the vehicle."

"No problem. The keys to your truck are on the bar. Judge Eaton has her purring like a kitten." Grant paused while Jade handed Mordiky a cup of coffee. "Find out anything?"

"There are three similar unsolved crimes in Mississippi."

"How old are the cases?"

"Ranging from 1988 to 2005."

Jade set a plate of food in front of Mordiky. "Do you think those cases are connected to Lacy Hanna's?" she asked.

"Thank you, ma'am," he said before answering. "I'm not sure if there is a connection. The only similarities I could find are the ages of the victims, all young mothers. And they all went missing and have yet to be found." He sipped his coffee. "I'll keep digging."

After breakfast, Jade cleaned the kitchen and ironed the kids' clothes. She looked forward to the afternoon in town. She'd get to see old friends and introduce her children to what made small towns special: political speeches, watermelon-eating contests, lawnmower races, and more. Her mind drifted to the Petty trial. Soon it would be over and they'd load up and drive back to Atlanta. She'd never admit it to Grant, but she wanted to move home more than ever. Maybe, she thought, her prayers would be answered.

• • •

The heart of America was on full display, Grant thought, as he, Jade, and the kids found a place to watch the parade in front of the *Greene County Herald* office. For the length of the little town, people were lined on both sides of Main Street, some sitting on tailgates of pickups. Grant and his family were in lawn chairs. The kids got excited as the high school band could be heard in the distance. Ladd stretched his neck to look, then turned to his mom and dad and said, "I see them!"

One of the town's highest honors was to be selected Grand Marshal for the occasion. Grant was excited for his friend, Justice Court Judge Walter Eaton, who'd been chosen to serve this year. Politicians weren't normally selected, but the committee made an exception since Eaton had already announced that he wasn't seeking an eleventh term.

"Where did Pete go?" Jade asked.

Grant pointed in the direction the parade would travel. "He walked that way. I guess he couldn't wait to see the parade."

The band members were dressed in their traditional red, white, and blue. Jade stood and walked closer to the street so the kids could get a better view. Grant chuckled when a band member gave Ladd a high-five as he marched past; Ladd grinned from ear to ear as he looked up at his mother.

The Grand Marshal's car followed the band. Mordiky had volunteered to drive Judge Eaton in his vintage red Thunderbird convertible. Eaton sat on the back of the car with his feet in the back seat. Eaton was waving at the crowd when Grant noticed another man sitting in the front seat with Mordiky, throwing candy. It was Pete Ball, riding shotgun.

The parade seemed to end as soon as it began. After a group of teenagers riding horses brought up the rear, the Hicks family walked to the courthouse lawn to wait on speeches and for a key to the town to be presented to Judge Eaton. A little boy had asked Ladd to throw a football and they were doing their best Peyton Manning imitations. Edwina had joined Jade and Ella Reese at the sno-cone stand.

Grant backed away from the crowd to avoid small talk. He'd never make it as a politician, he knew, because he abhorred boring conversations. He felt a tap on his shoulder and turned to find Wilson Coaker, the former sheriff.

"Hello, Sheriff," Grant said. He assumed sheriffs were like judges. Once a sheriff, always a sheriff. He'd known several attorneys who'd become judges and he never used their proper names again. And when a judge retired or left the bench, he or she was still referred to as Judge.

"Hello, Grant," Coaker said. "Big trial's in a few days, huh?"

"Yes, sir," Grant said. "I was planning to come see you next week."

"Oh yeah?" he asked. "How can I help you?"

"Sure it's okay to ask a few questions here?"

"Of course," Coaker said. "Go ahead."

"Why did you search Ben's trailer just before you left office?"

A man stopped and spoke to the former sheriff. After he left, Coaker turned to Grant. "Have you talked to Ronnie Hanna?"

Grant spotted Jade and Edwina talking to folks he recognized from the nursing home. He was glad they were occupied. "About Ben Petty?"

"Yeah," Coaker said.

"Not really. I've met him, but I haven't asked about the case. I didn't want to bother him."

Coaker nodded at another man who walked by. He turned back to Grant. "Ronnie called and asked me to search Petty's trailer and make sure it was clean."

"Was he a suspect?"

"Not to me, he wasn't," Coaker said. "But to be on the safe side, I tried to get a warrant. But the judge wouldn't sign it; we didn't have probable cause. Despite what some folks believe, even here you can't get a warrant based on a hunch."

"What did Ronnie Hanna say to you?" Grant asked.

"As I recall, he just wanted Petty's place searched," Coaker said. "Just in case."

"Hmm," Grant muttered. "Sheriff, you do know that a pair of Lacy Hanna's panties were found at Ben Petty's place, don't you?"

"I'd heard that. We could have missed them. We just looked around a little. We didn't disturb anything." He paused. "Grant, I may be a country bumpkin to some folks, but I know how to read people." He shook the hand of another man and said hello to the man's wife before focusing on Grant. "Ben Petty didn't kill Lacy Hanna. I'd bet my career on it." Coaker chuckled. "Well, I guess in a way, I did bet my career on it." He shook

Grant's hand. "I'd best get moving. Good luck."

Grant walked around the edge of the courthouse and leaned against a wall. So Coaker didn't believe Petty was guilty? And Ronnie Hanna wanted Petty's place searched. Why? Petty would be on trial *for his life* in nine days.

Grant stood straight. Tomorrow, he thought to himself, he'd pay a visit to Ronnie Hanna.

• • •

"Grant," Jade said after the fireworks were over, "Edwina is going to take the kids with her. She doesn't want to stay for the music."

Grant looked at Edwina. "You sure you don't want to stay?"

She pointed at the band. "Too many cowboy hats up there for me. Not my kind of music."

Grant chuckled. "Pete was planning on dancing with you, though."

"Huh," Edwina grunted. "That man can't handle dancing with Edwina. I'd give that cross-eyed toothpick a heart attack."

Grant helped Edwina buckle the kids into her car for the short drive to her aunt's house. He returned to the crowd and found Jade standing near the stage. The emcee introduced the first performer of the night: a little girl, not more than ten, sang "God Bless America." Local talent would play until a Leakesville native—now living in Nashville—would take over for the street dance.

Grant stood behind Jade with his arms around her waist, but his mind was elsewhere. The stage was only a few feet from the sheriff's office. He looked toward the barred window of what he thought was Ben Petty's cell. He knew Ben was probably lying in his bunk listening to the noises. Was he innocent? Grant tried to believe he was. He grew somber thinking of the task at hand and looked across the crowd. Some of these folks might be on the jury. He began to look at their faces and wonder if they'd have an open mind.

He returned to the present as he watched Marly and Jenna Hanna take the stage. He wondered what expression Jade had on her face as Marly looked in their direction. The girls performed three songs and had the hometown crowd cheering. Jade finally turned to him.

"The girls did well, didn't they?" she asked.

He forced a smile. "Yes, they did."

Grant's mind returned to Petty. Did he hear the emcee introduce the Hanna girls? If so, Grant thought, what expression was on his face? And what was Petty thinking now?

The crowd had grown larger by the time the main attraction took the stage. Grant reached for Jade's hand and led her to the street for a dance. He and Jade laughed and smiled as the band cranked up. Grant pulled her close and whispered in her ear that he loved her. She kissed him, and in that moment he knew he'd been kissed by the woman he'd always dreamed about.

Grant watched the crowd dance, laugh, and have a good time. Small towns, he thought, were special. He felt sorry for people who'd never have the chance to dance on a worn-out road, or laugh at an old man's feed store jokes, or watch an old warrior like Eaton tear up as he received the key to a place not big enough to be called a city.

CHAPTER 31

Sunday, June 29, 2014

"YOU AIN'T GOING to church?" Pete asked Grant after they watched Jade drive away with the kids.

"Not today," Grant said. "Jade's going to Mount Pisgah, where she grew up. They're having a homecoming service with dinner afterwards."

"You mind if I go to church?" Pete asked. "I was thinking of going to Big Creek Baptist since it's close by."

"Of course, Pete. You go ahead. I need to get some work done anyway."

"You be okay?"

"I'll be fine." Grant patted Pete on the shoulder. He turned to walk back into the house.

"Grant?"

He stopped and turned to Pete. "Yes?"

"I appreciate you trusting me enough to watch out for y'all. And I appreciate the money, but I'd do it for free."

Grant smiled. "I know you would, Pete. Enjoy the service today. I'll see you when you get back."

The Peter Bay

Grant watched Pete walk up the road with his Bible in his left hand. He had an old pickup, but he rarely drove the thing. The man preferred to walk. Grant thought about Forrest Gump. But instead of running and running and running, Pete walked and walked and walked.

Grant heard his cell ringing and went inside to grab it. George Brewer, the caller, was giddy that they'd receive the jury list tomorrow. The clerk had sent out a notice on Friday saying that she would provide them the names of 150 Grcenc Countians tomorrow at 9:00 a.m. Grant ended the call and pulled Petty's file from his briefcase. He wanted to review witness information and discovery answers one more time. He knew, though, that he was ready. In fact, he thought, he knew the state's case as well as the DA probably did.

Sleep would become more difficult as the trial approached. Despite his experience, Grant still became as nervous as he did before his first trial. A pang of anxiety shot through his stomach now. He knew Petty's trial would be the most important of his legal career. The consequences of losing had never been as high.

• • •

Jade made it home mid-afternoon after she and the kids stopped by the nursing home to visit Jade's grandmother. Grant helped her get them in the house before he left for Neely. He was nervous and wondered if he should have called Ronnie Hanna in advance, but he decided a surprise attack might work best.

The fork in the road was just as Grant remembered. Even though a stop sign was there, he slowed long enough to look both ways before the turn toward Neely. He never stopped at the sign growing up and still wondered why a yield sign wasn't there instead. He drove past a small store and noticed the old school across the road falling to the ground. Time was winning the battle against the abandoned building.

He turned down a county-maintained dirt road with pasture bordering each side. He looked at the fences and saw new barbed wire nailed to the old wooden posts. The rusted wire was still there, too. The road narrowed somewhat after the pastures ended, and the narrow lane divided a pine plantation from a pecan orchard. He noticed a mailbox ahead and slowed. The name on the box was one Grant didn't recognize. Perhaps like the Hannas, the people had moved from somewhere else to take advantage of the cheaper land prices.

After passing another mailbox he reached the Hanna place. The house was set off the road a hundred yards or so and situated in the middle of at least a five-acre yard. A dog started to bark as Grant approached. Before he could turn the engine off, though, Ronnie Hanna had already walked onto the wooden front porch. The white-painted house reminded him of *To Kill a Mockingbird* and Atticus Finch's old house.

"Hello, Mr. Hanna," Grant said.

"How can I help you?" Hanna asked without smiling.

"Mind if I ask you a couple of questions?"

Grant waited for Hanna to invite him inside but the man just stood there. Finally, the door opened and Marly Hanna walked out and stood by her father.

"Hello," she said. She turned to her father. "Daddy, want me to make some coffee?"

Hanna looked at his daughter, then back at Grant. "Come on in."

The front door opened into a foyer. To the right was what looked like the family room. To his left, Grant saw a dining room. He could see through a door to the kitchen.

"You have a nice place," he said.

"The bank and I own it," Hanna said. Grant could hear Marly pouring water into the coffee maker. A moment later she walked in and sat next to her dad. "Honey," he said, "mind if Mr. Hicks and I speak alone?"

She stood. "Okay, Daddy." She smiled at Grant. "Nice to see you, Mr. Hicks."

When she left the room, Grant turned to Hanna. "She's beautiful. And she and your other daughter can truly sing."

"Thanks," Hanna said. "Jenna's at a friend's. She likes to go a lot. Marly, on the other hand, is a homebody."

Grant's mind went to the morning of the kidnapping. He wanted to inspect the house but was afraid to ask. He decided instead to get to the point.

"Do you mind if I ask you a few questions?"

Hanna adjusted his weight. The couch squeaked as he did. "I figured you weren't here on a social call. Go ahead."

"Why did you ask Sheriff Coaker to search Ben Petty's trailer?"

"I thought he may have had something to do with it," Hanna said. "Apparently, I was right."

Grant knew it wouldn't be smart to debate Petty's innocence. "What caused you to suspect him?"

"He'd done some work here." Hanna paused when Marly brought them coffee, then cleared his throat. "I could tell he was attracted to her."

"What do you mean?"

Hanna was glaring now. "When she'd walk outside where we were working, I caught him looking a couple of times. You're married. You know if somebody is looking at your wife."

Hanna had a point. Grant saw the looks Jade received when they were out and knew the pride he felt because she was his wife. "Did he ever make a pass at her?"

"Not that I know of."

"Did Lacy ever mention that he made her feel uncomfortable?"

Hanna leaned forward. "I'd appreciate it if you would *not* refer to her as Lacy. You didn't know her, Mr. Hicks. And you're representing her killer." Hanna stood, and Grant knew it was time to leave. He got to his feet.

"I'm sorry. I didn't mean anything by it, sir." Then, on impulse: "Mr. Hanna, may I look at the bedroom where Mrs. Hanna was taken?"

Hanna's jaw tightened. He pointed at the door. "I think you best leave."

"Mr. Hanna, I—"

"I said leave." He gritted his teeth. "*Now*."

Grant walked out the front door and to his SUV. He'd wasted a trip, he thought, but he knew he needed to give it a try. The man was heartbroken and the jury would feel sorry for him. Perhaps, Grant thought as he backed out of the driveway, he wouldn't cross-examine Hanna after all.

CHAPTER 32

Monday, June 30, 2014

GRANT AND MORDIKY pulled into Judge Eaton's drive within seconds of each other. Brewer had picked up the jury list and was on his way. They'd planned to spend the day ranking the jurors. Grant was pacing in the den when he heard a car door shut outside.

"Very good," he said as he looked out the front window. "George is here right on time."

Brewer walked in and handed each of them a copy of the list. "Here you go, fellas."

Eaton had cleared his kitchen table. "Y'all have a seat. Coffee's made."

Brewer sat down and turned to Grant. "You a religious fella?"

Grant looked up from the list. "Me? Why?"

Brewer had put on his reading glasses and was peering over the top. "Yeah, you." He looked at the other men. "Don't y'all think we should pray over this list?"

"Can't be me," Mordiky said. "I haven't been to church in a while." He looked at Eaton. "Judge?"

"I don't pray out loud," Eaton said.

"Oh, hell," Brewer said. "I'll do it."

Brewer began to pray as the unlikely group bowed. The prayer stretched into its second minute and Grant became impatient. He peeked at the others and saw that Eaton and Moridiky had their eyes closed. Brewer was praying fervently and finally said amen.

"Okay," Brewer said after a sip of coffee. "There are 111 Caucasians and 39 African Americans. We have 79 women and 71 men."

"What do y'all want your jury to look like?" Mordiky asked.

"For me," Grant said, "I'm not worried so much about race or gender. I'm more interested in picking a fair-minded jury. People that are open-minded."

"You better be thinking about race or gender," Brewer said. "Because whether we admit it or not, that matters." He focused on Mordiky. "I'd like at least four African Americans. Whatever we do, though, we need to avoid a majority of white women. They'll hang Petty's ass."

Eaton looked at his list. "First name is Louise Bassett. She's a homemaker and fifty-two years old." He looked at the men. "She's from State Line. Her son works at the prison. I'd stay away from her."

"I know that old battle ax," Brewer said. "Extremely religious and closed-minded. Trust me, she'll think Petty's going to hell and believe it's her job to get him there as soon as possible."

"Harold Doxey," Eaton said.

"Works construction," Brewer said. "Probably won't be there. But if he is, put him on the good list. He'll be fair."

The Petty legal team was on juror 79 when Grant's phone rang. He stepped outside to take the call. The other men used the opportunity to take a break. Grant walked back inside two minutes later.

"That was Heather Sisco," he said. "Said she needs to meet with me about Petty's case."

"When?" Brewer asked.

"Right now. Said she quit the sheriff's office this morning."

"Well, what did you tell her?" Eaton asked.

"That I had to think about it," Grant said. "What do y'all think?"

"Go see what she wants," Brewer replied. "What do you think, Mordiky?"

Mordiky looked at Eaton. "Judge?"

"Tell her to come out here," Eaton said. "That way we don't have to worry about you putting yourself in a compromising position."

"She wants to meet alone," Grant said.

The men debated the wisdom of Grant meeting Sisco alone and weren't in clear agreement, but Brewer and Mordiky believed she might help with the case. Eaton gave in and suggested he drive Mordiky's truck. Mordiky tossed Grant the keys, and the men went back to work on the jury list as Grant walked out the door.

• • •

Grant pulled up next to Sisco's car and saw her leaning against the door. He was relieved that the meeting spot was in a grass-covered parking lot across from the high school. Although the road wasn't well-traveled during the summer, it had the feel of a public place. He killed the engine and walked to where she was now standing.

"Where'd you get the truck?" Sisco asked.

"It's a friend's," Grant said. Now that he was standing near her, he regretted meeting her. She was dressed in a low-cut blouse and wore more makeup than usual. He thought of Jade and was mad at himself that he'd ever been attracted to this lady in the first place. "What did you want to tell me?"

"Can we go somewhere and park?" she asked.

"No," Grant said impatiently. "I don't have time."

"I just don't want you to think less of me."

He already knew she was sleeping with the sheriff. He couldn't think less of her. He was hoping she would somehow redeem herself. She stepped closer to him.

"Grant, I'm extremely attracted to you."

Grant sighed. "I've got to go. I thought you had some information about the case."

She appeared confused that he didn't respond the way she thought he might, which was curious. Right then she received a text. Grant watched her respond. When Sisco looked up, she had an odd look on her face.

"Grant, let me be honest: Sheriff McInnis doesn't like you very much. He wants a conviction before the election next year, and he sees you as his enemy right now. He told me the other day that he couldn't stand you."

"Come on. Why would he dislike me?"

"He blames your dad for his daddy getting beat years ago," she said. "Plus, he's worried about Petty's trial. He's afraid you'll somehow get him off and hurt his chances to be re-elected."

"Well, to tell you the truth," Grant said, "I don't care for him a whole lot, either. Is that all you wanted to say?"

Her bangs had fallen over her eyes. She wiped them away and glanced over her shoulder before moving toward Grant. She pressed against him and kissed him on the cheek. He removed her hands and stepped away from her.

"Heather, don't," he said. "I'm very much in love with my wife. I think it'd be best if we don't meet again."

Grant drove off and left Sisco standing next to her car. He was furious that he'd let her waste his time—time better spent studying the jury list for Petty's trial, which was now only a week away. He'd been a fool to come out here, and a true idiot to have gotten flattered by Sisco's interest. It was a mistake, he thought to himself as he drove toward Eaton's, that he'd never make again.

CHAPTER 33

Monday, June 30, 2014

JADE DECIDED TO follow her instincts. She'd accepted Marly's invitation to meet her behind the old, abandoned school in Neely. Marly needed to talk, she'd told Jade, but couldn't risk being too far away from her home. Jade was nervous because she was unfamiliar with the place. Earlier, she'd driven to town and dropped the kids by Edwina's and prayed she'd not cross paths with Grant. When she pulled behind the old building, she was relieved to find Marly sitting on the abandoned back porch. Marly stood, and Jade hugged her before they sat down.

"Mr. Grant came to visit yesterday," Marly said.

"I know." Jade frowned. "He was afraid he made your dad mad."

"Daddy's just stressed, that's all. I think he felt bad for being so short with Mr. Grant."

"Grant understands," Jade said. "And trust me, we'll all be glad when this is over."

Marly's smile faded. "Mr. Grant wanted to see Momma's room."

Wow. Grant hadn't told her that. Jade wiped a wisp of hair from her eyes and waited for Marly to continue.

"Daddy hasn't slept in there since Momma was taken," Marly said. "He sleeps on the couch or in the guest bedroom."

Jade put her arm around Marly. "I'm so sorry." Marly wiped away a tear. "When this is over, if your daddy will let y'all, I'm taking you and Jenna shopping. Y'all need a girls' trip. Okay?"

"That would be fun." Then Marly's face changed. "Mrs. Jade, do you think Ben Petty killed my momma?"

Jade felt her heart sink. This was probably why the girl asked her out here. And Jade couldn't blame her, the way she'd acted like a surrogate aunt—or even mother.

"Baby, only God knows for sure. We'll just pray His will be done."

"I heard Daddy tell Mr. Grant that Ben Petty looked at Momma funny. Like he liked her. But I don't remember that."

"What do you remember, sweetie?"

"Ben Petty would work for Daddy some. Momma felt sorry for him and would occasionally give him things. I was with her one time when she dropped by his trailer and gave him some stuff from the garden."

Fearful, yet fascinated, Jade waited Marly out.

"In a way, though, I hope he *did* do it and he's found guilty. I'm tired of worrying all the time. I'm tired of jumping every time I hear a noise."

They were startled by a man in a pickup who had pulled behind the building to turn around. He waved at them like they somehow belonged there and drove away. Jade knew she needed to leave. Her nerves were frayed at having been seen by another person. She embraced Marly and held her as she whispered a prayer.

On the way back to Leakesville to pick up the kids, Jade began to cry. She didn't know if Ben Petty murdered Lacy Hanna. If he didn't, there were no indications that the crime would ever be solved. Jade found herself almost hoping Grant would lose next week. Perhaps, she thought, if Petty didn't commit the crime, he still needed to be the scapegoat. She didn't want him to be executed, just found guilty. Maybe that would allow everybody to move on with their lives. Maybe, she thought, the Hanna family would finally have some measure of closure.

CHAPTER 34

Friday, July 4, 2014

GRANT MADE SURE Pete was awake before he left for George Brewer's office. He found him outside stacking pecan tree logs and limbs under the homemade barbecue pit. When Jade told them of her plan to have a barbecue this afternoon, Pete decided he'd build a pit for the occasion. The morning was unseasonably cool for this time of year, and Pete had built a small fire to keep him warm from the morning dew. Pete jumped about a foot off the ground when Grant said good morning.

"I'll declare, fella," he said. "You scared the living daylights out of me."

It wasn't quite daylight and the wet grass had silenced Grant's steps, apparently. "Sorry. You need any help?"

"Paul Sumner's going to help. He's on his way."

"Good," Grant said as he sipped his coffee.

"Who all's coming?"

"Let's see," Grant said. "George Brewer, Judge Eaton, Mordiky and his wife, Edwina, her aunt and nieces and nephews, Paul Sumner, you, me, Jade and the kids. I think that's it."

"That's a lot of chicken."

Grant laughed. "It is indeed." He finished his coffee and stood. "I'm going to the office. Tell Jade we'll be here by lunch."

• • •

Grant drove the old Jeep to town, finally ready to leave the machine at the body shop and ride home with Brewer. He was looking forward to the new paint job and having windows without bullet holes.

The trial was only three days away. He'd met with Petty for the last time yesterday and the decision had been made that Petty *would* testify. Of course, like a lot of trial strategy, that decision was subject to change. Grant had prepared Petty by asking him questions the prosecutor would likely throw at him. Petty, Grant thought, would score a C-minus taking an oral exam. Grant knew it was a tremendous risk. But he felt it was worth the gamble.

Grant walked into the conference room in Brewer's office and saw names of potential witnesses in four columns on a white board. The first two were labeled State and Defense. Above those labels were the words: Guilt Phase. The next two columns were for the Sentencing Phase. He began to read the names of the jurors. They were so familiar to Grant that he believed he knew their favorite colors and what they ate for breakfast this morning. He put on a pot of coffee and was waiting for it to finish when Brewer walked in.

"Morning, Grant. Ready for the show on Monday?"

Grant smiled. "You know, I sort of am. Trials are a lot of work but it's hard to beat the adrenaline rush."

Brewer poured a cup of coffee. "Have to admit I'm kind of excited too." He paused. "I'm glad you asked me to help."

Grant chuckled. "I'm the one that should be thanking you. If you hadn't bailed me out, Judge Riley would have sent me back to Atlanta."

"I told Mordiky and Walter to meet us at your place for lunch. I hope that's okay."

"Sure. By the way, when will Petty's sister be here?"

"Mordiky will get her Sunday. We booked her a room at a hotel in Lucedale."

"Good deal. What about John Miles?"

"He'll be on stand-by," Brewer said. He set his cup down. "Now look, Grant, I didn't disclose our alibi defense to the prosecutor until two days ago. Troy Lee will raise hell Monday, but let me handle that."

"You think he'll be excluded as a witness?"

"No. Judge Riley will scold us but he'll be able to testify. Like I said, you don't say a word. I'll cover that. We'll turn the table on Lee."

Grant looked hard at the list. "There's a name missing."

"Who?"

"Heather Sisco."

Brewer frowned. "Is she testifying for the state? They didn't list her."

"No, she's testifying for us."

"I'm confused."

"I've been thinking about what she said about the jailhouse snitch. I don't think she's lying about him being a plant. We can call her to impeach him."

Brewer stared.

"We'll subpoena her if necessary," Grant added.

"But what if she's lying? What if you've misread her?"

Grant wrote her name on the board and turned to Brewer. "I haven't misread her. If she discredits the snitch, this is a circumstantial case. And our chances of getting a hung jury increases."

"But if she denies telling you that," Brewer said, "Petty's gone."

"Let's see how the trial is going. Her testimony may be what saves Petty's life."

Brewer grunted. "When will the Pentecosts be here?"

"I spoke to Paula last night. They're flying in Monday."

"Has she spoken to Ronnie Hanna?"

"I don't know," Grant said. "I booked them a room in Hattiesburg. They'll stay there till we need them to come to court."

Grant and Brewer developed strategy the rest of the morning. Brewer would handle the jury venire and Grant would tackle the pre-trial motions; Grant would give the opening statement and Brewer would close. They decided who would examine each witness and even decided what they'd wear (Brewer insisted on Grant appearing more like a small-town attorney than the Wall Street lawyer he usually resembled). Just before they walked out of the office to drive to the farm, Brewer stopped Grant.

"Do you think he's innocent?"

Grant paused before answering. "I do, George."

Brewer slapped him on the shoulder. "Well, that's good enough for me. Come Monday, let's get his ass acquitted."

• • •

The kids were playing kick ball when Grant and Brewer pulled into the driveway. Judge Eaton and Mordiky were sitting in lawn chairs watching Pete Ball and Paul Sumner tend to the chicken on the grill. The cool morning had given way to the traditional heat and humidity of the south. Grant smiled as he watched Ladd kick the ball and run safely to first base.

"Smells delicious," Brewer said, taking out his pocket knife and cutting a piece of sausage that had already been grilled.

"Well, boys," Eaton said, "y'all ready?"

"We think so," Grant said.

"Hell yeah, we're ready," Brewer said. "The DA thinks this'll be a lay-up. But we're going to make him work."

"George, do you know Paul?" Grant asked.

The Peter Bay

Brewer reached for Sumner's hand. "George Brewer. Have we met before?"

Sumner wiped his hands on a paper towel before shaking. "Paul Sumner. We may have. I lived here a few years ago."

"That's right," Brewer said. "You were the principal at the elementary school?"

"From 2004 to 2009. I took a job in Holmes County until I retired."

"You're mighty young to be retired," Eaton said.

"I got my twenty-five in and gave it up," Sumner said. "Today's kids and parents became too much of a pain to deal with so I decided to retire. Going to do something else but I haven't decided what yet."

Grant reached for a piece of sausage. "Paul moved into the old R.D. Lewis place." Wolf had walked up, and Grant gave him a piece of meat. "By the way, Paul, I've never asked. Why did you move back here?"

"The people," he said. "I've lived all over Mississippi but fell in love with Greene County. I hope to die here some day."

"This is a special place," Brewer said.

"I'd always wanted to move around some but spent my career in Hattiesburg," Mordiky said. "Where else did you live?"

"I started out in Okolona coaching and teaching. Got offered a principal's job in Friars Point, in the Delta," Sumner said. "Lived there for a while, then moved to Forest. I met the Greene County superintendent at a conference and applied for the job at the elementary school. I should have stayed here and finished my career."

"You're here now." Grant stood to help Pete remove the chicken from the grill and watched Wolf run to Ladd. "And I know Ladd is glad you moved back, or he wouldn't have met Wolf."

Eaton grunted. "Huh. Counselor, I don't know if I'd thank

him for that dog. That sucker's so ugly he'd have to sneak up on a bowl of water."

The men laughed as they walked around the house to where the ladies had set up tables under the shade of the red oaks. The collection of friends and neighbors spent time enjoying the meal and laughing. Brewer stood and made a toast to friendship. Grant looked around and realized how blessed he was. He thought of his office in Atlanta and realized he'd missed a lot of living after selling his soul to Rimes & Yancey.

After the meal Grant picked up the used paper plates and cups and dropped them in the garbage can. Jade and Edwina began serving homemade ice cream as he closed the lid and looked past the barn and into the field. He paused and remembered Petty standing and motioning with his good arm to come and play. He smiled and thought, *I wish we could, Ben. I wish we could.*

CHAPTER 35

Monday, July 7, 2014

JADE HAD THOUGHT about what Marly Hanna told her regarding Lacy Hanna's visit to Petty's trailer. She wondered if Grant knew. She wanted to tell him, but he'd be furious that she'd been secretly meeting with the girl after their fight.

Jade noticed that Grant had tossed and turned throughout the night. She decided to slip out of bed and make him breakfast. Grant normally didn't eat a heavy breakfast before a trial, and she didn't think he'd eat one today, either. But cooking was the only way she could show him how much she loved him. She smiled to herself. Well, it wasn't the *only* way, but she opted against making love to him this morning. His mind would not be with her; it would be on the trial.

"You're up early," Grant said as he entered the kitchen.

She walked over and kissed him on the cheek. "You need to eat."

He sat at the table. "Thanks."

Jade made bacon, scrambled eggs, and toast and joined him at the table. She put her hand on his. "Grant, I'm proud of you."

"For what?"

"For taking Ben Petty's case," she said. "You didn't have to."

He bit into a piece of bacon. "I hope we didn't forget to do something. I'll admit, this is new territory for me. A trial is a trial, but I don't know what I'll do if they give him the death penalty."

Jade waited him out.

"Losing a civil trial is mostly about money," he continued. "Ben deserves the best representation available. I'm just not sure I can give him that."

"Ben is lucky to have you," she said. "You're one of the best lawyers in the country and deep down you know it. You represent your clients with humility and professionalism. The jury will see that. And so will Ben."

Grant smiled. "Thanks for marrying me."

She got out of her chair and kissed him. "No, baby, thanks for marrying *me.*"

Jade was pleased that Grant ate most of his breakfast. She walked him to the door and kissed him goodbye. She chose not to tell him about Lacy Hanna's visit to Petty's trailer. Some things, she thought, were better left unsaid. Maybe Petty told him, or maybe Grant already knew. Plus, she thought, what difference could it make anyway?

• • •

Grant drove to the place that had become his harbor, the Hicks cemetery. He stepped out of the SUV and approached his father's grave, brushed off the iron bench, and sat down. He looked at his watch and knew he only had a few minutes. Several ant beds had sprung up throughout the cemetery; the family burial ground needed some attention. He'd do that, he thought, after the trial.

"Today's the big day, Dad," he said aloud. He stared at the

marker as if the granite would speak. He looked at his watch again and stood. He peered skyward. "I'd appreciate any help, and I know Ben would too."

Grant knelt at the headstone and wiped the frame which held the picture of his mom, dad, sister, and himself. He thought about his mom and sister. He decided he'd go see them both after the trial. He really meant it this time, he thought, as he drove away from the remains of his ancestors.

• • •

Grant was surprised to see Brewer's pickup in the parking lot. Brewer, it seemed, had finally beaten him to the office. Grant walked into the bathroom and looked in the mirror. He'd tried to tone down his dress but didn't have an outfit that fit Brewer's recommendation. He thought about Troy Lee and knew the DA would look like a *Gentleman's Quarterly* model. Grant leaned closer to the mirror. He noticed the imperfections, the gentle marks of time. He stood tall and straightened his tie. It was time.

He and Brewer were looking out the window of the hallway when Mordiky walked in. "She must be good looking," he said, laughing.

Brewer didn't move. "We're watching our jurors walk into the courthouse."

"Morning, Mordiky," Grant said, turning to him and shaking his hand. "I really appreciate all you've done. You're one hell of an investigator."

"No thanks necessary," Mordiky said. "I'd do anything for Judge Eaton."

Brewer turned to Mordiky. "Where's the judge, anyway?"

"I had coffee at his place this morning," Mordiky said. "He said to wish y'all good luck and that he appreciates y'all helping Ben."

Grant felt the ensuing silence become awkward. Brewer turned to them and smiled. "Let's go have some fun, boys."

• • •

Grant knew the three of them looked mismatched as they approached the courthouse steps. Brewer was a few inches shy of six feet, and his face and gut were the only places he'd gained weight over the years. He had an infectious smile, and the man sure carried a twinkle in his eye. Mordiky was well over six feet, and Pete Ball was right, Grant thought, that Mordiky looked like Chuck Connors (who'd played Lucas McCain in *The Rifleman*). Mordiky usually wore his cowboy hat, but not today—he looked like he was headed to church.

Grant walked next to Brewer as they slowed to speak to a group of people leaning against the rail and smoking. "Let's try to get one of those smokers on the jury," Brewer whispered after they were inside. "People who'll smoke in public these days ain't scared of shit." Grant smiled. He'd not heard that strategy before. He and Brewer walked into the judge's chambers while Mordiky lingered with the large crowd of people standing outside the courtroom (most of which, Grant could sense, didn't want to be there).

"Morning, George," Judge Riley said with a smile. "When was the last time we picked a jury together?"

He laughed. "I think it was about ten years ago when that coonass sued Piggly Wiggly."

"I guess it was." She looked at Grant. "Relax, Mr. Hicks. You look like you've seen a ghost."

Grant smiled. "Oh, no, Judge. I was thinking about the jury."

The district attorney and his entourage walked into the small office. After greetings were exchanged, Riley stood. "Okay, folks, if you're not an attorney, wait outside."

The room was cleared. Soon, only Grant, Brewer, Troy Lee,

and Molly London remained. Riley looked up.

"George, which one of y'all will conduct voir dire?"

"I will, Your Honor," Brewer said. "Grant will handle the opening and I have the closing. We'll alternate taking the witnesses, but Grant will handle most of them."

Riley looked at Lee. "Troy?"

"I'll handle voir dire and the opening and closing. I'll take most of the witnesses. Molly will take a witness or two."

Riley stood. "Let's go. I can't wait to hear the excuses for avoiding jury duty today."

The first part of the selection process was governed by Riley. Grant was impressed at how she handled the jury venire. One potential member, in an attempt to avoid jury duty, said he couldn't serve because he didn't trust lawyers. She told him she was a lawyer too, and he said, "Well, Judge, I don't reckon I trust you neither." The courtroom filled with laughter as Riley told the man to sit back down.

She excused people for various reasons: a few senior citizens elected to take their statutory exemption, there were folks who'd recently served, some with medical conditions, and one very pregnant lady. Riley then explained that the jury would hear from the attorneys. Grant quickly discovered how Troy Lee had been able to get elected at such a young age. Lee worked the crowd with precision. When he was finished, it was Brewer's turn. Grant's stomach ached as he watched the veteran walk to the podium and face the jury.

Brewer took his reading glasses off and, using the right frame temple, twirled them in his right hand. "Morning, folks. I won't plow the same ground that's been plowed already. But I do have a few questions to ask y'all." He looked at the crowd. "First of all, I don't want to get too personal with y'all but this is necessary." He let that sink in a moment. "I've read your questionnaires and we'll be meeting with some of y'all individually in a little while. But by show of hands, how many of you would consider yourselves active voters? In other words, you never miss an election?"

Grant watched Brewer and wondered what his strategy was. He took notes and began to enjoy the process. He noticed the marked difference between Lee and Brewer; the DA was campaigning throughout the process. Brewer, on the other hand, was asking questions that were so interesting that Grant started answering them to himself. Brewer asked about politics and restaurants and music and books. Brewer was good, Grant thought. Very good.

"I have one final question," Brewer said, and pointed at Lee. "How many of you will hold it against Mr. Lee due to the obvious fact that I'm a much better-looking man than he?" The crowd laughed. Grant, smiling, watched Brewer turn to Judge Riley and tell her that he had no further questions. Riley was also smiling; she clearly liked Brewer. Grant glanced back at the smiling jury venire. They appeared to like him too.

• • •

The judge released the jury at 12:30 that afternoon and told them to return at 2:00. The Petty legal team hurried across the street to Brewer's office. When they walked in, the secretary handed Grant a brown envelope with his name printed across the front. She told him that it was taped to the door when she got back from her morning post office trip. He opened it and pulled out a handful of snapshots. The first was Jade sitting on a blanket on the ground. The next was Jade sitting on the front steps holding Ella Reese. Others showed Jade with both kids. All were recent. He grabbed his phone and called her. She answered on the first ring.

"Jade, are you okay?"

"Yes, I'm fine," she said. "Why?"

"Where's Pete?"

"He and Paul are building Wolf a doghouse," she said. "Is everything okay?"

"I'll be there in ten minutes. I need to show you something."

Brewer flipped through the pictures while Grant was on the phone. He handed them over when Grant ended the call. "Everything okay?"

"I don't know," he said. "I'll be back."

Grant sped toward the farm, hitting 100 miles per hour as he crossed Big Creek. He turned onto Herndon Road and houses flew past—he imagined what he'd say to one of McInnis's deputies if he got pulled over. He finally turned down Hicks Road, topped the hill, and his house came into view. The dust boiled past the Range Rover as Grant came to a sliding stop. He walked inside to find Jade, Pete, and Paul Sumner sitting at the kitchen table. He slid the pictures across to Jade.

"Somebody's been watching you," he said to Jade.

"Watching me?" she asked as she thumbed through the photos. "Why?"

"I don't know," Grant said as he looked at his watch. "I want you to come with me."

"I can't," she said. "Ella Reese is asleep."

Sumner spoke. "Grant, if it'd make you feel better, I could stay and help Pete keep an eye on things around here."

Grant glanced at Pete, then back to Sumner. "Are you sure?"

"I don't mind a bit," Sumner said.

Ladd had walked into the room with Wolf on his heels. "Daddy, do you want to see Wolf's doghouse?"

Grant rubbed the top of his son's head. "I can't right now. I have to get back to court. But I will when I get home from work."

Sumner and Pete assured Grant that Jade and the kids would be protected. Jade walked Grant to the Range Rover and made him promise that he'd concentrate on Ben Petty. He kissed her goodbye and sped back to town. However this trial turned out, he was going to have a long talk with Sheriff McInnis.

And maybe include his father, the former sheriff and a man Grant trusted.

CHAPTER 36

Tuesday, July 8, 2014

AFTER TWO LONG, tedious days, the jury was seated just before five o'clock. Judge Riley apologized for having to sequester them, but explained why it was necessary. Minutes later, two rented vans left the courthouse en route to Lucedale, the nearest city with a hotel. Grant had become more and more dependent on George Brewer—the meticulous manner in which he'd picked the jury was unlike any Grant had seen before.

Grant walked into the sheriff's office and a found a young male dispatcher in Heather Sisco's spot. The new guy looked barely out of high school and was still fighting acne. Grant tapped on the plexiglass, and the dispatcher looked up. Grant leaned over to speak through the opening at the bottom.

"I'm here to see Ben Petty," he said. "I'm Grant Hicks."

"Just a minute, sir." The young man walked down the hall. A minute later he opened the door. "Sheriff says you'll have to meet in the holding room."

Grant wasn't going to argue with the new guy. "Can I see the sheriff, please?"

McInnis and Troy Lee walked into view right then.

"Grant, we don't have enough officers for y'all to meet in the yard today," McInnis said. "You're going to have to meet in the holding room."

"Is there a recording device in there?"

Lee laughed. "Jeez, Grant. Now why would he do that?"

Grant didn't answer. He was suddenly in a bad mood. He'd grown leery of the sheriff and didn't trust the DA, either. He had plenty of reasons not to trust McInnis, but Lee, on the other hand, was an ambitious politician. And an ambitious politician with the ability to indict was a dangerous animal.

Grant sighed and walked into the room where he and Petty had their reunion over four months ago. Petty was brought in a second later. Grant pulled out a legal pad and told Petty to write down anything he didn't feel comfortable saying aloud.

"I'll bring you some clothes to change into tomorrow morning," Grant said. "I think we've picked a good jury."

Ben scribbled on the note pad: "Will they be fair?"

Grant wrote back: "Yes. Do you have any questions?"

Petty pulled the note pad closer. "When will I testify?"

Grant: "Depends on how long the state takes to put on its case. My guess is Friday."

Petty didn't reach for the pad this time.

Grant wrote again. "Need anything?"

Petty reached for the pad. "Can you bring me a sausage biscuit in the morning?"

Grant smiled. "I'll bring you a full breakfast in the morning," he said. "From Ward's."

Petty wrote: "Thanks for everything. I wish I could pay you."

"Just being my friend is payment enough," Grant said as he stood. "I'll see you in the morning."

Grant waited until the deputy had led Petty back to his cell before he left. Troy Lee was nowhere in sight, but McInnis was leaning against his squad car talking to two deputies when Grant walked past.

"Good night, Counselor," McInnis said.

Grant paused and glanced at the deputies, then smiled at the sheriff. "Get some rest, Sheriff. You'll need it for when I cross-examine you."

McInnis stood straight. "You trying to intimidate a witness?"

"I guess that depends on you," Grant said.

Grant didn't normally try to act cocky, but the smirk on the sheriff's face ticked him off. He backed out of the parking lot and drove toward the farm. Brewer and Mordiky were coming over tonight to discuss the jury and prepare for tomorrow. A flood of adrenaline had shot through his veins at the little joust with McInnis. The stage was set, battle lines had been drawn. And tomorrow, the first shots would be fired.

•••

Jade and the kids were in the bedroom watching a movie while the men met in the den. She'd made a pan of brownies and had fixed each a cup of coffee before she'd excused herself. She'd told Grant that she felt safe with Pete Ball (and now Paul Sumner) standing guard. But Grant wanted to be with her and Ladd and Ella Reese after dark, so he'd insisted they meet here.

Grant was pleased that Judge Eaton had joined them. The old judge had been an enormous help in preparing them for jury selection. Grant was anxious to hear Eaton's opinion on the twelve selected. Greene County was the least populated of the three counties in Judge Riley's circuit court district. The judge, district attorney, and the assistant DA all lived in Jackson County. The fact that Brewer was local helped him understand the people better than Lee. Even though the county prosecutor assisted Lee, it was evident that he was only there to provide a local presence.

"Who'd we end up with?" Eaton asked.

"We have ten white jurors and two black," Grant said. "Seven women and five men."

"I like the jury," Brewer said. "I think we have a fair chance to hang it up."

"Who do you think will be foreman?" Moridiky asked.

"Either Gabe Tucker or Phillip Thornton would be my guess," Brewer answered.

Eaton was still looking at the list. The others waited for him to finish. "Bernadean Benjamin and Cregg Polkey are the two y'all need to present your case to," he said.

"What do you mean?" Grant asked.

"I agree," Brewer said. He turned to Grant. "Benjamin's grandfather was murdered in Natchez during the civil rights movement years ago. They never solved the crime."

"How will that help?" Mordiky asked.

"They didn't *attempt* to solve the crime," Eaton said. "She'll be suspicious of law enforcement."

"What about Polkey?" Grant asked.

"A Coaker supporter," Eaton said. "Word on the street is that Coaker's gonna take on Mcinnis next year."

"What about the other ten?"

"We should try this case for three people, Grant," Brewer said. "Benjamin, Polkey, and hope like hell that Gabe Tucker's the foreman." He tossed his list on the coffee table. "Tucker's open-minded and folks tend to follow him."

They spent another half hour discussing the jurors. Eaton gave them an overall C-plus. Considering the fact that they were in one of the most conservative counties in the south, Eaton told them they'd done the best job that they could under the circumstances. They then discussed the likely order in which Troy Lee would call witnesses. Grant could tell that he'd impressed the men with his preparation. He asked for pointers on his opening and told them he would put the final touches on it after they left.

Mordiky, who'd been quiet, finally spoke up. "Men, can I change the subject a bit?"

"Sure," Grant said.

"Petty's sister wants to see him."

"When?"

"Tomorrow morning before trial."

Grant stood. "I don't think that's a good idea. That may upset him. And we don't need him looking guilty."

"Okay," Mordiky said. "After court tomorrow?"

Brewer stood. "Fine with me. Who knows? Her being here may help him."

"Where is she now?" Eaton asked.

"A hotel in Lucedale," Mordiky said.

Brewer had stuffed a brownie into his mouth but didn't wait to chew or swallow. "Which hotel?"

"The Holiday Inn."

Brewer looked at Grant. "Oh, shit. That's where the jury is staying."

CHAPTER 37

Wednesday morning, July 9, 2014

A SURPRISE COLD FRONT passed through south Mississippi overnight, bringing somewhat cooler temperatures and a ton of rain. By daylight, the large windows couldn't hide the gray gloom peeking into the drafty courtroom.

Grant and Brewer sat at Counselor's table and waited on their client. Grant had delivered breakfast to Petty from Ward's just like he'd promised. He watched his client devour the grits, eggs, bacon, and biscuit and didn't discuss the trial (or much of anything) with him. He left Petty with a new set of clothes and told him he'd see him in the courtroom.

Grant busied himself with the bankers box full of files on the floor beside his chair. He saw Troy Lee whispering to Molly London and the bailiff, who was seated next to the door behind the bench, sipping coffee from a Styrofoam cup. The clerk and her assistant were at a table against the wall to his left, directly across the room from the jury box. Grant wasn't surprised that the courtroom was full of curious locals. Sheriff McInnis was seated on the front row next to Rob Woods, the DA's investigator. The room was eerily quiet. Grant glanced at the clock on the wall. It was almost 9:00.

The door opened then and three deputies walked in with Petty, whose hands and ankles were bound. Grant and Brewer stood as the deputies removed the cuffs and shackles. They waited for Petty to sit between them before they took their seats. Brewer patted Petty on the shoulder. The bailiff stood and directed the room to rise as Riley stepped behind the bench. She told everyone to be seated. She looked at Troy Lee.

"Is the state ready?"

The district attorney stood. "Yes, Your Honor."

She looked at Grant. "Is the defense ready?"

"Yes, Your Honor," Grant said, standing.

"Will the rule be invoked?"

Both attorneys answered in the affirmative. This meant that any witnesses or potential witnesses had to leave the courtroom. After they shuffled out, Riley waited for the door to close. Then she told the bailiff to bring in the jury. The attorneys stood as the twelve men and women who would determine Petty's fate marched in and sat down. Most of the jurors, Grant noticed, stole glances at Petty. Riley made some short preliminary remarks to the jury and audience. She then instructed Lee to begin his opening statement. The DA stood and walked to the center of the courtroom, where he faced the jury.

"Ladies and gentlemen of the jury, we've met, but I want to introduce myself again. I'm Troy Lee, your district attorney." He pointed at London. "And this is my assistant district attorney, Molly London." Lee waited until he had their attention before continuing. "On December 13, 2010, after Lacy Hanna's husband left to go to work and the Hannas' little girls, Marly and Jenna, got on the school bus, Lacy Hanna was kidnapped and murdered."

Grant shifted so he could watch the reactions of Bernadean

Benjamin and Cregg Polkey. Each member of the jury was concentrating on Lee's every syllable.

"Lacy's murderer, in premeditated fashion, entered her home, bound her, carried her to a deserted place, and in cold-blooded fashion murdered her," he continued. "He took her away from her beloved husband and her precious children." Lee paused and pointed at Petty. "She was murdered by that man, the defendant." Lee now moved closer to the jury. "And he *almost* got away with it."

Grant listened as Lee walked them through the evidence that he expected to present. It pointed to one conclusion: Petty was guilty. Grant glanced at the clock. Lee's opening was approaching thirty minutes and Grant thought he'd perhaps gone too long. A couple of jury members had shifted in their seats. Lee finally neared the end.

"After the evidence is presented, there will be one conclusion, and one conclusion only: Ben Petty, beyond any reasonable doubt, kidnapped and murdered Lacy Hanna." Lee moved to within a foot of the jury box. "Thank you for your attention. Thank you for your service to our country. And, most of all, thank you for your service to Lacy Hanna."

Riley looked at Grant and nodded. Grant stood and walked over to the jurors. He paused and looked into the eyes of each member. The rain was falling harder; he heard it ping against the windows. A clap of thunder rolled through the room, rattling the windows. He waited for quiet before beginning his opening statement.

"Ladies and gentlemen, we also met during the selection process, and as you know, my name's Grant Hicks." He turned toward Brewer. "This is George Brewer, whom you've also met. Sitting next to George is our client, Ben Petty."

The jury, for the first time, looked directly at Petty. He nodded slightly at them. Petty's dark blue sport coat and white shirt fit nicely. He was freshly shaven and looked as if he should be sitting *with* the jury as opposed to being judged by them.

"The district attorney provided you the framework of the state's case," Grant continued. "And as I sat listening, one word continued to come to mind: *coincidence*. Ben is being prosecuted for not a *large* number of coincidences, but a *few* coincidences. I'll detail those for you now."

Grant paused to make eye contact with each juror. All were tuned in to his words.

"Ben Petty lived here briefly when he was a child, and because he loved this place he returned as an adult," Grant said. "He lives only a few miles from the Hannas and occasionally worked for Mr. Hanna. He grew to—and still does—respect Mr. Hanna. He also grew to respect Lacy Hanna and the Hanna children. Ladies and gentlemen, Ben Petty is not a murderer. Far from it."

Grant was pacing slowly in front of the jury box. Twenty-four eyes, he saw, were watching his every move.

"As the witnesses testify and the evidence is presented, I want you to remember that one word I mentioned earlier," he continued. "You know what that word is: coincidence. I looked up the definition. It means a striking occurrence of two or more events at one time, apparently by mere chance." Grant paused again. "The state's responsibility is to present evidence that convinces you that my client kidnapped and murdered Lacy Hanna. And not by a striking occurrence of two or more events ... no. The state is *required* to prove every element of the crime and *not* by a preponderance of the evidence. Not by clear and convincing evidence, *but beyond a reasonable doubt.*"

Grant turned to look at Petty and paused. He sensed that the jurors did too. Petty, Grant thought, appeared harmless with his good arm resting atop the table. His crooked arm, of course, hung limp along his right side. Grant started toward Petty and turned to face the jury from within several feet of his client.

"Folks, some of you remember my dad," Grant said. "And all of you remember Brandon Smallwood. A little over four years ago, I returned home to watch Brandon die. We mourned for him. And we buried him."

Brandon Smallwood, as he hoped these people knew, had been wrongly convicted by a jury that sat in the very chairs this jury now occupied. The small community still wrestled with the guilt of that collective decision. Grant was proud of how they rallied around the Smallwood family during his sickness and death, though, and he hoped the reminder would cause these twelve Greene Countians to realize that innocent people get prosecuted. That innocent people go to prison, and that innocent people sometimes look guilty but are as innocent as the morning dew.

Grant stepped toward the jurors and pointed at Petty. "Brandon sat at that table and in that chair. And with only a few coincidences, twelve of our neighbors sent Brandon Smallwood to prison, where he'd spend the best parts of his life even though he was an innocent man. Why? Because of a striking occurrence of two or more events at one time apparently by mere chance. Because of coincidence." Grant paused to let this sink in. "Ladies and gentlemen, you have an important task ahead. And as you listen, I know you'll listen actively." A clap of thunder jarred the windows once more. Grant waited for the sound to fade. "And the sound you'll hear in the end will not be the sound of thunder or the sound of guilt beyond a reasonable doubt, but the sound of innocence. The sound of Ben Petty's innocence."

Grant walked toward the jurors and stopped. He again made eye contact with each one. "Thank you for listening. And thank you for serving."

• • •

The state called Mississippi's medical pathologist as its first witness. The expert had another trial in Biloxi the next day, so

The Peter Bay

Lee elected to take him out of sequence. He spent two hours testifying about the science of identifying the remains of the long-ago departed. He'd examined and reexamined the skeleton of the decedent, Lacy Hanna. He testified as to the height of the victim and the body structure and size of the skeletal frame. He concluded that the skeleton matched the size of Lacy Hanna.

Grant asked few questions. He didn't dispute the identity of the victim. He knew the remains were Lacy Hanna's, but he refused to stipulate to that fact. After all, he thought, there was always a chance that a miracle could happen. Riley recessed for lunch and directed the parties to be back at 1:30.

Brewer's secretary had lunch waiting on them at the office. When they were at the conference table, Mordiky asked how things were going—like the other likely witnesses, he had to leave the courtroom.

Grant looked up. "We're tied right now. I wonder who Troy Lee will call as his next witness."

"My guess is the dental expert," Brewer said. "Let me see their list of witnesses."

Grant handed it to him. Mordiky's cell rang, and he stepped into the hall. A minute later he rejoined them. "That was the investigator at Clarksdale," he said. "They got an anonymous tip and think they might have discovered the remains of their missing person."

"Refresh my memory," Brewer said.

"When I went on my fishing expedition, I discovered that there'd been three other unsolved disappearances, all women and all between the ages of twenty-five and thirty-five. One was in Coahoma County."

Brewer chewed a mouthful of fried chicken, clearly wanting to speak. He swallowed and looked at Grant. "Have you mentioned that to Troy Lee?"

Grant looked puzzled. "I don't talk to him, you do."

Brewer looked at Mordiky. "What time were you going to bring Petty's sister to see him?"

"I'll go get her when y'all recess for the day."

"Grant will go get her," Brewer said. "I want you to head to Clarksdale."

CHAPTER 38

Wednesday afternoon, July 9, 2014

THE STATE'S DENTAL expert spent most of her time explaining the science behind her expertise. Grant noticed one of the male jurors fighting to keep his eyelids open for the last half hour of the testimony. The expert, though, positively identified the remains to be those of Lacy Hanna. Again, Grant asked few questions. His goal was simply to keep his presence before the jury.

After a mid-afternoon recess, Judge Riley entered the courtroom and instructed Troy Lee to call his next witness.

"The state calls Wilson Coaker," Lee said.

Coaker was in khaki pants and a black shirt. He had the reputation of walking slow and talking slower. The clerk swore him in and Grant watched him nod and smile at the jury as he sat down.

"Afternoon, Mr. Coaker," Lee said. The former sheriff returned the gesture before Lee continued. "You were the sheriff when Lacy Hanna disappeared, weren't you?"

"I was indeed."

"Do you remember that day? The morning of December 13, 2010?"

Coaker shifted in his chair. "Of course."

"Can you tell us what happened that morning?"

"Best I can recall," he said, "it started off as a normal day. Then, a 911 call came in from the Hanna home."

Lee had walked to the edge of the jury box and was leaning against the railing. He'd positioned himself so that the jury would focus on Coaker. "Do you know who called 911?"

"I do," he said. "I believe she was the niece of Mrs. Hanna."

"What time was that call?"

Coaker squinted and looked toward the ceiling. He then looked at Lee. "Around 7:15 that morning, if memory serves."

"Tell us what happened next," Lee said.

"The child couldn't speak to the dispatcher, but we knew the location of the call. One of my deputies was nearby so he got there first. I showed up about five minutes after he did."

"What did y'all discover?"

"The little girl was hiding in the pantry in the kitchen, scared to death," Coaker said. "She was still holding the phone to her ear."

"Do you remember the girl's name?"

"No, sir. It may have been Karen. Or Carrie."

Grant found it interesting that Lee didn't correct the sheriff. He apparently didn't know Caroline's name.

"How old was she?" Lee asked.

"I believe she was five. Maybe six."

"Was the little girl able to tell you anything?"

Grant knew he could object based on hearsay, but he decided to let Coaker answer the question. The answer, he thought, could be helpful to Petty.

"She just said a man took her aunt," Coaker said. "Or something like that."

"Was she able to describe the man?"

"No, she wasn't. We tried everything and the girl couldn't help us."

"Mr. Coaker," Lee said. "I have a six-year-old daughter and she talks ninety to nothing. Can you explain to the jury why this six-year-old couldn't talk a whole lot?"

"She has a disability."

"What kind of disability?"

"Down Syndrome." The sheriff smiled. "She's a pretty little girl."

The former sheriff continued to summarize the events of that horrible day. He testified that he called in the Mississippi Highway Patrol and the Mississippi Bureau of Investigation for help. Coaker told the jury that they weren't able to find fingerprints or DNA; there were too many tire tracks on the dirt road to lift any exemplars. In short, they had no definitive leads.

Troy Lee tendered the witness at 4:45, and Riley informed the jury that they'd recess after Coaker's testimony. She then instructed Grant to proceed. He stood and walked toward Coaker.

"Good afternoon, Sheriff," Grant said, smiling. "Good to see you again."

Coaker smiled. "Good to see you too, Mr. Hicks."

"Before we get started, sir, the little girl's name is Caroline."

"That's right," Coaker said. "I remember now. She was a precious child."

"I won't ask you to repeat any of your testimony. But I do have a question or two. Correct me if I'm wrong, but you liked being the sheriff, didn't you?"

Lee stood. "Objection, Your Honor. Relevance."

"Overruled," Riley said promptly.

"You can answer, Sheriff," Grant said.

"I loved it," he said. "It was an honor to serve Greene County."

"And you did everything professionally you could, in order to find Lacy Hanna's killer, didn't you?"

"I did," Coaker replied. "I stayed up at night worrying about that case."

"Sheriff, do you know my client?" Grant pointed at Petty.

"I do."

"Did Ronnie Hanna call you and ask you to search Ben's trailer?"

"He did."

"When?" Grant asked.

"About a month before I left office. A little over a year after Lacy went missing."

"Did Mr. Hanna say *why* he wanted you to search Ben's trailer?"

"Said he just wanted him checked out. Ben Petty had done some work for the Hannas a week or so before Mrs. Hanna disappeared."

"Did you have a search warrant?"

"No, sir," he said. "Judge Eaton wouldn't give me one."

Grant expected an objection, but Lee said nothing. "Did you go to Ben's trailer anyway?"

"I did. Me and a deputy went and asked him if we could look around."

"Did you look around?"

"Yes, sir," Coaker said. "He gave us permission. I mean, it wasn't a search or anything. I just wanted to gauge his behavior."

"Sheriff," Grant said as he approached Counselor's table and stood next to Petty. "Did you ever consider Ben Petty a suspect?"

Coaker looked at the jury before turning to Grant. "No, sir."

Lee's effort at rehabilitating Coaker on redirect fell short, and the day ended on a high note for the Petty team. Grant and Brewer were excited that the last thing the jury heard before leaving for their hotel was that Coaker *didn't* consider Petty a suspect. But they knew tomorrow would be the most difficult day of the trial.

Sheriff McInnis wouldn't be as cooperative. Grant was as sure of that as he was the sun coming up tomorrow. And part of that, he couldn't help but think, was that McInnis didn't like *him*.

CHAPTER 39

Wednesday evening, July 9, 2014

BRIGHT SUN WAS out by day's end. Grant had picked Jade up at Edwina's, and they were on their way to the Lucedale hotel where Petty's sister, Elaine Doss, was waiting. Brewer had made arrangements with the sheriff for Petty to meet with his sister in the jury room (Petty still did not know Doss was coming). Three deputies were working overtime to accommodate the visit. The sheriff had balked at first, but Judge Riley had insisted.

Grant ended a call with Mordiky, who'd made it to Clarksdale. Mordiky's friend, the local investigator, asked that he spend the night at his place so they would have ample time to review the evidence. It was a long shot, but they hoped to find something that would help Petty.

"Trial go okay today?" Jade asked.

"I think so," Grant said. "The jury knows it was definitely Lacy Hanna's remains that were found. No surprise there. And they know Sheriff Coaker never considered Ben a suspect."

"Are you relieved this is almost over?"

Grant glanced at Jade before turning back to the road. "I am.

Starting tomorrow, though, I want to leave the kids with Edwina's aunt. I'd feel safer if you were in the courtroom with me."

"Are you sure?" Jade asked. "I feel safe with both Pete and Paul at the house."

"Yes. When I had that early-morning knock at the door—and then we had the mysterious gunfire—I can rationalize those as random acts or, at best, aimed at me. But those pictures of you scare me."

"What did the sheriff say?"

"He said they'd *investigate*," Grant said, spitting the word. "But I have zero confidence in him."

"Who do you think would do this?"

"There's no question in my mind it's tied to this trial. Either someone is trying to intimidate me apart from the sheriff's office or, worse, there's a coverup McInnis has something to do with."

Jade took his hand. "It'll be alright. When do you think the trial will be over?"

"I bet the state will rest Friday. Depending on how many witnesses we call, the jury could be deliberating by Saturday night."

• • •

Grant hurried inside the hotel while Jade waited in the Range Rover. The jury was sequestered and he wanted to get in and out as soon as possible. Moments later, Elaine Doss followed him out the sliding glass doors to the SUV. Doss wore blue pants and a white, long-sleeve blouse. She looked thinner than Grant remembered. The stress of a brother on trial for his life certainly had something to do with it.

"Elaine," Grant said, "this is my wife, Jade."

"Pleased to meet you," Doss said.

Jade reached for her hand. "It's my pleasure. You finding everything okay at the hotel?"

"Yes," she said. "Everyone's very nice. But it gets kinda

boring being stuck there all day."

Jade was surprised that Doss didn't have a car and had been there since Sunday. Grant explained that Mordiky was supposed to chauffeur her, but he had to go to Clarksdale. After Jade scolded Grant for not telling her, Doss came to his rescue.

"The hotel's been ordering my food, thanks to your husband," Doss said. "And I brought some word puzzles to work. I'm fine. Mr. Hicks," Doss continued, "Ben know I'm coming?"

"No," Grant said. "We didn't tell him, as you requested. He knows I'm meeting with him to talk about tomorrow. But that's it."

Little was said the rest of the way to Leakesville. They pulled into the parking lot of the courthouse as Grant ended a call with one of his partners in Atlanta. Petty, Brewer, and the three deputies were in the jury room awaiting their arrival.

Jade and Doss waited in the hallway while Grant joined the legal team. The three deputies left and positioned themselves outside the doors. There was Petty, who looked as if he were waiting at a train station for a ride to nowhere. Brewer stood a few feet away.

"Hey, guys," Grant said. "Ben, you okay?"

"Been a long day."

"Someone wants to see you."

Petty squinted. "Me? Who?"

"Your sister," Grant said.

Petty stared, saying nothing.

"Elaine is here, Ben."

"How'd she find out?"

"We had to research your background for the trial," Brewer said. "Mordiky, our investigator, found her."

Petty looked down at the table. Grant waited him out, and he finally looked up. "I reckon I can see her."

Grant looked at Brewer as they stood. He put his hand on

Petty's shoulder. "We'll wait outside."

"Grant, uh, will you stay in here?"

"Sure, man," he said. "If that'll make you feel more comfortable."

Brewer left and shut the door. Doss entered a moment later. Her hands were shaking as she walked toward her brother. Petty looked up and they stared for a moment. She sat in the chair next to Petty with her hands in her lap.

"Hey," she said.

Petty reached to scratch his nose with his left hand. "Hey," he said. "You doing alright?"

Grant watched as tears suddenly rushed down Doss's cheeks. She wiped them away with nervous hands. But more came, and more after those. Grant turned away and tried to appear invisible. When he looked up, a tear was running down Petty's cheek. Doss rose from her chair and embraced her brother.

Grant watched the siblings hold each other. Their chests shook as they wept together. He watched Petty attempt to hold the sister he hadn't seen since they were children. Grant wiped a tear from his own face, then slipped out of the room, shut the door, and held Jade close.

CHAPTER 40

Thursday morning, July 10, 2014

"ARE YOU OKAY, Grant?" Brewer asked, handing him a cup of coffee.

After he'd watched the reunion between Petty and his sister last night, Grant felt embarrassed for his uncharacteristic display of emotion. Especially in front of Brewer and the deputy standing guard.

"I'm fine," he said. "Who do you think will be the first up today? McInnis?"

"My guess is Rob Woods."

"Think they'll rest today?"

"You scored some points with the jury yesterday," Brewer said. "So I wouldn't be surprised if Troy Lee doesn't go for blood. He's not a good loser."

"He hasn't lost yet."

"No, but I promise you he wasn't in a good mood after Coaker's testimony."

Grant and Brewer walked to the courtroom half an hour before the trial was to resume. The crowd was growing. Grant saw

Pete Ball and Paul Sumner in the back and walked over to them.

"Morning, fellas," he said.

"Morning, Grant," Pete said. "Since Mrs. Jade is here, we thought we'd watch. That okay?"

"Absolutely. And thanks for looking out for Jade and the kids."

"No thanks necessary, neighbor," Sumner said. "Glad to do it. We'll be pulling for you back here."

Grant thanked him and walked to the front and sat next to Jade. Edwina had taken off work today and joined her. Grant wondered if he should be spending these last valuable minutes studying witness information. But deep down, he knew he was ready. He just needed a witness, he thought, as he gripped her hand before moving to Counselor's table.

Soon, the deputies escorted Petty into the room. He sat between Grant and Brewer. Troy Lee and Molly London walked in next and didn't exchange the usual morning pleasantries. That was okay with Grant, though. He wasn't in the mood either.

"All rise!" the bailiff yelled as he walked in. Judge Riley was right behind. Grant closed his eyes and whispered a quick prayer. Then the jury entered. He looked at each member. They seemed tired, and the trial was only entering its fourth day. Riley, not waiting around, instructed Lee to call his first witness.

"Your Honor, the state calls Rob Woods."

Woods was sworn in and sat in the witness box. The state's investigator was a pleasant man in his mid-fifties. He had gray, thinning hair and a salt-and-pepper mustache. He smiled often, and Grant thought if he was a bit heavier he'd make a perfect Santa Claus. Troy Lee led Woods through an introduction to the jury, including his experience and qualifications.

"Mr. Woods, when were you first brought in to investigate Lacy Hanna's murder?" Lee asked.

"I've been involved since the beginning."

"When Lacy first disappeared, were there any leads?"

"Not really," Woods said. "Lacy's niece saw the man, but she wasn't able to help establish an identity. She did tell us he was white, though."

"What methods did you employ to extract any meaningful information from ... I believe her name is Caroline?" Lee asked. Grant fought the urge to shake his head.

You idiot. You still can't remember her name?

"We had her meet with two experts and they weren't able to get her to identify the killer. She has Down Syndrome, and at her age and communication ability she just wasn't able to help."

Lee then had Woods discuss (in painstaking detail) the efforts made to investigate the Hanna death. It lasted over an hour, and Grant felt the jurors drift a bit. Grant finally sensed Lee wrapping up. Then Lee paused and let the tension build.

"Mr. Woods, how much time passed between the time you got the call from Sheriff McInnis, who informed you that the remains of who we now know to be Lacy Hanna were found, and the time it took you to get to the crime scene?"

Grant started to object to the form of the question. The question was entirely too long and could lead to confusion. But he decided to let Woods answer.

"Probably about forty-five minutes."

"Who was there when you arrived?" Lee asked.

Woods continued to discuss the location and details surrounding the crime scene. Grant watched the jurors. Most were attentive, but a couple seemed bored. Lee walked to the court reporter's table and retrieved a pocket knife which had been previously marked into evidence. Lee approached Woods.

"Investigator Woods, do you recognize this knife?"

"I do," he said. "I found it at the crime scene."

"What did you notice about this particular knife?"

"It had gotten a bit rusty. But on the handle, I noticed some initials."

"Can you read those initials?"

"B.F.P."

"During your investigation, were you able to determine the defendant's full name?" Lee asked.

"Yes. Benjamin Franklin Petty."

"Last question, and for the record, what are the defendant's initials?"

Woods looked at Petty, then turned to the jury. "B.F.P."

"No further questions, Your Honor," Lee said as he retrieved the pocket knife and placed it on the evidence table next to the court reporter.

Grant didn't wait on Riley. He strode to the exhibit table, picked up the knife, and handed it to Woods. "Mr. Woods, who made this pocket knife?"

Woods looked at the knife, then at Grant. "It's an Old Timer."

"Did you search Petty's trailer?"

"I didn't. Sheriff McInnis and one of his deputies did."

"Do you know if there were any other pocket knives found at Ben's trailer?"

"I'm not sure."

"If I told you that Ben collected Barlow pocket knives, would you have reason to doubt me?"

Lee stood. "Objection, Your Honor."

"I'll withdraw the question, Judge," Grant said. "Mr. Woods, when was the last time that you visited Caroline Pentecost? The little girl who was in the house when Lacy disappeared."

Woods shifted in his seat. Grant detected a hint of unease from him now. "I guess it was a year or so ago. But I called her mother a day or two after we found Mrs. Hanna's body."

"Now, Mr. Woods," Grant replied, a tiny bit coy. "We don't need you to guess. Was it more than a year ago that you actually spoke to Caroline or not?"

He squinted. "It was."

Mordiky had told Grant many times that Woods was a good man, but occasionally got lazy. And maybe this was one of those times. Grant never asked open-ended questions on cross-examination, but he decided to and prayed Mordiky was right.

"Mr. Woods," Grant said, pointing at Petty, "my client is sitting there accused of capital murder, sir. So why in the world haven't you talked to the only witness to the crime since Lacy Hanna's body was found?"

Woods glanced at Lee for an instant, then back at Grant. "I told you I called the girl's mother. And she told me the answer to my questions would have been the same."

Grant hesitated. He looked at Brewer, who was staring back and gave him an almost imperceptible nod. He turned back to Woods. "Mr. Woods, have you shown a *picture* of Ben Petty to Caroline?"

Woods, for a moment, almost seemed to smirk at the question. Grant pounced.

"Do you think this is funny, sir?"

"Of *course* I don't think it's funny!" Woods snapped. "Sheriff McInnis, his deputies, and I turned over every stone there was to look under. And I know beyond a shadow of a doubt we have the right man on trial for Lacy Hanna's murder."

"Did you show Ben Petty's picture to Caroline, yes or no?"

"I did—"

"Louder, Mr. Woods. Where we can hear you, sir," Grant said with an edge in his voice.

"I did not," Woods said after a pause. "We showed her hundreds of pictures before trying to get a sketch. She couldn't help us."

Grant stood between Woods and the jury and gave the red-faced investigator a long, cool look. "No further questions, Your Honor."

Once again, Lee attempted to rehabilitate his witness on

redirect. When he was finished, Grant looked into the DA's eyes. Lee's cordial demeanor was long gone, and Grant could feel the anger. He glared right back.

• • •

A covey of lawyers showed up from Jackson County for a civil matter after Woods completed his testimony. Riley recessed for half an hour to handle the situation, and Grant watched the group of eight lawyers and envied them. There was collectively over two *thousand* dollars an hour in attorney fees standing around waiting to see the judge, he knew. He wondered who their client was and what litigious issue had brought them here. He snapped back to reality, though, when Brewer told him that Mordiky needed them to call.

They walked downstairs and into the chancery clerk's office. The friendly clerk allowed them the privacy of her office and even poured them coffee. Grant dialed Mordiky's cell. He answered on the first ring.

"It's Grant. George is with me. You're on speaker."

"How's the trial going?" Mordiky asked.

"I wish you could see Grant in action," Brewer said, laughing. "He's kicking Troy Lee's ass. I kid you not, man."

"I wouldn't go that far," Grant said. "Find anything?"

"Nope," Mordiky said. "All we have is bones in a shallow grave. No leads on a suspect."

"You headed this way?" Brewer asked.

"Not yet. Get this: I just got a call from Scott County. They had another anonymous tip which led to their missing person's bones. I'm driving there now."

"You really think there's a connection?" Grant asked.

"I'm trying to find one," Mordiky said. "I'll keep looking."

CHAPTER 41

Thursday afternoon, July 10, 2014

RILEY CALLED COURT back to order before noon. She announced that they'd break for lunch after the next witness or at 1:00, whichever came first. Grant spotted Ronnie Hanna sitting on the first row behind Lee.

Molly London stood. "Your Honor, the state calls Ronnie Hanna."

Grant looked at Brewer. They hadn't been sure Hanna would be called as a witness. They'd offered to stipulate that the panties found in Petty's trailer were Lacy's, but Lee obviously wasn't going to take their offer. Brewer was prepared to cross-examine Hanna because Grant's visit to the family home didn't go well. If the jury sensed that Hanna didn't like Grant, they'd certainly dislike him too.

Ronnie Hanna was sworn in and sat in the witness chair. The jury appeared more alert and curious than they'd been to this point. Grant watched London approach a podium that had been placed in front of the state's counsel table. She had a yellow legal pad with notes written in blue ink. Grant knew she wasn't a seasoned attorney. How could she be? She looked right out of law school.

"Can you state your name for the record, please?" London asked.

"Ronnie Hanna," he said, leaning into the microphone.

"And where do you live?"

"In Neely."

Hanna wore crisp Levi jeans, a starched white shirt, and snakeskin cowboy boots. He was a couple inches shy of six feet and had a full head of black hair. Grant noticed that he still wore his wedding band.

"How long have you lived in Neely?"

Hanna told the jury when he and his family moved to Greene County. He wiped his eyes as he explained how he had to talk his city-loving wife into moving to the country. It was clear that he blamed himself, at least partially, for her death. She fell in love with the people here, taught Sunday School and volunteered at the girls' school, he explained.

Grant watched as three female jurors wiped their eyes when Hanna described his daughters. Grant nudged Brewer at one point to object—parts of Hanna's testimony were speculative and contained hearsay—but Brewer didn't make eye contact and simply waved him off with a flick of his hand.

"Mr. Hanna," London said, "can you tell us about the morning that Lacy ... went missing?"

Hanna didn't break eye contact. "It started out as a normal day. I left for the shipyard at five like I always do. Lacy fixed us breakfast and we ate together. I remember that morning she'd made pancakes and—"

Hanna paused, then began to cry. London handed him a box of tissues. Grant watched the jury react and wasn't pleased with what he saw: at least eight members were wiping tears away. Cregg Polkey, one of their hopefuls, was clearly shaken. Grant turned and found Jade. He could tell she was fighting a lump in her throat, too.

"I'm sorry," Hanna said.

"That's okay, Mr. Hanna," London said. "Do you need a break?"

Grant knew that Lee had made the right move in allowing London to examine Hanna. She was soft-spoken and handled him with gentle perfection. The only upside to Hanna's testimony, Grant thought, was that he wasn't the state's final witness. He didn't want Lee to rest after such emotional testimony.

"No, ma'am," Hanna said. "I'm okay."

"Do you remember anything abnormal about that morning before you left for work?"

"No, ma'am. It was a typical day. Lacy would see me off, then get the girls ready for school. She'd lay down after they left."

"What time did the school bus usually pick up the girls?" London asked.

"Most the time about five minutes till seven."

"Now, according to previous testimony, your niece Caroline was there too?"

"Yes. She'd spent a couple nights with us. Lacy's sister, Paula, had gone on a business trip with her husband."

Hanna explained Caroline's situation to the jury, telling how her Down Syndrome caused some communication problems. His testimony was similar to what Coaker and Woods provided. And, like those men, Ronnie Hanna had pretty much given up on her identifying the killer.

London walked away from the comfort of her notes and stood next to the jury box. "Mr. Hanna, we're almost done." She paused as he wiped his nose. "You know the defendant, don't you?"

"Yes."

"When did you first meet him?"

"I needed someone to help me around the place," Hanna said.

"I told a fellow at church that I was looking for somebody and he recommended him to me. I guess that was around 2008."

"So at least two years before Lacy's death?"

"Yes, ma'am. I'd say that."

"Mr. Hanna, did Ben Petty ever give you pause? Did he ever make you feel uncomfortable with him being around your wife or daughters?"

Brewer stood. "Object to the form of the question."

Riley sustained the objection and asked London to rephrase.

"Mr. Hanna, did Ben Petty ever act inappropriately toward your wife?" she asked.

Hanna still hadn't looked toward Petty. He focused on London as he answered. "I saw the way he looked at her."

Brewer stood. "Move to strike, Your Honor. Improper foundation. We ask that his statement be stricken from the record."

"Overruled," Riley replied, and Brewer sat.

"Was she afraid of him?" London continued.

Brewer started to stand again but Grant put a hand on his shoulder. Brewer shot Grant a puzzled look before turning his attention back to Hanna.

"I believe she was. And to this day," he said as he started to choke up again, "I wished I'd never brought that man to my home."

• • •

Riley decided to break for lunch before Brewer could cross-examine Hanna. Brewer's secretary had ordered sandwiches for the Petty team and put them in the conference room. Jade met Grant and Brewer there, and Grant noticed her being quiet. He knew how emotional she was and assumed she was still upset after watching Ronnie Hanna's testimony.

"Grant," Jade said, "we need to talk."

"I'll step outside," Brewer said.

"No, George," she said. "I think you need to hear this, too."

Grant put his fork down and leaned back in his chair. Jade wiped a strand of hair from her face and took a deep breath. "I'm going to tell y'all something, but Grant, will you promise not to get mad?"

Grant felt his blood pressure increase. "Why would I get mad?"

"He won't get mad, Jade," Brewer said. He looked at Grant. "Will you, son?"

Grant didn't take his eyes off Jade. "No, I won't. So tell us."

"Mr. Hanna testified that Lacy was afraid of Ben," Jade said. "Well, that's not true."

"What makes you say that?" Brewer asked.

"Lacy felt sorry for Ben," she said. "She actually brought him food from time to time."

Grant stared at her. "And how do you know this?"

"Marly told me. Please don't get her in trouble."

Grant stood and walked to the end of the conference table. He turned to Jade. "When did she tell you this?"

"Last week," she said. "Grant, I know you told me not to contact her, but she needed someone to talk to."

"Did Ronnie Hanna know this? That she was confiding in you?" Brewer asked.

"I honestly don't know. Marly didn't say."

"When and where did you see Marly Hanna?" Grant asked.

Jade hesitated. "I met her at the cemetery a couple of times. And I met her in Neely once."

Grant walked to the door, turned, and pointed at Jade. "I *told* you to stay away from her. And you did it anyway."

"Calm down, Grant," Brewer said. "She didn't have to tell you, but she did. And we needed to know—Ben needed us to know. She's trying to help us."

Grant walked out of the conference room, down the hall, and

out the front door. He was angry and hurt. Jade had lied to him, having chosen the well-being of another person over his wishes. What else had she done behind his back? He looked at his watch and walked back to the courtroom. He'd deal with Jade later. His client was in the fight of his life, and the last thing Grant needed was to lose his focus.

A few minutes later, Brewer joined him at Counselor's table. "Grant, don't be upset with your wife," Brewer said under his breath. "She means well."

"She lied to me," Grant snapped.

"Maybe she did. But some lies have to be told."

"I've never lied to her."

Brewer leaned closer and smiled. "I'm calling bullshit on that one, buddy."

"This isn't an innocent half-truth. I *forbid* her from contacting that girl."

"She's a grown woman," Brewer said. "You can't forbid her from doing anything. In case you haven't looked at the calendar lately, we're living in the United States of America in the twenty-first century."

After the deputies returned Petty to his place between his attorneys and the jury was seated, Ronnie Hanna was reminded that he was still under oath. Brewer walked to the center of the room, folded his arms, and began his cross-examination.

"Mr. Hanna, I'm George Brewer. I don't believe we've had the pleasure of meeting, and I'm not happy that it's under these awful circumstances. I have a few questions for you if you don't mind."

"Okay," Hanna said.

"Prior to your wife's disappearance, when was the last time Ben Petty was at your home?"

"I don't remember the exact date," Hanna said. "But it was a week or so."

"You testified earlier that you believed Lacy was afraid of Ben?" Brewer asked.

"Yes. I believe she was."

"Did Lacy ever bring Ben any food to his trailer? Leftovers and such?"

Hanna leaned into the microphone. "I can't recall if she did, but I don't believe so."

"Did y'all have a garden?"

"Yes we did."

"Did you ever give any vegetables to your neighbors?" Brewer asked.

"On occasion."

Grant could tell that Hanna was being guarded with his answers. He paused slightly after each question, as if trying to discern any hidden tricks. Grant turned to see if Jade was in the courtroom—she wasn't. He was still angry, but now he was worried for her safety. He hoped she was in Brewer's office. A shot of guilt hit him in the stomach for abandoning her.

"Now, Mr. Hanna, I need you to give me a direct answer this time and we'll be finished," Brewer said more firmly. "Did Lacy, to your knowledge, ever bring any vegetables or meals to Ben Petty at his trailer?"

Hanna glanced at London before sitting upright to face Brewer. "I don't think so."

"Yes or no, Mr. Hanna," Brewer said.

London stood. "Objection, Your Honor. Asked and answered."

"Overruled," Riley said.

"Yes or no? Did Lacy deliver vegetables or food to Ben Petty's trailer?"

"No," Hanna said after the tiniest of pauses. "She did not."

CHAPTER 42

Thursday late afternoon, July 10, 2014

GRANT ASKED FOR a five-minute recess before the next witness was called to the stand, then walked into the hallway and dialed Jade's number.

"Hello," she said quietly.

"Where are you?"

"Does it matter?"

"Of course," he said. "I can't talk long. Where are you?"

"At Edwina's with the kids," she said. "I think I'll stay here the rest of the day."

"You can come back."

"I just need a break," she said. "Grant?"

"What?"

"I know you're upset with me. And I'm sorry. But please don't get Marly in trouble."

Brewer opened the door to the courtroom and motioned for Grant to hurry. He whispered that he was almost finished.

"We'll talk tonight, Jade," Grant said. "I just had to know you were safe."

• • •

Riley, it turned out, had extended the court's recess and requested that the attorneys meet her in chambers. The clerk had baked a lemon pound cake for the jury's afternoon break.

"Troy, how many more witnesses?" Riley asked.

Lee was standing in the corner of the office, leaning against a wall. "We'll call Sheriff McInnis. If necessary, we'll also call the deputy that was with him when he executed the search warrant. We also plan to call Jeremiah Shelly, the inmate Petty confessed to."

"I wouldn't call Shelly if I were you," Brewer said.

"Who I call is none of your business," Lee snapped.

"Judge, do you mind if Grant and I meet alone with Troy and Molly?" Brewer asked.

Riley stood and told the bailiff to join her for some cake. They left the room, and Brewer spoke after the door closed.

"Troy, if you call the snitch," he said, "we're going to have to embarrass the sheriff ... and your investigator."

"What in the *hell* are you talking about?"

"We have someone ready to testify that Woods and McInnis planted the informant."

Lee laughed. "Let me guess," he said. "Heather Sisco?"

"Maybe," Brewer said.

Lee whispered in London's ear. She nodded and walked out of the office. A minute later she stepped back in holding a manila folder. Lee opened it, removed a stack of eight-by-ten photos, and tossed them on the desk.

"Y'all may want to look at these."

Grant, from the smug look on the DA's face, knew this was trouble. Sure enough, the first picture was Grant sitting on his porch swing with Sisco. The second was Sisco walking into Grant's house with a time stamp indicating it was 10:30 p.m.

The third was Sisco kissing Grant on the cheek with her body pressed close to his.

"You son of a bitch," Grant said, moving toward Lee with clinched fists.

Brewer grabbed his arm and stopped him. "Troy, I'm surprised at you. We catch you with your pants down and you resort to blackmail?"

"Blackmail?" Lee said with a nasty little snort. "You plan to call a witness to the stand to lie about my investigator and the sheriff. And you have the audacity to accuse *me* of blackmail? I'm just doing my job." He opened the door and stared at Grant. "Call Miss Sisco. We'll impeach the hell out of her."

Grant pulled away from Brewer and walked over to Lee. "Do what you have to, you slimy bastard. I'm not throwing my client under the bus to avoid a little embarrassment. Go ahead, tough guy, put Shelly on the stand."

He paused, a cocky smile playing at the corners of his mouth now. Lee opened his mouth but apparently thought better of whatever he was going to say.

"And you may want to tell Paul McInnis to let his wife know that he's been screwing his dispatcher."

• • •

"Call your next witness," Riley said.

"The state calls Sheriff Paul McInnis," Lee replied. Grant couldn't help but note the confidence in the DA's voice. After McInnis was sworn in, he smiled and nodded at the jury. He sat down and got comfortable in the witness chair. Grant heard McInnis's leather holster rubbing against the wood.

The district attorney and sheriff spent several minutes discussing McInnis's qualifications and background. Grant thought the discussion was more appropriate for a campaign ad than a murder trial. Lee finally focused on the reason they were there.

"Sheriff, talk about the day Lacy's remains were discovered, on February 25, 2014," he said. "Tell us what happened."

McInnis, in painstaking detail, summarized the day's events. He was told by his dispatcher that a skeleton was found near the Chickasawhay River by a local hunter; he and two of his deputies drove there and confirmed the find. He called the DA's office and the Mississippi Bureau of Investigation. When the investigators arrived, he helped them search the area.

"And what did you find?" Lee asked.

"There was an old bed sheet and pieces of masking tape near the bones," McInnis said.

"Let me stop you there." Lee looked at the jury. "Were you able to confirm where the bed sheet came from?"

"Yes. It came from the Hanna home."

Grant stood. "Move to strike, Your Honor. No foundation."

Riley sustained the objection. Lee spent five awkward minutes attempting to use McInnis to authenticate the sheet and failed. Riley then instructed the court reporter to remove McInnis's earlier answer from the record. Grant felt this was huge and knew Brewer did, too.

"Okay, Sheriff," Lee said, "what else did you find?"

"We searched the surrounding area and Rob Woods found a pocket knife about twenty feet from the tree," McInnis said patiently. "There's a huge cypress tree that's hollowed out down there. The body was hidden in the base of that tree. The knife was barely sticking out of the dirt. You could hardly see it."

Lee retrieved the knife from the exhibit table and handed it to the sheriff. "Is this it, Sheriff?"

"That's it."

"And whose initials are on the knife?"

"Ben Petty's," McInnis said.

Grant stood. "Objection, Your Honor. There's no proof that the knife is Ben Petty's."

"I'll rephrase," Lee said before the judge could rule. "What are the initials on the knife?"

The sheriff, like Investigator Woods, testified that the knife belonged to a person with the initials B.F.P., then said that Petty's initials matched. Grant watched the jury and didn't like the body language he saw. Sheriff McInnis went on, explaining that a few hours later they were able to get a search warrant for Petty's trailer.

"Was Petty there when you searched?" Lee asked.

"He was," McInnis said.

"Tell the jury what you found."

"In his bedroom, stuffed between his mattresses, was a pair of panties and a picture of Lacy Hanna."

Grant fidgeted in his seat as the sheriff confirmed the panties that Ronnie Hanna had earlier identified were the ones McInnis found. Lee then asked Riley if he could approach the witness. She allowed it, and he handed a picture to McInnis.

"Sheriff, can you identify the person in that picture?"

"It's Lacy Hanna," McInnis said.

Like the knife, the picture had been previously entered into evidence. Lee asked Judge Riley if he could pass it among the jury members. This, too, was allowed, and Grant watched each member look at the photo of Lacy in a pair of panties and bra. He guessed the picture had been taken for her husband, probably as an anniversary or valentine gift. Grant was embarrassed for her—he knew she never imagined the photo being looked at by strangers. But she never imagined herself being kidnapped and murdered either.

"No further questions," Lee said. "I tender the witness."

Grant didn't wait on Riley to recognize him. "Mr. McInnis, you haven't been sheriff long, have you?"

"I'm in my first term."

"And how many murder investigations have you conducted?"

"This is my first one," he said. "But I've been to training. I know what I'm doing."

He sounds defensive. Good sign. "Were you able to find DNA on the pocket knife matching Ben Petty?"

"Uhh, we couldn't—"

"Is that a no?"

"No," McInnis said, frowning now. "We didn't find any DNA."

Grant walked toward Counselor's table, but before he sat down he looked at Brewer and Petty. Then he glanced at Lee and London. Riley, he noticed, leaned up in her chair.

"Do you have any further questions, Mr. Hicks?" she asked.

"Just one more, Judge." Grant approached McInnis and stopped a few feet from the witness. The sheriff's bravado was gone—he had to know the lack of DNA had badly damaged the prosecution of Ben Petty. "Mr. McInnis, who is Heather Sisco?"

McInnis froze for an instant, then glanced at Lee. Lee started to his feet, then changed his mind and settled back in his chair. McInnis looked back at Grant.

"She's my dispatcher," he said carefully. "Why?"

Grant turned and walked to his chair and sat down. "No further questions, Your Honor."

Lee stood, apparently not sure where to go next. But he chose not to ask any questions on redirect. He and London whispered a minute. Then they both stood and looked at Riley.

"The state rests, Your Honor," the DA said.

CHAPTER 43

Thursday night, July 10, 2014

GRANT ARRIVED AT Judge Eaton's ahead of when Brewer and Mordiky would arrive, wanting to speak to him alone. He'd made sure that Jade, Ladd, and Ella Reese were settled in for the evening; Paul Sumner had gone to Lucedale and bought pizza for supper, and Grant and Jade were both grateful because they were exhausted. Sumner and Pete Ball would stand watch until Grant got home later in the evening.

"Come in, Counselor," Eaton said.

Grant shook Eaton's hand and followed him inside. "Judge, it didn't go well today."

"I heard," he said. "Can you tell me how Lacy Hanna's panties and her picture ended up in Ben's trailer?"

"Not unless he waives attorney-client privilege, I can't."

"Possibility that they were planted?"

Grant stared at the old judge. Eaton got the message. "Well, I was afraid of that," he said as he poured coffee. "Can you salvage the case?"

"I think we're in trouble."

"I do thank you for taking Ben's case. You've done a good job, Grant."

He smiled. Eaton rarely called him by name. "I'm glad I did."

"George tells me there's some tension at home?"

Grant sighed. "A little. Jade and I will work it out after the trial. She means well." He walked to the bar, lifted the lid of the cookie jar, and grabbed a Fig Newton. "Judge, you were right."

"About?"

"Heather Sisco. They set me up."

"How do you know?" Eaton asked.

"They used her to get me in a vulnerable situation and I bit. Hook, line, and sinker."

"Don't tell me—"

Grant waved his hand as he swallowed the cookie. "I didn't sleep with her. But they took pictures of us, and if Jade sees them she'll believe I did."

"What did they have to gain?"

"McInnis is so afraid of getting beat next year he wanted to blackmail me into throwing Ben's case." Grant grabbed another cookie. "That's my hypothesis, anyway. I don't believe the DA is involved."

Eaton went to the coffee pot and refilled his cup. "So the snitch wasn't a plant?"

"I still think he was," Grant said. "Or else Lee would have used him as a witness. Thank God Mordiky found out Sisco was sleeping with the sheriff. Or my marriage would be in trouble, too."

Eaton looked fierce for the moment. "I'll get those pictures. Get this over with and concentrate on Jade. You'll be fine."

The front door opened. Brewer walked in, followed by Mordiky. "Shit, I'm glad that part is over," Brewer said.

"Mordiky," Grant said, "give me some good news. What did you find out?"

Mordiky hung his cowboy hat on the back of a chair, then hung his head. "There were no clues. Only bones. The investigators from Coahoma and Scott Counties are trying to find a connection. I'll talk with them again in the morning."

"Grant, I still don't think it's a good idea for Ben to testify," Brewer said.

"He wants to."

"We don't always get what we want. The Rolling Stones even knew that."

"The man could very well be sentenced to death by Saturday night," Grant said. "He has a right to make that call."

"Did the snitch testify?" Mordiky asked.

"No," Brewer said. "We bluffed a little beforehand and Lee opted not to call him. It's now a purely circumstantial case."

"You think that helps?" Eaton asked.

"Nope," Brewer said. "But it doesn't hurt."

The men spent two hours debating the order of witnesses. Before the meeting concluded, a strategy was agreed upon and the men hugged before they left for the night. As bad as the circumstantial evidence was, none of the men spoke of Petty's guilt or innocence. Grant knew what he had to do tomorrow. He'd represent Petty to the best of his ability. And he'd fight till the end.

When Grant returned home, he found Pete Ball and Paul Sumner sitting outside. Grant had become attached to Pete. At first, he admitted to himself, he looked after Pete out of pity. But he now admired Pete's childlike trust and faith. Grant was also grateful for Paul Sumner. He was happy to be in a place where a person's neighbors became like family.

Grant was tired and needed rest. He walked into the house and found Jade asleep on the couch. He almost touched her but was afraid he'd awaken her. He stared at his wife a moment before he walked to the kids' rooms and checked on them.

He finally lay down in bed and did something he never would

have considered several years ago—he closed his eyes and said a silent prayer. Comfortable in his faith now after years of being angry at God for the hypocrisy he saw in others around here (and weakness in his father), Grant asked God to be with all of them in the courtroom tomorrow, especially with those whose decisions would save or end Ben Petty's life.

Then he slipped into a deep sleep. A sleep without dreams. A sleep without Ben Petty.

CHAPTER 44

Friday, July 11, 2014

GRANT TOLD BREWER the next morning that he'd meet him in the courtroom. Up till now, Grant and Brewer had waited at Counselor's Table as Petty was led in by the deputies. But today Grant would make the trip across the lawn with his childhood friend. He'd walk with his client.

He opened the door to the sheriff's office and saw Heather Sisco back at the dispatcher's desk. Rage blew through him as she ignored him; the very thought of the woman becoming a lawyer made him sick to his stomach. He knew he shouldn't mouth off, but he couldn't help himself. He moved close to her window.

"I'll be writing the law school to make sure they know the kind of person you are," he growled.

Sisco looked up and smirked. "Who said anything about going to law school? But I do wonder what sweet little Miss Jade would do if she thought you screwed me in her bed. I'm sure she'd like that."

A deputy walked into view. "Here to see your client?"

Grant nodded, walked into the small room, and looked around. Hopefully he'd never see these walls again. At some point today or tonight, most likely, the jury would decide Petty's fate. The door opened and Petty walked in, dressed for court. Grant saw the deputy standing in the hall with his back to the door.

"Ben," Grant said softly, "We don't think you should testify."

"Why?"

"The jury's not going to believe your story about the panties. Or the picture."

"They already think I'm guilty," Petty said. "I want to testify. I owe them an explanation."

Grant placed his hand on Petty's shoulder. "Let's see how it goes today."

• • •

A few minutes later the jury was ready. Judge Riley instructed Grant to call his first witness.

"The defense calls John Miles," he said.

Miles was a tall, slender man with bad posture. His hair was shoulder length and he wore faded jeans and what appeared to be water boots. He had on a red t-shirt with a front pocket that held a pack of cigarettes. After the clerk swore him in, Grant stood and walked to the center of the room. He rested his elbow on top of the podium and put his right hand in the front pocket of his suit pants—a habit he'd had while in court for years.

"Please state your name," he said.

"John Miles."

"Where do you reside, Mr. Miles?"

"I live in Buffalo."

Grant smiled. "You don't mean Buffalo, New York, do you?"

Miles laughed. "Oh, no sir. The community of Buffalo. Between Neely and McLain."

"How long have you lived in Greene County?"

"All my life," he said. "I'm on the property my parents inherited from their parents."

"Mr. Miles, do you know my client? Ben Petty?"

"I know who he is," Miles said. "I've seen him around."

"Are y'all friends?"

"No sir. I just know who he is."

"Mr. Miles, does the date December 13, 2010, ring a bell?"

"Yeah it does."

"What do you remember about that date?"

Miles shifted in his seat and addressed the jury. "That was the day that Mrs. Hanna went missing."

"Now," Grant said as he moved closer to the jury, "that's almost four years ago. I have no idea what I was doing that day. Why do you remember?"

"Cause we a small county. We usually never have no murders or nothing. Especially no kidnappings. Usually only drug arrests and such."

"Do you remember where you were the morning of December 13, 2010?" Grant asked.

"I was deer hunting." Miles looked at the jury. "I know it was between gun seasons and all. Guess you could say I was hunting out of season."

Grant heard a jury member chuckle. "Did you see anybody while you were hunting?"

"Yes, sir. I saw Ben Petty."

"Are you sure it was Ben?"

"Can't miss a fellow with an arm like his. I was in my tree stand and he came walking through. He had a rifle. Looked like he was squirrel hunting."

"Objection," Lee said. "Speculative."

Riley sustained the objection so Grant moved on. "Do you recall what time of day it was?"

"I'd say before eight that morning, probably closer to

seven-thirty."

"And you're a hundred percent sure that you saw Ben Petty hunting on the morning that Lacy Hanna went missing?"

"A thousand percent sure," Miles said.

"And it was before eight?"

"Yes, sir."

Grant thanked Miles, then tendered the witness. Troy Lee bounced from his seat.

"Your Honor, may I approach the witness?" Riley nodded yes, and Lee walked to Miles and handed him a piece of paper. "Mr. Miles, this is your arrest record."

Grant objected and asked to approach the bench. He and Lee had a spirited, whispered debate about the admissibility of Miles's previous criminal record; Riley allowed Lee to question Miles about recent, prior convictions ... but not arrests. Grant felt he'd won a small victory.

"Mr. Miles, have you ever been convicted of a crime?" Lee asked.

"What do you mean?"

"Have you served any time?"

"In the jail here, or in state prison?"

Grant watched helplessly as Lee spent thirty minutes destroying Miles's credibility. Lee also managed to get Miles to admit that he wasn't exactly sure if his times were correct on the morning Lacy Hanna was murdered. Grant was relieved to hear the DA say that he had one final question.

"As a convicted felon, Mr. Miles, you do know you were violating the law that day by carrying a firearm. Don't you?"

Miles pointed at George Brewer. "The statute of limitations has run on that," he said testily. "Ask Mr. Brewer over there."

• • •

The Petty legal team caught a break when Riley recessed for

half an hour to deal with an emergency matter. Grant hurried them to Brewer's office to talk strategy.

"Well," Brewer said, "that went about as well as an enema."

"We need to subpoena Marly Hanna," Grant said.

"You discussed that with your wife?" Brewer asked.

"No," Grant said. "She'll be pissed, but she'll get over it."

"Where is Jade, anyway?" Brewer asked.

"She's in the courtroom. Sitting in the back."

"Okay," Brewer said. "If you think that's best."

Grant prepared a subpoena and called Mordiky to have it issued and delivered. At this point, he knew, Petty's chances of acquittal were dim. Perhaps it was time to throw a Hail Mary.

• • •

Jade wasn't there when Grant walked back into the courtroom. Nervous, he pulled out his cell to call her. Her phone had begun to ring when he noticed her enter through the back of the courtroom and sit down. Relieved now, he watched her pull her phone out and look up when she saw it was him calling. He ended the call before she could answer and nodded at her.

He called Dr. Mark Boyd as his next witness. Dr. Boyd took the stand and Grant inquired into his background and credentials in pediatrics and speech and language pathology. After he concluded, Troy Lee got up to ask Dr. Boyd a few questions of his own. Judge Riley then accepted Dr. Boyd as an expert, and Grant resumed his direct examination.

"Dr. Boyd, have you had the opportunity to examine Caroline Pentecost?" he asked.

"No," he answered. "I did speak to her mother on the phone, however."

"Did you review Caroline's medical records?"

"I did."

"And what is her condition?" Grant asked.

"Caroline is a healthy young lady with Down Syndrome."

"Dr. Boyd, it's no secret that Caroline witnessed a horrible event. She saw her mother's sister being taken from her home. Can you explain how her having Down Syndrome could affect her ability to recall that event?"

"First of all, I'm of the opinion that Caroline having Down Syndrome has very little, if anything, to do with her inability to recall the event."

Grant felt his heart leap. "Can you explain?"

"She was a six-year-old child that witnessed a traumatic event," Boyd said. "It is my professional opinion that she suffers from a severe case of Post Traumatic Stress Disorder, or PTSD."

"Would Down Syndrome exacerbate PTSD?"

"It could, sure."

"Dr. Boyd, in your opinion, do you believe Caroline would be able to identify the man that abducted her Aunt Lacy?"

"Yes I do," Boyd said firmly. "If she saw him, I believe she'd recognize him."

Grant ended there. Troy Lee spent an hour dissecting Boyd's testimony on cross-examination, clearly attempting to undermine the man's opinion. Grant thought the jury seemed bored and confused. Lee finally ended his questions, and Grant spent little time on redirect. It seemed that Boyd had accomplished what Grant hoped he would. And that was a good thing, after the way John Miles had been torn apart.

CHAPTER 45

Friday, July 11, 2014

JADE HAD DRIVEN to Edwina's to check on the kids. Both were fine—Jade knew Ella Reese enjoyed the attention from Edwina's nieces and nephews. Ladd and some neighborhood boys were playing video games in the den. Jade kissed them goodbye and left to meet Edwina for lunch.

"He still mad?" Edwina asked, digging into a cheese steak.

"He makes me so angry sometimes," Jade said. "He's such a pouter."

"He should be proud you gave him the information."

An acne-faced boy brought Jade's salad, topped off their tea, and walked away. Edwina frowned. "That's just nasty. You know he's back there picking them pimples."

"Edwina, hush. He may hear you."

"Not his fault. Whoever owns this place ought to keep him in the back."

They ate in comfortable silence. Edwina looked up after finishing her sandwich. "Jade, you think Ben Petty killed her?"

"I don't know," she said. "But it looks bad for him."

"I told y'all from the beginning that pervert killed her ass. No telling what all he done to her."

"If he did, I hope he's found guilty," Jade said. "But I don't want him getting the death penalty."

"Why not? Eye for an eye."

Jade's cell rang. She reached into her purse, pulled it out, and saw Marly Hanna's name on the screen. Unease went through her. "Hello, Marly," she said cautiously.

"Mrs. Jade, why did you tell?" Marly asked. Jade could hear the sniffles and knew Marly was crying.

"What? I don't—"

"Daddy's mad at me."

Oh, no. "Do you want me to talk to him?" Jade asked, and regretted the words the second they left her lips.

"A man delivered me some papers. I have to go to court." Jade heard another sniffle. "I'm scared."

"I'll go see Grant right now. Maybe I can stop this."

"I got to go. Daddy's blowing the horn."

• • •

Jade marched into Brewer's office and stormed past the receptionist. Grant and Mordiky were sitting across from Brewer at the conference table.

"Howdy, Jade," Brewer said.

She ignored him and looked hard at Grant. "Why'd you get Marly mixed up in this?"

Grant stood. "I didn't. *You* did!"

"Why didn't you get my opinion before you scared her to death with a subpoena? Now her dad may never forgive her!"

"In case you haven't noticed, Jade, we are representing a man that could get the *death penalty*!" he shouted. "And you want to know what else? I don't care what the hell Ronnie Hanna thinks."

The Peter Bay

Furious and now humiliated, Jade turned and stomped out of the office. She got in her car and drove while trying to calm down. She was angry at Grant, angry at herself, and angry that her husband ever agreed to represent Ben Petty.

CHAPTER 46

Friday, July 11, 2014

"You okay, Grant?" Brewer asked once Jade was gone. "Want me to handle the witnesses?"

"I'm fine," Grant said quietly. "I'll handle them. Sorry about that, y'all."

Judge Riley called court back to order, and Paula Pentecost took her oath and sat down. Her beauty was striking. Grant watched a couple of the male jurors lean forward in their chairs and pat down their hair. It made him want to smile, which he needed after the confrontation with his wife.

"Please state your name for the record," he said.

"Paula Pentecost."

"Mrs. Pentecost, where do you live?"

"Austin, Texas."

"And who do you live with?" Grant asked.

"My husband Calvin and our daughter, Caroline."

"Is she your only child?"

"Yes."

Grant pointed at the jury. "The members of the jury have

already been told that Caroline has Down Syndrome. Is that accurate?"

"Yes."

Grant could sense she was being guarded with her answers. "Mrs. Pentecost, I know the answer to this question, but what relation were you to Lacy Hanna?"

She looked at the jury for the first time. "My sister."

Grant rested his elbow on the podium. "Did you volunteer to come here today?"

"Not exactly," she said. "You sent me a subpoena."

Grant nodded and smiled. "Mrs. Pentecost, let's talk about the morning Lacy disappeared. Caroline was with your sister's family?"

"Yes. She was spending a few days with them. I had gone out of town with my husband."

"I see," Grant said. "And I'll make this as brief as possible. Has Caroline ever been able to identify or describe the man that kidnapped Lacy?"

"No."

"Do you think she would recognize him if she saw him?"

Pentecost shifted in her seat. She glanced at the jury. "Yes. I believe she would."

"Mrs. Pentecost, how old is Caroline now?"

"She's ten."

"Do you think she remembers that morning?"

"Of course she does," Pentecost said. "That's why we moved to Austin. She kept telling us—"

"Objection!" Lee said. "Hearsay."

Riley leaned up in her chair and looked at Grant. "Sustained."

"Mrs. Pentecost, without telling us what Caroline said, why did y'all move to Texas?"

"Caroline kept looking for the *bad man*. We thought she might stop looking if we moved."

"Has she stopped?" he asked gently.

Pentecost hesitated before answering. Grant saw the tears in her eyes. She took out a tissue and wiped them. "No, she hasn't."

"I need to ask a question I asked earlier. Mrs. Pentecost, do you believe that Caroline would recognize the man that was in your sister's home that day?"

"I do."

"No further questions, Your Honor," Grant said.

Lee stood and carefully asked Paula Pentecost a few questions. Grant knew he was trying to be careful and felt Lee's cross-examination went nowhere—he didn't appear to have prepared for Caroline. When he finished, Grant didn't ask questions on redirect, as there was no need. She'd served her purpose.

• • •

Judge Riley removed the jury from the courtroom while holding a competency hearing to determine whether Caroline Pentecost was able to testify. The courtroom was filled to capacity, though, so Riley told her court reporter to set up in her chambers. Only Grant and Troy Lee were allowed inside.

Caroline was in a light blue dress with her hair in a headband. Grant noticed that her ears were pierced and saw two gold-studded earrings. She wore a gold necklace with a cross. Her eyes were big, and she was fidgeting with her hands.

"Caroline, how are you today?" Riley asked.

She briefly made eye contact with Riley before looking at her hands. "Okay," she whispered.

"How old are you?"

She held up ten fingers.

"Can you answer out loud for us, sweetheart?" Riley asked as she pointed at the court reporter. "That lady needs to write down what you say."

Caroline looked at the court reporter, then back at Riley.

"Where's Momma?"

"She's right out that door," Riley said gently. "You want me to get her?"

Caroline shook her head yes. Grant opened the door and motioned for Paula Pentecost to come into Riley's office. Caroline hugged her when she walked in.

"When can we go, Momma?"

Paula Pentecost cupped her daughter's face and smiled. "Sweetie, can you answer their questions?"

"Why?"

"They need to ask you about Aunt Lacy."

Caroline turned and looked at Judge Riley. "Okay."

Riley asked Paula Pentecost to take Caroline outside. Then she looked at Grant. "I don't think I'm going to allow her to testify."

"Judge, I promise I won't keep her on the stand long," Grant said. It was a struggle to hold his temper now. "Less than five minutes."

"Judge," Lee said. "There's no question her testimony will be a disaster. I agree. She's not competent."

"Then I'll file an emergency interlocutory appeal with the Supreme Court," Grant snapped. "My client is being tried for capital murder and the only person who witnessed the crime is not allowed to testify? Come on, Judge."

"Y'all get out," Riley snapped. "Give me a few minutes."

• • •

The jury waited as Caroline was led to the witness stand by her mother. Since Grant and Lee had agreed that Paula Pentecost would not be recalled as a witness, she was allowed to stay in the courtroom. Grant looked on as Caroline watched her mother sit on the first row and give her daughter a big smile.

Riley leaned over the judges' bench and spoke. "Caroline, do you remember who I am?"

"You're the judge," she said.

Grant peered at the jurors and saw them smiling. Caroline had their hearts ... and their attention.

"Yes, I am," Riley said. "Do you know the difference between telling a lie and telling the truth?"

"Yes, ma'am," she said. "If you tell a lie, you'll go to the devil."

Riley chuckled. "That's a good way of putting it. Caroline, the two men you met in my office have a couple of questions for you. That okay?"

Caroline shook her head yes.

"And sweetheart, will you answer out loud for us? Okay?"

Caroline looked at the court reporter, then back at the judge. "Yes, ma'am."

Riley looked at Grant. "Mr. Hicks, you may proceed."

Grant walked close to Caroline. "Caroline, do you remember me?"

She shook her head yes. She then remembered Riley's instruction. "Yes, sir."

"A long time ago, do you remember spending the night at your Aunt Lacy's?" he asked gently. Caroline looked at the judge, then the court reporter. She looked past Grant and into the crowd. He waited while she scratched the bridge of her nose.

"Do you remember spending the night at Marly and Jenna's house?" Grant asked.

"A bad man took Aunt Lacy."

"Do you remember what he looked like?"

Caroline shrugged her shoulders.

"Can you answer out loud, please?"

"Okay."

"Do you remember seeing the bad man?"

"Yes, sir."

Grant pointed at Troy Lee. "Was that the man?"

She shook her head and responded. "No, sir."

Grant hesitated. The moment of truth was at hand. Caroline was staring past him at her mother. Grant looked at Petty, who sat erect in his chair.

"What about him, Caroline?" Grant pointed at Petty. "Is *he* the bad man?"

Caroline looked at Petty and at Brewer before turning to Grant. She shrugged her shoulders. Grant motioned for Petty to stand.

"Is he the bad man that you saw, Caroline?"

She glanced at Petty again. She found her mother in the crowd and didn't respond.

"Sweetheart," Grant said, pointing at Petty. "Is *he* the man that you saw take Aunt Lacy?"

Caroline looked again at Petty and shrugged. "I don't remember."

Grant hoped the wind leaving his chest and the wobble in his knees wasn't detected by the jury. He thanked Caroline for coming, and Troy Lee asked no questions. The bailiff led Caroline to her mother and they left the courtroom. Grant was relieved that Riley recessed for fifteen minutes. He needed to gather his composure, and he was delighted when the judge decided after the recess to adjourn for the day. It was already 5:30 and the day had been taxing for everybody. Riley informed the jury that the taxpayers of Greene County would be paying for some Rocky Creek Catfish to be delivered to their hotel tonight.

Then her gavel fell and the wounded Petty legal team left the courthouse.

CHAPTER 47

Friday night, July 11, 2014

GRANT GOT HOME and discovered a note taped to the front door explaining that Jade and the kids were staying at Edwina's until the trial was over. She apologized for breaking her promise by contacting Marly Hanna; she hoped he'd eventually understand that Marly needed a friend. She told him that she loved him and, despite what she'd said, was proud he took Petty's case. She ended by saying that she was praying for him. Her postscript told him his dinner was in the refrigerator.

Grant walked inside and fixed himself a drink. Jade wouldn't permit him to keep beer in the refrigerator. But he kept a bottle of rum in the bottom drawer of the guestroom dresser for emergencies. Tonight qualified as such an occasion.

He walked outside and sat in his favorite spot, the top step. He was secretly glad the trial was almost over. Petty continued to insist that he testify ... so tomorrow he'd get his chance. Grant thought about the jury. They knew the body was Lacy Hanna's. They knew that a man abducted her. A knife found at the crime scene had Ben Petty's initials. A pair of Lacy Hanna's panties, along with a picture of her in lingerie, was crammed between the mattresses where Petty slept. Grant sipped from his drink and knew a conviction was likely. After a minute he pulled out his cell and dialed Mordiky.

"Hello, Grant," Mordiky said. "You okay?"

"Doing the best I can," he said. "Look, I don't think there's a chance of an acquittal or a hung jury. We need to get ready for the sentencing phase."

"Agreed."

"What evidence do we have to present to the jury to try to save Petty's life?"

"His sister. We have his DHS records; he was lost in the system for years. We have most of his school records, his medical records. His IQ is in the low 90s so he's not intellectually disabled."

"There really aren't any aggravating factors other than the kidnapping," Grant said. "Fortunately for him, there's no proof he raped or tortured her or anything."

"True," Mordiky said. "But I have a question. I'm not a lawyer, but it seems to me that if Petty testifies, then the DA could make him look like a pervert. And he had that voyeurism charge as a teenager. You think it's a good idea to expose him to the jury in that way? I mean, that may push them toward the death penalty."

"I believe I can keep the voyeurism charge from getting into evidence." Grant paused as he thought. Mordiky waited him out. "Hell, you may be right. I'll meet with Ben and George in the morning and see what they want to do."

"Sounds like a plan," Mordiky said. "Oh, I almost forgot to tell you. Rob Woods told me today that he was contacted by the Mississippi Bureau of Investigation this morning. They've listed Ben Petty as a person of interest in the Clarksdale and Scott County cases."

"Shit," Grant said. "I was hoping we'd get some good news."

"Me, too. See you in the morning."

• • •

Grant tried to sleep but couldn't. He texted Jade and told her he was sorry. She said she was too, and that she'd be in court tomorrow. He told her he loved her. She said she loved him, too, and he thought their reconciliation would relax him. It didn't. He tried to think of how he'd react to the jury's verdict. What would he say to Ben Petty?

He rarely watched television but turned it on for the company. *Pawn Stars* was on when he heard a knock at his door. Grant felt his heart surge and wondered where his gun was—he cursed when he remembered it was under the seat in his Range Rover. He crept to the door and turned on the porch light. He pulled back the curtain ... and found Pete Ball smiling at him.

"Hey, Pete," Grant said, relieved. "Come on in."

"Where's Mrs. Jade?"

"She stayed in town tonight."

"She mad?" Pete asked.

"She was. I think she's okay now."

"Paul told me she seemed madder than a wet setting hen today, for some reason." Grant didn't respond. "Anyway, I saw the TV on and thought I'd say hey."

"Pete, you still live in your momma's old house?"

"Yep. Been there all my life."

"I rode by there the other day," Grant said. "Looks like it needs a new roof."

"It leaks a little, but it's fine."

Grant stood and walked him to the door. "When this trial is over, how about you and me move the camper to your place and you stay there while we get that roof repaired."

Pete stuck out his hand. "I appreciate everything, Grant. But

I don't take no handouts."

"Handout?" Grant asked. "Won't be no handout. I'm hiring you to help me get this place in tip-top shape. Deal?"

Pete hugged Grant and backed away. "That's a deal. And Grant?"

"Yes?"

"You don't know how much this means to me. I don't have no family or nothing."

Grant walked out on the porch with Pete. "You're my friend. And for me, that's the same as family."

Hours later, Grant set his iPhone on the night stand and plugged in his earbuds. He found the *Pink Floyd* channel on Pandora and at some point fell asleep. And to his surprise, he slept well.

CHAPTER 48

Saturday morning, July 12, 2014

GRANT PARKED THE next morning and looked toward the courthouse. It was 7:45. Riley informed them yesterday that court would start promptly at 8:30, instead of the usual 9:30. She knew that the longer a sequestered jury was kept from their families, the more likely problems could occur. Especially on weekends.

Brewer pulled up next to Grant in his pickup. They walked into Brewer's office to talk strategy for the last time. At least for the guilt phase of the Petty trial.

"Get any sleep?" Brewer asked.

"I actually slept well," Grant said. "You?"

"Not much. I wanted a drink, but I was afraid if I started I wouldn't stop."

Brewer turned on the coffee pot, then leaned against the counter and folded his arms. "Who are we calling next?"

"What do you think?"

"We can rest now, but they'll find him guilty in less than an hour."

290

"What about the Hanna girl?" Grant asked. "Think we should call her?"

"I'm not sure. If it looks like we're pitting her against her dad, the jury may not like us much. As for Petty, I've been opposed to him testifying, but we may as well go out firing."

"Mordiky made an interesting point last night," Grant said. "He said if we call Ben, Troy Lee will make him look like a pervert and may just expedite his trip to death row."

"He's right, Grant. Let's just see what the temperature is when we get there."

• • •

True to her word, Riley called court to order at 8:30 and directed Grant to call his next witness.

"The defense calls Ben Petty," he said after getting to his feet. He heard a tiny tremor in his voice. He also heard movement from the crowd as Petty walked toward the stand. Each jury member watched him raise his crooked arm and swear to tell the truth, the whole truth, and nothing but the truth, so help him God.

Grant turned and saw Jade in the back, sitting between Pete Ball and Paul Sumner. She smiled a bit and he returned the gesture. He looked at Brewer, who nodded his head. He felt a bit weak-kneed as he saw how innocent Ben looked in the witness chair. Like the flash of a falling star, the memory of Ben walking out of the woods as a nine-year-old little boy shot past.

"You may proceed, Mr. Hicks," Riley said.

"Thank you, Your Honor." He looked at Petty. "Can you introduce yourself to the jury?"

"My name's Ben Petty."

"Where do you live?"

"I live about twelve miles from here. Towards McLain."

"How long have you lived in Greene County?" Grant asked.

"This time, about ten years. I lived here when I was a kid, for about two years."

"Did you know Lacy Hanna?"

"Yes, sir. I had done some work around their place. Like Mr. Hanna said, off and on he'd hire me to do stuff like put up fence. Work around the place some."

Grant spent a few minutes discussing the various projects that Petty worked on for the Hannas. Petty said he enjoyed working for them. Grant glanced at the jury, then walked close to Petty.

"Ben, where were you the morning Lacy Hanna went missing?"

"I was squirrel hunting," Petty said calmly.

"Did you kill any squirrels that morning?"

"I killed a couple, I think. But I missed a few more."

"Did you see John Miles when you were hunting?" Grant asked.

"No, sir. He must've been hid real good."

"When did you learn that Mrs. Hanna had gone missing?"

"Next day," Petty said. "I don't take no paper or have a TV or nothing where I get the news."

"How did you find out?"

"I'd stopped by the store in Neely and people was talkin' about it."

"Did you go see Ronnie Hanna when you found out?"

"No, sir," Petty said.

"Did you consider Ronnie Hanna a friend?"

"I just worked for him some. We got along. But we didn't hang out or nothing. But I thought a lot of Mrs. Hanna."

Grant had told Petty over and over to *only* answer the question asked. Petty had strayed from those instructions, and Grant adjusted his strategy to try to minimize the damage.

"What do you mean, Ben?"

"She was always nice to me."

"Did you ever eat a meal with the Hanna family?"

"No, sir. Not really. I mean she'd bring me something to drink or eat if I was there during lunch or dinner. But I ain't never went inside and sat at the table."

"Do you recall Sheriff Coaker coming to your house a year or so after Lacy Hanna went missing?" Grant asked.

"Yes, sir. I told him they could look around."

Grant walked to the edge of the jury box. "Ben, did Lacy Hanna ever visit your trailer?"

"She did a time or two."

Grant caught movement from the corner of his eye. He could tell the jury was listening intently. "Did she come inside?"

"No, sir. I wouldn't let her," Petty said.

"Why not?"

Petty looked down, then back at Grant. "I was too embarrassed. My place is kinda rundown."

"Was she by herself?"

"One time she brought me some winter clothes. I think she was by herself that time." Petty paused. "But another time she brought me some vegetables. Her daughter helped her unload the stuff."

"Ben, you heard Mr. Hanna say that he thought Lacy was afraid of you. In your mind, did she act afraid around you?"

Lee stood and objected. Riley overruled him, thankfully, and Grant repeated the question.

"Not at all," Petty replied. "She was always friendly."

"Ben, you also heard the investigator, Rob Woods, testify about a pocket knife found at the crime scene." Grant walked over and picked up the knife and handed it to Ben. "Is that yours?"

"No, sir."

"But it has your initials."

"That don't make it mine," Petty said calmly. "That's not the kind of brand I like. I wouldn't have anything but a Barlow."

"Do you remember a few months ago when Sheriff McInnis showed up at your house?"

"Yes."

"You heard him testify that he found a pair of Lacy's panties and a picture of her under your mattress. Is that true?"

"Yes, sir."

Grant could sense discontent from the jury. "How did those items get there?"

Petty didn't blink. "I put them there."

"How did they come to be in your possession?"

Petty glanced at the jury, then back to Grant. "I took them."

"*How* did you take them?"

"I ain't gonna lie. I thought Mrs. Hanna was a pretty lady. I ain't never had no woman. I stole the panties out of a clothes hamper."

Grant's stomach turned. Petty had stumbled again and Grant knew it. He quickly tried to move past the damaging admission. "What about the picture?"

"Well, one day me and Mr. Hanna was replacing a window in their bedroom. I had to hold it from the inside. I saw a book sticking out from underneath the bed. While Mr. Hanna was digging in his toolbox, I saw the book was full of pictures of Mrs. Hanna. I wanted to look at them so I put them under my shirt. I wanted to return them. But I never got a chance."

Grant walked close to Petty. "Ben, I want you to look at that jury and tell them if you killed Lacy Hanna."

Petty looked at the men and women. All, Grant saw, looked straight at him. "Ladies and gentlemen, I ain't killed nobody. I'd never hurt anybody, especially someone as nice as Mrs. Hanna."

Grant looked at Judge Riley. "I tender the witness, Your Honor."

Grant felt every eye on him as he returned to his seat. He

looked at Jade and read her lips—she silently told him that she loved him. He nodded and sat next to Brewer in the chair normally occupied by Petty. Brewer shook Grant's hand. Grant looked up just in time to see Troy Lee start in on Petty.

"You were sexually attracted to Lacy Hanna weren't you, Mr. Petty?"

"No, I just thought she was pretty."

"What kind of man takes a woman's panties, then steals intimate pictures meant only for her husband?"

"I didn't mean no harm."

"What did you do with her panties?"

Petty glanced at the jury and back to Lee. "I just kept them, that's all."

Mordiky turned out to be right, Grant conceded. Lee seemed to succeed in painting Petty as a deviant who was infatuated with Lacy Hanna, as a man with a dangerous crush which led to her kidnapping and murder. Grant looked at the jury and prayed that at least one of them believed his client was innocent.

CHAPTER 49

Saturday late morning, July 12, 2014

JUDGE RILEY MET with the attorneys and finalized the jury instructions. Grant thought she was uncharacteristically sentimental when she thanked them for their professionalism. Then she stood and followed them into the courtroom. They took their places and the jury was brought back in and seated. Riley called on Troy Lee to begin his closing statement.

"Ladies and gentlemen," he said, "I know this week has been stressful for you and your families. But you should be proud of your service. You've sat here and listened to the evidence with attention to each detail."

Grant listened as Lee meticulously walked the jurors through the evidence that he believed pointed to one conclusion: Ben Petty kidnapped and murdered Lacy Hanna. Grant watched a couple of jurors nod in agreement. He focused on Bernadean Benjamin and Cregg Polkey—both were concentrating on Lee's words. He noticed a notepad in Benjamin's lap. He hoped she'd be the one to save Petty's life.

Lee's closing lasted half an hour. It was powerful, Grant

thought; Lee knew what he was doing. After he asked the jury to perform its civic duty and find Petty guilty, he sat down. Riley then looked at Brewer and nodded, and the old warhorse walked to within a few feet of the jury.

"Like Mr. Lee, on behalf of Ben Petty, Mr. Hicks, and myself, I'd like to thank you for your service," he said. "To me, one of the most patriotic duties as a United States citizen is to answer the call to serve on the jury. It's a noble duty."

Brewer's pace slowed as he spoke. "I know y'all remember that during Mr. Hicks's opening statement he mentioned the word *coincidence*. As I sat through this trial, I was struck at the number of unfortunate coincidences that have brought us here today. And those coincidences have Ben Petty on trial for the kidnapping and murder of Lacy Hanna.

"You heard the testimony of Sheriff Coaker, who was the sheriff when this terrible crime occurred. He searched Ben's home and found nothing. In fact, he was the sheriff for over a year *after* Mrs. Hanna's disappearance and he never considered Ben Petty a suspect.

"The prosecutor would have you believe that three items warrant you to ignore the rest of the evidence and find Ben Petty guilty." Brewer held up three fingers on his right hand. "Let's talk about those three items. First, the knife." Brewer walked close to the jury. "Ben collects knives. But not *Old Timer* knives. He collects Barlow knives. Now, I agree that the fact that the initials on the knife match Ben's initials doesn't look good. But folks, that's a simple coincidence. Only God knows whose pocket knife that is. And maybe one day, he'll reveal that to us. But for now—make no mistake, ladies and gentlemen—there has been *no direct evidence* linking that knife to Ben Petty. None. Zero."

Brewer raised two fingers on his right hand. "Let's discuss the second and third coincidences: the panties and the picture." He paced slowly in front of the jury. "As for those items, Ben Petty chose to face you and tell you the truth. He told you that he took them. Again, that doesn't look good and it was wrong." Brewer paused and seemed to focus on Bernadean Benjamin. "But make no mistake, those two facts are simply two more coincidences that, accompanied with a single pocket knife, do not look good." Brewer paused to allow his words to sink in as he made eye contact with each juror. "But, folks, *not looking good* is not the test. The jury instructions which you will follow require you to determine whether Ben Petty kidnapped and murdered Lacy Hanna beyond a reasonable doubt. Not whether the evidence doesn't look good, not whether there were a few coincidences.

"Ladies and gentlemen, the state's case has too many holes. Too many dots unconnected." Grant watched Brewer smile at the jury. "Folks, I've been around the world twice and to a rooster fight, and I ain't never seen nothing like this. Things just don't add up."

Two male jurors smiled at Brewer's last comment. Grant peeked at Judge Riley and sensed she was enjoying Brewer's remarks. He looked next at the DA. Lee was sitting with his legs crossed as if the whole trial was a mere formality. Grant's stomach churned, which reminded him how much he hated to lose, especially to an attorney that he felt was an inferior opponent. Grant turned his attention back to Brewer, who'd walked to the end of the jury box.

"Who else did you hear from?" Brewer asked. "You heard from John Miles. Despite the fact that he had to admit to the whole world that he'd broken the law when he went hunting, he came forward nonetheless. Why? He doesn't know Ben Petty. They're not friends. The reason he came forward was that he couldn't sit back and let an innocent man be found guilty of a crime *he wasn't there to commit.* You heard him. At the time of the crime, he saw Ben hunting that morning. Ben wasn't even near the Hanna home. Not even close."

The Peter Bay

Brewer walked from one end of the jury box to the other before continuing. "You also heard from Dr. Mark Boyd. He explained that little Caroline, by witnessing such a traumatic event, now suffers from Post Traumatic Stress Disorder. Most importantly, you heard from her mother, Paula Pentecost. Paula testified that she believed Caroline would recognize the bad man that came into the Hanna home that morning." Brewer lowered his voice. "And when Mr. Hicks pointed at Ben Petty, Caroline *didn't recognize him* as that bad man."

Brewer walked to the center of the room and faced the jury. "Ladies and gentlemen, jury duty is hard. Especially in a circumstantial evidence case like this one. There is *no* direct evidence connecting Ben Petty to this crime. None. There is *no* witness, not one. So you must exclude all other reasonable hypotheses before you can convict Ben Petty." Brewer clasped his hands together and leaned toward the jury. "Please, please don't convict Ben Petty based on three mere coincidences. Find him not guilty. Thank you."

Grant reached across Petty and shook Brewer's hand when he returned to the table. Brewer had given his best. And Grant had too.

The prosecutor spent ten minutes rebutting Brewer's closing. It was noon when Lee finished. The jury would eat, then determine Ben Petty's future. Grant couldn't remember a time when he'd been more nervous. After the jury went off to deliberate, two deputies escorted Petty back to the jail to wait on the verdict.

Grant hugged his old friend before they led him away.

CHAPTER 50

Saturday afternoon, July 12, 2014

THE PETTY LEGAL team gathered in Brewer's conference room and stared everywhere but at each other. Lunch had been served, but the food went untouched. They were still sitting in silence when Jade, Pete Ball, and Paul Sumner walked in. Grant stood and hugged Jade. Brewer told them to help themselves to the food, and Ball and Sumner did.

Grant took Jade's hand and led her into the hall. "I'm sorry about last night."

"Me, too, baby," Jade said. "I promise never to do anything like that again."

"And I promise not to throw a temper-tantrum when I don't get my way."

"How long will the jury take?" she asked.

"Hard to tell. The longer they stay out, the better for our side."

"So will you wait here?"

"Yes," Grant said. "We have to be close by in case they reach a verdict."

"I'm going to Edwina's, then, and wait with the kids. Can you let me know when the verdict is reached?"

Grant kissed her. "You bet. I love you, Jade."

"I love you, too, Grant Hicks."

• • •

Pete decided to stay with Grant and Brewer. Grant looked at his watch and saw that it was already 2:30. The jury had been deliberating at least an hour, he thought. He decided to walk over and sit in the courtroom. He left Brewer and Pete in a discussion about which river had the most fish: the Chickasawhay or the Leaf.

A few people were sitting in the courtroom, but most had scattered. Grant didn't speak to anyone. He doodled on a notepad and fiddled with his phone to pass the time. He stared at the empty jury box, then looked at the door which they were gathered behind. He'd give anything to be a fly on a wall in that room. He was startled by a hand on his shoulder and looked up to find Calvin and Paula Pentecost behind him.

"I'm sorry," Paula said. "Didn't mean to sneak up on you."

Grant stood. "That's okay." He shook their hands. "Paula, I'm sorry I had to bring you here." He nodded at Caroline, who was sitting on the front row. "How is she?"

"She's actually pretty good," Paula said, turning to look at her daughter.

"Grant," Calvin said. "We just wanted to thank you." Grant couldn't hide his surprised expression. "We were able to visit with Ronnie and the girls this morning. I think we've mended some fences."

"Good. I'm happy to hear that."

"Calvin and I are taking Caroline, Marly, and Jenna out to Ronnie's," Paula said. "The girls don't want to be here, and we feel it's time to let Caroline know it's okay to be there. We want her to get reacquainted with her cousins."

"I appreciate y'all telling me this," Grant said. "Nice meeting you folks."

Grant watched the Pentecost family leave the courtroom. Perhaps, he thought as he sat back down to wait, there was a silver lining in every cloud. Maybe a time and place for everything.

• • •

At 4:00 the bailiff notified Judge Riley that a verdict had been reached. Court would be called to order in fifteen minutes, and Grant texted Jade to let her know. He then called Brewer. Five minutes later, Petty was brought in by the same two deputies who'd served as his escorts for the week. Ronnie Hanna sat on the first row on the far side of the courtroom, the pastor from Big Creek Baptist Church alongside.

The courtroom door flew open and Brewer walked in breathing hard. "Hell, I'm out of shape," he whispered as he sat down.

Grant didn't respond. He nervously shook his knees and watched for Judge Riley to enter. He checked his phone; Jade hadn't returned his text. Then he realized his battery was just about dead. He looked over his shoulder and couldn't find her in the crowd. The bailiff's voice echoed through the courtroom then and Grant stood. After the jury was seated, Riley looked at them.

"Has the jury reached a verdict?" she asked.

Jury foreman Gabe Tucker stood. "We have, Your Honor."

Riley looked at Petty. "Will the defendant please stand?"

Grant and Brewer stood with Petty. Grant fumbled while trying to button his coat, and he finally dropped his arms to his side. The bailiff delivered the written verdict to the judge. She read it, eyes giving away nothing, and handed it back to the bailiff.

"Madame Clerk, will you read the verdict?" Riley asked.

The clerk stood as the bailiff handed her the sheet. She put on her reading glasses and looked it. She cleared her throat. "On the charge of capital murder with the underlying felony of kidnapping, we the jury find Benjamin Franklin Petty *guilty*."

The courtroom remained strangely quiet. It was like they had already reacted, Grant thought. Or maybe they just weren't surprised. Brewer asked that the jury members be polled individually, and one by one each member stood and stated that he or she agreed with the verdict—it was unanimous. Riley adjourned court until first thing Monday morning, when the jury would decide whether Ben Petty would receive the death penalty or spend the rest of his life in prison. Grant tried to comfort Petty as the deputies led him from the courtroom, but his friend seemed to be in a daze.

After Petty was gone, Brewer put his hand on Grant's shoulder. "We did all we could do," he said. "Let's meet tomorrow afternoon and discuss sentencing. Maybe we can at least save his life." Brewer didn't carry a cell phone, and a young lady from the clerk's office handed him a message. He frowned as he read it, then looked up. "Mordiky wants us to call. Says it's an emergency."

Grant reached for his cell, but the phone was now dead. "Battery's spent," he said. "Let me check on Jade. I'll call you as soon as I can."

CHAPTER 51

Saturday late afternoon, July 12, 2014

JADE WAS BITING her fingernails in Edwina's den when her phone vibrated with a text. She'd hoped it was Grant telling her the jury had reached a verdict, but it was from Marly Hanna.

MARLY: Hey, it's Marly.
JADE: Hello, you okay?
MARLY: Yes, ma'am. Aunt Paula, Uncle Calvin, and Caroline brought us to the house. We didn't want to be at the courthouse.
JADE: I understand. I hope you're not too mad at me for talking to Grant.
MARLY: I'm not mad. I was hurt at first but I'm okay.
JADE: Maybe we can get together soon.
MARLY: I'd like that. Ttyl.
JADE: See you soon.

While going back and forth with Marly, Jade missed a text from Grant. By the time she saw the numeric indicator and read the text, ten minutes had past. She called Paul Sumner, who was already on his way to pick her up. Ella Reese was playing on the floor as Edwina watched television, and Jade kissed her daughter and told Edwina she'd be back soon. Edwina wanted to go, but her aunt was napping and she needed to watch the kids.

Jade was standing by the road watching Ladd and his friends play baseball when Sumner pulled up at the curb. She waved at Ladd and jumped in the passenger seat of Sumner's Camry. Sumner hit Main Street and headed toward the courthouse, and Jade prayed she'd get there before the verdict was read.

. . .

Grant pulled into Edwina's driveway and saw Ladd and two boys playing in the yard. He hugged his son and walked inside. Edwina was holding Ella Reese and reading to her.

"Hey," he said. "Where's Jade?"

"Went to the courthouse a few minutes ago. With Paul Sumner."

"Hate I missed her," Grant said, reaching for the door handle. "Thanks."

"Guilty?" Edwina asked.

"Yep."

"Well ... I'm sorry."

"We did the best we could," Grant said. "We'll be back to get the kids in a bit."

. . .

Grant drove back to the courthouse and saw that the parking lot had emptied. Only a few locals were standing outside talking as he drove around the building. He didn't see Sumner's car and wondered if he'd missed them along the way. His phone had been on the charger, and he picked it up and turned on the ringer. He'd missed several calls and tried to reach George Brewer first but got no answer. He didn't recognize the second number but from the prefix he knew that it came from Neely. He dialed and identified himself when a man answered.

"Grant, this is Calvin Pentecost. We have something you need to know."

There was urgency in the man's voice. Grant could feel his heart race. "What is it?"

"We brought Caroline out to Ronnie's to see if we could help her get past her fears," Calvin said. "Marly pulled out the old school annuals from when she and Jenna were at Black Creek Elementary to show Caroline what they looked like at her age."

Grant still hadn't seen Sumner's car (a Toyota, he thought) on his way back to Edwina's. He wanted Calvin to get to the point so he could try Jade on her cell.

"Anyway, when Caroline was looking through one of the annuals, she started screaming and pointed at a man."

Oh, wow. "Who?"

"It was the principal, Grant. Guy named Paul Sumner," Pentecost said. "Caroline said *he* was the bad man."

• • •

Grant felt his heart drop. He disconnected from Pentecost and called Edwina—Jade hadn't returned there. He called Jade and got her voice mail. He called Sumner and got *his* voice mail. Speeding toward the farm and frantic now, he called Brewer's office ... and no one answered. He was about to call 911 when he saw Mordiky's name flashing on the screen.

"Grant," Mordiky said breathlessly, "where's Jade?"

The SUV seemed to be floating as the speedometer bumped 120 miles per hour. "I don't know!" Grant said, panic setting in. "I can't find her!"

"Paul Sumner is the killer," he said. "I called McInnis to let him know."

The Peter Bay

"I just talked to Calvin Pentecost— where the hell is Jade?"

"I called George, and he's looking, too," Mordiky replied. "I just left Scott County, man. I'll get there as soon as I can."

• • •

Jade wasn't at the farm. Grant drove the short distance to Sumner's and found no one there, either. He thought about Lacy Hanna and what Sumner must have done to her. Then he reached under his seat, found the revolver, and put it in his lap. He prayed aloud as he drove to the only other place he thought they might be.

The Peter Bay.

CHAPTER 52

Saturday evening, July 12, 2014

A THUNDERSTORM HAD PASSED through earlier and the dirt road was slippery. But Grant saw fresh tire tracks and sped up. He dearly hoped he could remember where Judge Eaton had taken him to show him the place where Lacy Hanna's body was found. He came upon a sharp curve, though, and hit the brakes to make the angle. The wheels wouldn't turn in the thick mud and sent the Range Rover into the ditch.

Grant grabbed the revolver and ran. Another storm was approaching, the thunder getting louder. He heard lightning crackle in the distance and saw the wind moving high in the trees. He made it to the old pipeline and started toward the cypress trees. Briars pulled the skin from his hands and ripped at his pants.

Near the end of the clearing and tucked behind a briar thicket was Sumner's Camry. Grant felt fear slice through him and picked his pace up. He ran through high weeds and brush and didn't see the stump hole until it was too late—his right ankle gave as his upper body shot forward. He screamed in pain, partly because his gun slipped and disappeared in the thick bushes. He forced himself up and hobbled toward the swaying trees. Tears rolled down his face as he screamed Jade's name.

He could see her face, her innocence, the love she had for people. The love she showed her family, the love she showed Marly Hanna, and the neighborly love she showed Paul Sumner, a man who'd apparently killed Lacy Hanna and had befriended the Hicks family. Grant kept moving forward, not sure what he would do if he found Sumner. He'd lost his only weapon.

The pipeline clearing ended, and a steep hill led into the swamp. Grant gripped trees and limbs to keep his balance and clutched a small oak to hold him up as he rushed down the hill.

The tree was rotten and snapped, though, and Grant fell and rolled to the bottom and into a water-filled puddle next to a cypress knee. He pulled himself up again. Pain shot through every nerve in his body. He located the top of the massive cypress where Lacy Hanna's body was found and moved in that direction.

He froze when he heard a shot fired, then another. He began to weep as he pulled himself forward. "Dear God, please help Jade! Please," he gasped. He could hardly put weight on his right ankle but hurried toward the gunfire and finally saw movement in the distance.

"Jade!"

His world stopped cold when he saw Jade lying on her stomach and a man standing over her. The man turned, and Grant realized it was George Brewer.

"She's alive, Grant," he said.

He knelt beside Jade, who was unconscious but breathing. He held her and stroked her hair, then looked up at Brewer. "Where's Sumner?"

Brewer pointed behind the large cypress. Pete Ball was kneeling next to a body.

"He alive, Pete?" Brewer called out.

Grant heard sirens in the distance.

"Feller's deader than a door nail." Pete stood and walked over. "How's Mrs. Jade?"

"She'll make it," Brewer said. "Judging from the bruise on her face, he knocked her out cold."

Grant only now noticed that her hands were handcuffed behind her back; her belt and shoes were on a sheet a few feet away. Grant took her into his arms. Buttons were missing from her shirt, and her bra had been pulled down below her breasts. Brewer and Pete looked away as Grant dressed her the best he could.

"We got here in time, Grant," Brewer said with his back still turned. "He didn't get to do what he'd planned on."

Pete had gone through Sumner's clothes by then and found the keys to the cuffs. He knelt beside Jade, unlocked them, and tossed them away. Then he dashed to the pipeline to meet the paramedics when he heard the ambulance approaching. Brewer helped Grant to his feet.

"Thank you, George," he whispered. "Thank you so much."

"You bet, man." Brewer paused. "Where's your damn revolver?"

Grant wiped his face. "I lost it when I fell back there."

"Well," Brewer said. "Maybe you won't need it again."

CHAPTER 53

Monday, July 14, 2014

GRANT HAD BEEN at the Hattiesburg hospital with Jade since they'd arrived Saturday afternoon. He'd had surgery to repair his ankle, and the surgeon said the break was clean and that he would be back to normal in a few weeks. Jade, though, had been in a medically-induced coma. She had a cracked jaw, loose teeth, a concussion, and multiple bruises on her neck, face, and arms. Grant was asleep in the fold-out bed when he heard the voice he'd been waiting to hear and snapped to attention.

"Grant?" Jade whispered.

"Hey, baby," he said. "Hold on. Let me get us some light."

"Where are the kids?" she asked.

"Edwina has them," he said. "They were here—" Grant fumbled for his watch. "Well, it's Monday now. They were here last night."

"Where are we?"

"Hospital in Hattiesburg."

"Oh, baby, your leg?" Jade asked.

"Ankle. Stepped in a hole. It's going to be fine."

Grant sat on the edge of her bed and looked into her eyes. "I love you so much. I almost lost you." Her eyes filled with tears, and Grant gathered her into his arms and held her. He whispered in her ear. "I love you so much."

"All I could think about ... when he had me ... was you and the kids ..."

"You're safe now, honey," he said. "I'll never let you go."

• • •

Grant heard a light knock on the door several hours later. He assumed it was someone from the hospital staff, but when no one entered, he pulled himself up and eased to the door. Jade was sleeping peacefully. He found Ben Petty and his sister Elaine Doss standing in the hall. Petty was holding flowers.

"Hey, Ben," Grant whispered. "Elaine. Y'all come in." They followed Grant inside and waited until he was seated and gotten his ankle propped up. "I'd offer y'all a seat if I had one."

Petty walked close to Jade. Doss didn't move. Grant watched the siblings through the silence. Petty wore the outfit Grant had bought him for trial. Doss had on the same pants and shirt she wore on the day he and Jade picked her up at the Lucedale motel. Doss took the floral arrangement from Petty and found a spot on the table next to the bed, then stepped away. Grant would have felt awkward in the moment—what was there to say at this point? But he was too tired to force conversation.

Petty, thankfully, was a free man. George Brewer and Troy Lee had stood before Judge Riley as she granted Brewer's motion to set aside the verdict. Brewer had called Grant with the news on the cell he'd bought the day before—it was his first cell phone. Grant had smiled when Brewer asked if he would teach him how to use the damn thing when they got home from the hospital.

Petty turned to Grant. "We got to go," he whispered. "Mr.

The Peter Bay

Mordiky is waiting to take us to Columbus."

Grant hobbled out in the hall with them. "When will you be back, man?"

"Don't know. Elaine asked me to stay with her a while."

"I can get him a job at the store where I work," she said, and smiled. "I hope he moves up there. We have a lot of catching up to do."

Grant grinned at Elaine before turning to his old friend. He patted Petty on the shoulder. "We do, too, old buddy."

"We do, don't we?" Petty's smile faded. "Grant, thank you for everything."

"Oh, Ben," he said, waving this away. "No thanks necessary. Wish I'd have done a better job."

"I'll always remember what you and Mr. Brewer did for me. Maybe when I come get my stuff from the trailer in a few weeks, I can come see y'all and thank Mrs. Jade."

"We'd love for you to visit." Grant turned to Doss. "Y'all can stay with us at the farm."

Doss hugged Grant. "You and George Brewer are the first lawyers I've ever liked."

They all laughed. Petty reached in his pocket and retrieved a pocket knife and handed it to Grant. It was a cream-colored Barlow.

"I want you to have this," Petty said. "It's my favorite."

Grant hugged Petty. "Thanks, friend. I'll take good care of it."

Grant watched Petty and Doss walk to the elevator. He heard the light ding which announced the door's opening. Petty and Doss waved and disappeared. He looked at the knife and back down the empty hall. Then he smiled and opened the door. Jade was still asleep. The flowers were beautiful and were patiently waiting for Jade to welcome them to her room.

CHAPTER 54

Tuesday, July 15, 2014

"READY TO GO home?" the doctor said to Jade.

"Yes," Jade replied. "I was beginning to think you were going to make me stay another day."

The doctor looked up from the clipboard she was reading. "Not a chance. I hear you have two little ones waiting to see you. You'll be home by lunch."

The doctor gave Grant some paperwork and brief instructions before she left the room. Minutes later an orderly walked in pushing an empty wheelchair. Jade sat down and Grant followed them out of the room. He was getting used to the crutches and moved almost as well as he did before. The cast would come off soon. Then he'd be in a boot for a month or so.

George Brewer was leaning against the Range Rover when they came outside. He opened the front passenger door and helped Jade inside. Grant sat in the back with his leg stretched across the floor. Brewer put Jade's bags and Grant's crutches in the rear and jumped in the driver's seat.

He looked at Jade. "Where to, my lady?"

The Peter Bay

Grant saw her smile. "Home."

• • •

Grant and Jade had discussed parts of the ordeal which almost took her life. He figured she'd learn the details soon enough. They stopped at a red light, and Grant watched a car idling next to them. A little boy stared, and he waved. The little boy waved in return. The light turned green and the car pulled away.

"George," Jade said after they merged onto Highway 98, "tell me what happened."

Brewer glanced at Grant in the rearview mirror before answering. "After the verdict was announced, I'd gone back to my office to call Mordiky. He told me that Paul Sumner was the killer. I tried to call Grant and couldn't get him. So I took off for the Peter Bay."

"How did Mordiky know?"

"He remembered a conversation we had at y'all's place on the Fourth of July," Brewer said. "It hit him that the other three unsolved crimes had occurred near places where Sumner had lived. He called the investigators and shared his hunch, and after some digging, all the victims had children that attended schools where Sumner worked. The kidnappings occurred within a year after Sumner had moved *away* from each place."

Grant was shaking his head. "How did you know to go to the Peter Bay?" he asked.

Brewer smiled. "Our friend Pete Ball. As I was running to my truck, he jumped in. I told him you were in danger, Jade. Pete said to go there—he was sure of it."

"How'd he know?"

"Said Sumner talked a lot about that place." Brewer looked at Jade. "I guess Pete Ball is not as dumb as we thought."

"I wonder whose pocket knife was found by Lacy's body," Grant said.

Brewer looked in the rearview mirror. "Get this: Mordiky learned that Sumner's maternal grandfather's name was *Benjamin Franklin Purcer*. We think the knife came from him."

"Where was your pickup?" Grant asked, still trying to get his mind around the fact that Paul Sumner, a man they thought was their friend, tried to kill Jade. "I don't remember seeing it when I was running down the pipeline."

"There's another road that'll get you there faster. I came from that direction."

Grant thought again about how close he'd come to losing Jade as Brewer turned onto Highway 57. Now they were only fifteen minutes from the farm.

"What did he do to me?" Jade asked.

"You want to know the details?"

"Please."

"It's fine, George," Grant said. "Go ahead."

"Well, he had already knocked you out and cuffed you. When we got there, he had just ripped your shirt open and pulled down your bra," Brewer said. "But that's all he was able to do."

Jade looked out the window. Grant could see her wiping away tears. Brewer and Grant made eye contact but didn't speak. Minutes later Brewer reached Hicks Road. Jade asked him to stop the vehicle.

"Before we get to the house," Jade said, reaching to hug Brewer, "I want to thank you. I'm about to hold my children, and if it wasn't for you I never would have hugged them again."

Brewer smiled. "Speaking of your kids," he said in a husky voice, "I believe they're waiting on you."

When the Range Rover topped the last hill and the farm came into view, a large banner read: *Welcome Home Momma*! Grant saw Ladd pointing in their direction. Brewer stopped and hurried around to open the door for Jade. Grant watched Ladd run to his mother and kiss her. Ella Reese wasn't far behind.

The Peter Bay

Edwina and Pete Ball were busy setting the picnic tables, which were covered with food. Mordiky walked up and Jade wiped a tear away as she hugged and thanked him. Judge Eaton followed close behind. Jade laughed as Edwina scolded her for being late for lunch. Grant knew Jade's best friend would never show affection in front of the others. And he also knew how much Edwina loved her.

Grant's mother and his sister's family had joined the welcoming party for Jade. Despite the occasion, Grant was happy to have his mother and sister on the same ground that they'd spent the best years of their lives together. He thought of his dad and hoped somehow he was there, too. Then he saw Pete Ball walk around the back of the house. Grant looked for his crutches and saw Ladd acting like he had a broken leg. He grabbed them and found Pete on the back steps of the house, crying. Grant sat next to Pete and put his arm around him.

"Hey, Pete," he whispered. "You did good, man. Thank you."

A moment later a small twig snapped. Grant looked up and saw Jade. He stood and made room for her. Jade sat next to Pete and hugged him. Grant smiled through his tears as he walked back toward everyone.

Grant looked into the sky and saw a lone cloud, a small puff of white against a clear blue canvas. He thought about clouds once more. They *were* like people. Some, he thought, did bring warning. Some came with darkness and fear. But most were harmless and inviting. Most could be trusted. Grant watched the small cloud float away. Clouds like that were special, he thought. They were like that one true friend every person needed. And for Grant, Pete Ball had become that friend.

• • •

"I'd like to propose a toast," Judge Eaton said and raised his glass. The others raised theirs. "To Jade, Grant, Ladd, and Ella

Reese ... for blessing our little community with your presence and friendship."

"Hear, hear," Brewer said as they tapped glasses. He emptied his water glass and set it on the table. "Mordiky, can you help me a second?"

The two men walked to Brewer's pickup and unloaded a large object covered by a sheet. They returned to the table and stopped in front of Jade and Grant. Grant held Jade's hand as Brewer called Ladd over to assist.

"Young man, pull the sheet off," Brewer said.

Mordiky helped Ladd remove the sheet. A sign appeared that read: HICKS AND BREWER, ATTORNEYS AT LAW. Grant watched Jade cover her mouth with her hand. She looked at him with tears in her eyes.

"This is our home," he said to her. "And I want to live the rest of my life with you, right here."